THE
LEAST
AMONG US

Also available by Gwen Florio

The Truth of It All

Lola Wicks Mysteries

Under the Shadows
Reservations
Disgraced
Dakota
Montana

Nora Best Mysteries

Best Laid Plans
Best Kept Secrets

Standalone

Silent Hearts

THE
LEAST
AMONG US

A NOVEL

GWEN FLORIO

CROOKED
LANE

NEW YORK

Published in the United States by Crooked Lane Books, an imprint of The Quick Brown Fox & Company LLC.

Crooked Lane Books and its logo are trademarks of The Quick Brown Fox & Company LLC.

Library of Congress Catalog-in-Publication data available upon request.

ISBN (hardcover): 978-1-63910-068-2
ISBN (ebook): 978-1-63910-069-9

Cover design by Meghan Deist

Printed in the United States.

www.crookedlanebooks.com

Crooked Lane Books
34 West 27th St., 10th Floor
New York, NY 10001

First Edition: December 2022

10 9 8 7 6 5 4 3 2 1

In memory of my daughter Kate, who abhorred injustice and worked with hopeful anticipation toward a more equitable world.

CHAPTER

1

JULIA GEARY CAME across all kinds of stupid in the course of her job as a Peak County public defender, but Ray Belmar pushed fuckup into a whole new dimension.

The justice of the peace looked down her long nose and read the charges facing Ray—public disturbance, lewdness, indecent exposure—then turned to him and put them into appalled plain English.

"You ran into the middle of the St. Patrick's Day Parade stark naked?"

On the Monday after the parade, the courtroom reeked of stale alcohol sweating its way through overworked pores. It was packed with still-hungover miscreants awaiting initial court appearances on all manner of misbehavior that had crossed a legal line. The snoozers among them—there were many—snapped to wakefulness.

Julia spoke up. "With respect, Your Honor, my client wasn't naked. He wore a sock. The charge of indecent exposure doesn't apply."

The judge turned her glare upon Julia.

"A single clad foot doesn't negate the charge, Ms. Geary. As you well know."

Julia cleared her throat.

"Your Honor." She waited a beat. "It wasn't on his foot."

The courtroom erupted.

Ray turned to face the gallery and took a bow. "A sock," he mouthed, spreading his hands apart to indicate extra-long.

"Mr. Belmar!" The judge slammed her gavel.

Julia cast an ostentatious glance at the courtroom clock and, behind her back, rubbed her fingers together, knowing that Claudette Greene—Peak County's lead prosecutor—would see the gesture from her table on the other side of the well.

As they'd walked together into the courtroom, Julia had bet Claudette ten dollars she'd have the courtroom in stitches three minutes into Ray's case.

"You're on," Claudette said. "They're all still too wasted to hear anything other than it's their turn to say, 'Not guilty.'"

"What are you doing here today, anyway? Isn't this a few steps below your fancy new pay grade?"

Julia knew the answer, even as she asked. Claudette, her former partner in the Public Defender's Division, had moved to the dark side—into a job as acting prosecutor—when the former chief prosecutor resigned. But now Claudette faced an election and needed all the press she could get. The charges against Ray, all misdemeanors, normally wouldn't have rated Claudette's attention, but videos of Ray's antics at the parade had predictably gone viral and Claudette was in court to throw the book at him and squeeze one more story out of the whole escapade.

Chance Larsen, the crime reporter for *The Bulletin*, sat in the back of the room, dutifully scribbling as Claudette outlined all the reasons Ray should spend some time behind bars to contemplate the error of his ways. "He jumped onto the Rotary float! Flaunting his . . . *sock* . . . in front of a child!" Chief among Ray's misfortunes was the fact that one of the Rotarians had invited his sixteen-year-old granddaughter to accompany him on the float.

Julia appreciated Claudette's motivation, but it pissed her off anyway. Jail time would be bad enough, but the indecent exposure charge, if it stuck, could see Ray labeled a sex offender because of the granddaughter's age. She had an inches-thick file containing the paperwork on Ray's various brushes with the law, but even during the worst of his alcohol-fueled misbehavior, he'd never crossed that particular line.

She gazed out the tall courthouse window during Claudette's wearying recital. Red and blue lights still flashed from the cop cars lining the creek bank two blocks away. where an early-morning jogger had a found a "popsicle," the derisive term some cops applied to transients who succumbed to Duck Creek's frigid winters.

Claudette thundered her windup.

"Your Honor, I'd ask that you deny bail to Mr. Belmar, or impose one in a high enough amount that guarantees he'll remain incarcerated until his trial. He's clearly a threat to the community."

Julia rose in defense of her hapless frequent flier. "Your Honor, if this indecent exposure charge is to remain against my client, half this room must face similar charges, given the amount of public urination on the streets that day. My own little boy commented on it."

The judge didn't need to know of Calvin's utter delight at the sight. Julia had to grab his hand to stop the five-year-old from pulling down his pants and attempting to imitate the mighty arcing streams splashing against Duck Creek's storefronts as the high school band marched past, merrily tootling "The Rakes of Mallow."

"Additionally, if I count correctly, some thirty people were arrested on charges of public drunkenness, a dozen for simple assault, and five for felony assault, including a couple of sexual assaults." Julia heaved a mournful sigh. She'd learned a little something about theatrics in the brief time she'd shared an office with Claudette. "St. Patrick's Day in Duck Creek continues its ignoble tradition."

Duck Creek owed its existence to silver mines, which before they were dug dry had attracted scores of Irish immigrants, whose descendants—helped by a yearly infusion of students from the university in the next county—celebrated in notoriously uninhibited fashion. In addition to being obviously hungover, several in the room wore visible signs of their weekend revelry in the forms of black eyes, cuts and scrapes, and more than one arm in a sling.

Ray himself sported a purple goose egg on his forehead, a swollen jaw, and a bandaged hand. More worrisome, given a recent commitment to sobriety after his brash demonstration of impressive sock length, he'd slumped in his chair seemingly even more hungover than the others, his skin gray and papery, eyes scary-monster red, with an occasional whole-body tremor.

"Those Rotary folks kicked the shit out of me before they threw me off their float," he'd said in response to Julia's startled look—a detail intentionally omitted as she pleaded Ray's cause.

"My client recently completed a three-month sobriety program," she said, hoping the judge focused on the papers in front of her and not Ray's appearance, which made her fear for the sobriety she was so vigorously touting. "For the first time in years he has a job, washing dishes in one of our local establishments. By all accounts, he's an excellent employee." By which Julia meant she hadn't heard otherwise. She took a breath and finished her spiel.

"Until Saturday, a day on which—I repeat—far worse behavior abounded, he's had no recent encounters with the law. To impose such an outsize and unfair bail, and to hold him in jail until this case is resolved, would interrupt the tremendous progress he's made. He attends Alcoholic Anonymous meetings three times a week and counseling sessions twice a month, and hasn't missed a single one, nor has he failed any of his regular alcohol and drug tests. I'd ask that he be released on his own recognizance so that he can continue his hard work toward becoming a productive member of society."

She sat as Claudette argued a final time for a high bail.

"Hey." Ray tugged at her arm. "I need to talk to you. It's important."

Julia didn't dare look at the bench but sensed the judge's attention.

"Okay," she whispered out of the side of her mouth. "As soon as we're done."

"No. Not here. Someplace where—" He looked around the room. "Not here."

She understood. Since his transformation into an approximation of a solid citizen, Ray had styled himself as something of an informant, tipping Julia off to extenuating circumstances that could benefit her clients, many of them his former compatriots in petty crime, although in some cases she'd get a text with a name and a simple warning: *Let his ass rot in jail.* But the courthouse was populated by attorneys, clerks, cops, sheriff's deputies, wrongdoers, and those who'd been done wrong, any of whom might be interested in Ray's tidbits, or so he believed.

Julia wasn't so sure. His number had lighted up her phone a half dozen times in the days before the parade, but a little bit of Ray went a long way and she was especially disinclined to talk with him after seeing various videos of his parade high jinks. Now, though, he had her cornered.

The court reporter asked Claudette to repeat something she'd just said. Julia took advantage of the general distraction to stall.

"How'd you get out, anyway?" Normally, people who couldn't afford to post bail were held in jail until their initial court appearances, but Ray had dragged himself into court a free man.

"Jail was too full. They kicked a bunch of us low-level cases out Sunday morning. How about coffee later?"

"Colombia?" It was just a couple of blocks from the courthouse. "Around four?"

He shook his head. "Tomorrow. Say, noon. Starbucks."

She blinked. Duck Creek's lone Starbucks was on the edge of town and, unlike Colombia, presented little risk that anyone from the courthouse would see them. Whatever Ray wanted to tell her might actually be important.

"Okay, but I'll have to keep it quick. The funeral's at two. I can't miss it."

Leslie Harper, a state legislator from Duck Creek, had been found dead in her home a few days earlier. The first police reports had hinted at suicide or maybe an unfortunate combination of booze and sleeping pills. Over her years in the legislature, Harper had sponsored—sometimes even successfully—bills to ease penalties and fees for nonviolent offenders, and members of the Public Defender's Division would be at her funeral in force.

To see Ray, Julia would have to give up her lunch hour, a laughable concept anyway among the perennially overburdened public defenders.

"Quick is all I need. I'll be at the funeral too. Harper was good people."

Julia turned to him in surprise. "You knew her?"

"There's a lot about me you don't know." He gave a wan grin and she kicked him under the table, reminding him of the seriousness of the occasion.

Ray pasted on a somber expression just in time to hear the judge acquiesce to Julia's request to release him on his own recognizance, with the condition that he be tested daily, rather than weekly, for alcohol and drug use at his own expense.

He gathered enough strength for a jaunty wave and sauntered from the courtroom.

Julia smiled and settled back to wait for her next case. She'd just bested Claudette, who had years of experience on her, in a courtroom skirmish—a minor one, to be sure, but satisfying nonetheless.

She was still riding high from her success the previous year in proving the innocence of a teenager charged with sexually assaulting a classmate. And she was looking forward to her dinner this evening with Dom Parrish, the principal of Duck Creek High, with whom a shy flirtation during that case had turned into an unexpectedly satisfying relationship.

She'd finally emerged from the despairing years of mourning after an IED in Iraq killed her husband, a loss that still had the power to blindside her with occasional gasping, stop-in-her-tracks agony, albeit losing a shade of strength with each blow. These days she looked forward, not back, and sunshine suffused the view.

She put Ray's file aside, picked up another, and turned her attention to her next client.

"Sonofabitch!" An outcry in the hallway outside interrupted the proceedings. A few people rose and peered through the door's glass window.

The judge rapped her gavel. "Be seated."

A crash sounded outside, followed by a torrent of strangled profanity.

"Order!"

But everyone in the gallery was on their feet now, jostling toward the door.

The judge let her gavel fall a final time. "Ten-minute recess."

Julia joined the pack fleeing the room.

"What's going on?"

"Damned if I know," said Claudette. "You okay with taking that ten dollars in the form of a couple of lattes from Colombia? Tomorrow after the funeral? Wish I could get the barista to add a shot of whiskey. I'll need it." She and Leslie Harper had been close, a friendship they'd maintained even after Claudette moved into the chief prosecutor's job, whose previous occupants had not looked kindly upon the criminal justice reforms that Claudette had continued—with Leslie's help—to champion.

Two women elbowed past them to join the fast-growing crowd in the rotunda. Julia stood on tiptoe, but even raising herself up to five feet two was useless given the jostling mass before her.

"More than okay. Ray's dragging me to Starbucks tomorrow. It'll take more than two lattes to get that taste out of my mouth. I'm going to have to give up my lunch hour to listen to his latest conspiracy theory."

Claudette, whose height gave her the vantage point Julia lacked, looked to the far side of the rotunda. "No, you won't." She raised her voice. "Prosecutor coming through!"

Julia scuttled behind her in the space that magically appeared, stopping cold at the sight of two sheriff's deputies wrestling a screaming Ray Belmar to the marble floor.

"I didn't do it! Whatever it is, I didn't fucking do it!"

Julia shouldered past Claudette. "Hey! Don't hurt him. He's my client. Ray, what's going on?"

The deputies knelt over Ray, one with his knee against the side of Ray's head, mashing his face against a floor filthy from the traces of melting snow and mud. The other dug a knee into Ray's back as he forced handcuffs around his wrists.

Ray bucked beneath them, then fell still. His eyes rolled wildly toward Julia.

"I don't know," he gasped.

"Get off him. I'm his lawyer, dammit. Get off him." Julia pulled her phone from her blazer pocket and aimed it toward the scene. The deputies grunted to their feet, roughly pulling Ray up with them.

Julia recognized one. Unlike some cops and deputies, he'd never seemed to view public defenders' efforts as an insult to his own work.

"Wayne, what the hell?"

He jerked his head toward the window. "That guy they found down by the river this morning?"

She followed his gaze. The cop cars were still there, along with the coroner's van, but they'd finally turned the lights off. "What about him?"

"He didn't freeze. Well, maybe he did, but only because somebody beat him to a bloody pulp first."

"Who?"

A harder man might have laughed. Wayne's glance was all pity.

From the corner of her eye, Julia saw Chance Larsen beside her, his phone held toward Wayne, the record light blinking.

"Come on, Julia. Now is not the time to start being stupid."

The other deputy started to drag Ray away.

"That's not possible. Ray wouldn't hurt anyone."

Wayne's face hardened.

"He didn't hurt anyone. He killed him."

CHAPTER

2

Light shone through the frosted glass of Julia's office door, laying a bright path down the dark hallway that led to the warren
of offices housing the public defenders.

"Damn." She was sure she'd turned it off before she went to
court. She'd hear about it from Deb, the meddlesome office manager
who made it her business to ensure the office was pinching every
possible penny.

Julia counted herself fortunate to finally have an office to herself after Claudette's departure to the far-better-paying position of
county attorney. She didn't want to risk her newfound luxury by
running afoul of Deb—a futile effort, she realized seconds later
when she opened the door.

A young woman stood inside, a tape dispenser in one hand, a
stapler in the other. Two open file boxes sat atop Claudette's desk,
and Julia's own desk contained a stack of files that hadn't been there
before. A long wool herringbone coat hung beside Julia's puffy parka
on the coatrack.

"Who the hell are you?"

Julia knew she should apologize for her rudeness. But it didn't
appear to have rattled the interloper.

"Marie St. Clair. I'm your new intern."

She was taller than Julia—but then, everyone was—with a
broad, pale face, wispy pale hair, and pale eyes that bulged froglike,
all of it giving her the appearance of someone who existed below

ground, in a place devoid of sunlight. Her expression suggested she rarely smiled.

Julia had planned to transfer her own things into Claudette's desk, slightly larger than hers and in marginally better condition, and then move her old desk out entirely, making the space appear less like a repurposed closet and more like an actual office. She'd never gotten around to it and apparently had missed her chance.

"I didn't ask for an intern. And what are you doing here now, anyway? Aren't internships a summertime thing?"

"I asked if I could start early. I'm doing well enough in my classes that they said I could work a few hours a week during the semester."

Marie placed the stapler and tape dispenser on the desk, aligning them precisely with a stack of Post-it notes and an in/out box. "Sounds like we—"

We?

"—are going to have a homicide trial on our hands."

"Not likely." Julia sat at her desk and logged on to her computer in an attempt to look purposeful. The office windows, grimy from years of inattention, let in precious little light, and even that was fast fading. She'd come back to the office planning only to grab her coat and go home, eager to close the door on this day, but didn't want to cede the office, *her* office, to Marie, who was hovering beside her with an expectant expression on her face and a question on her lips.

"What do you mean?"

"He didn't do it."

"They all say that."

Ah, the arrogance and certainty of law school. Lawyers got a bad rap on both counts, but nothing beat baby lawyers for being the smartest people in the room.

Julia nudged the files littering her desk. They were her own, both old and pending cases. "What are these doing here?"

Marie looked toward the file cabinet. "Deb told me to clear out a couple of drawers for myself, so I did."

Julia had always thought the references to blood boiling mere colorful hyperbole. Now hers surged hot through her veins. She wondered whom she hated more at the moment, Marie or Deb.

Marie lingered oblivious, rearranging the already perfectly aligned items on her desk. "Have you ever tried a homicide before?"

"No."

A mix of disappointment and irritation chased the eagerness from Marie's face. "They'll probably assign someone with more experience, then."

Julia logged off with a loud clack of keys and grabbed her coat from the rack. Marie could spend all damn night lining up her office supplies for all she cared.

"They're not going to need to assign anyone. Ray Belmar didn't kill that man."

She closed the door behind her, then opened it again.

"Get your shit out of my file cabinet. Leave the stuff on my desk where it is. And if you ever touch my files again, I'll ship you back to law school before you can say *habeas corpus*."

* * *

A blast of warm air, redolent of tomato and garlic and simmering meats, greeted Julia when she pushed open the door of Dom Parrish's house.

Her spirits soared. "Sunday gravy? But it's Monday."

Parrish appeared in the kitchen doorway, a wooden spoon in one hand, his other cupped beneath it to catch drips. He held the spoon to her lips. "Taste."

"Mmm. Perfect. I'd rather have this than a glass of wine—and I really need a glass of wine."

"In there." He pointed to the living room, where two chairs had been pulled close to the fireplace, two glasses of wine on a table between them. "Dinner can wait."

She unwound her scarf, kicked off her shoes, draped her coat over the back of one of the chairs, and stood before the fire, hands outstretched.

"What's the occasion?"

"For starters, Calvin and Elena demanded tacos yesterday. Remember? And today's a teacher in-service day. No school for the kids and early out for us. I knew you had Ray today—hence, Sunday gravy. Cures all ills, even better than chicken soup."

Dom was the first and only man Julia had dated since Michael's death. Their relationship had proceeded slowly, cautiously, its tentative pace imposed in part by the combined realities of Dom's teenage daughter, Julia's young son, and the fact that Julia still lived with her mother-in-law. Sex involved the sort of scheduling maneuvers worthy of air traffic controllers. They'd fallen into a pattern of two weeknight dinners at his house, timed to his daughter's evening volunteer shifts at a local refugee center, and weekend outings of varying success with one or both kids.

She'd persuaded him to try cross-country skiing, the low-rent alternative to the glitzy ski resort on the outskirts of town, and Dom—whose last name, Parrish, was the anglicized version of Parisi, the name bestowed on him by an indifferent clerk at Ellis Island—in turn had introduced her to the Italian tradition of Sunday gravy: the meaty, long-simmered sauce that warmed them through upon their return from their excursions.

They lifted glasses, clinked, and sank into the chairs.

"How'd it go with Ray today? Was he up to his usual shenanigans?" In the months they'd been together, Dom had heard more about Ray than any of Julia's other clients.

Julia's sip turned into a gulp. She rolled the stem of the glass between her fingers.

"Pretty much." She set her wine aside and recounted the story of the sock, spreading her hands far apart in imitation of Ray's theatrics, eliciting a spit take from Dom.

"Even the judge laughed. It was all fun and games until they arrested him for homicide."

She was thankful Dom hadn't taken another sip of wine.

"What? Did somebody at the parade have a heart attack at the sight of that sock flopping around? You're kidding, right?"

"Afraid not."

A log collapsed into the fire, sending up a starburst of sparks. A few bounced through the screen and landed on the rug. Julia ground her toe against them, heedless of the damage to her striped wool sock.

"I'd no sooner finished getting Ray out from under the insane bail Claudette wanted than they arrested him. They say he killed that guy they found down by the river. I just can't believe it."

"From everything you've told me about him, that doesn't sound like Ray."

"It's not. And then they stuck me with this obnoxious intern . . ."

Julia was off and running, indulging in one of the forgotten pleasures of being in a relationship—namely, shoveling the day's unpleasantness onto someone else's shoulders.

Dom, as usual, did the right thing, making sympathetic noises and refilling her glass, until he finally took it from her and wrapped her hands in his.

"You know what? You're far too tense to give that gravy the attention it rightly deserves. Dinner can wait."

He didn't need to say more. Julia practically ran ahead of him to the bedroom, where everything that came next banished all thoughts of Ray Belmar from her head.

Maybe it was the wine. Or maybe it was her need to block out the shock and frustration of Ray's arrest, followed by the insult of the unwanted intern.

Julia took the lead, pushing Dom onto his back, her movements fast, almost rough, her moans drowning out the sounds of the key in the front door, the footsteps down the hall.

"Yes!" she yelled, just as the bedroom door flew open and a shocked voice intruded upon her consciousness.

"Dad?"

3

E NOUGH OF THE mortification of Elena's unexpected intrusion
lingered the next morning that Julia didn't even flinch at the
sight of an email from her boss when she scrolled through her work
email before leaving the house.

Drop by my office when you get in.

Typical Li'l Pecker—the office shorthand for chief public
defender Bill Decker—who specialized in opacity. Probably wanted
to give her the belated news about the intern. Well, she had a few
things she wanted to let him know, too, starting with the fact that
the last thing she needed was an intern.

What she needed was some sort of drug that would erase forever
the memory of Elena's wide and staring eyes, the way she'd stood
frozen in the doorway as Julia scrambled from her perch and into
her clothing.

Pipe burst at the refugee center, Dom had texted later by way of
explaining his daughter's earlier-than-expected return. *Probably best
to lie low for a while.*

Julia was fine with that, especially if lying low meant a fissure that
would open in the earth and swallow her whole. Elena was sixteen,
and Julia assumed she knew Julia and her father were having sex.

But she and Dom had never spent so much as a night together,
and she'd always been careful to leave his house long before Elena
returned home from her volunteer work so as not to present the girl
with the evidence of their sated expressions, their languid, relaxed

gestures. Which, in retrospect, would have been infinitely preferable to the sight of a naked Julia bouncing around . . . *God*. Even now, safely alone, she blushed hot recalling the moment.

She went straight to Decker's office, not even stopping by her own to drop off her coat. The quicker she got this over with, the better.

Decker didn't stand when she came in. Of course not.

For her part, Julia waited a moment longer than necessary after he gestured for her to sit, trying to underscore his rudeness, a move almost certainly lost on him. But at least he didn't invite her to take her coat off, meaning their meeting would probably be brief.

Decker leaned back in his chair and served up his most avuncular smile. Julia knew that expression well. It was, along with his reassuring appearance—the silvery mane, the trim frame, the dark suits and crisp white shirts—one of his most potent weapons. Julia revised her estimate of the meeting's length and wished she'd ditched the coat.

"This matter that's just dropped in your lap. You've never handled a homicide case, correct?"

Of course she hadn't. Neither had anyone else in the office for the last few years. Duck Creek's low crime rate ranked just a few steps below the ski hill north of town as one of its prime attractions.

"No. But I'm quite familiar with this defendant. His recent history has been impressive—rehab, meetings, counseling. I'm certain of my ability to handle another big case," she said, a none-too-subtle reminder of her success the previous year in proving her client's innocence.

"Your work was excellent." Another Li'l Pecker special: the compliment designed to soften the blow that would inevitably follow. She braced herself.

"But our former colleague Claudette will go all out on this one. Now that she's gotten a taste of that top job, she wants to hold on to it. We can't afford to lose."

Julia refrained from reminding him that Claudette went all out on every case. "The curse of being a Black woman," Claudette often reminded her. "You're always expected to be less than. Anything other than balls to the wall and people go full *I told you so*."

Julia knew Decker's response went beyond every attorney's natural competitiveness. The man had his eye on a judgeship—his father, Big Pecker, had been a federal judge—and so took every high-profile case personally. Judges in their state were elected, and the voting public generally preferred tough-on-crime prosecutors. If an accused murderer went free because of a successful defense by Decker's office, the defense needed to be airtight and the community proud of justice served.

Julia mentally ran through the other public defenders in the office, assessing which one might be Decker's chosen replacement and marshaling arguments against each.

"I've asked Tim Saunders to come in on the case."

"Tim Saunders?" Julia's voice came out in a damnable squeak. This she hadn't seen coming.

Saunders was an associate in Duck Creek's most prominent law firm, an up-and-comer seen as the obvious successor to Dan Tibbits, the best—and by far the most expensive—defense attorney in the region. Julia had once hoped to work there until she'd gotten crosswise with Tibbits during her last big case. She'd seen Saunders around the courthouse. He was hard to miss. His nickname, Adonis, bestowed by the women and men alike, was richly deserved.

"But why?"

"As I just told you." Decker switched to principal-talking-to-a-recalcitrant-student mode. "We need to handle this one just right. Given the circumstances, Mr. Belmar will likely plea to a reduced charge of negligent homicide, Tim Saunders will have done his pro bono work, and you'll get to notch another success." Not to mention the fact that the case would be out of the public eye.

"I wouldn't view a negligent homicide plea as a success. Ray didn't do it."

Decker stood. Their meeting was over.

"Exactly why I've asked Saunders to come in. Geary, I'm surprised at you. Any other woman in the office would be beside herself."

A remark so infuriating that Julia left without another word, only through superhuman effort stopping herself from slamming the door behind her and realizing too late she'd forgotten to object to her new intern.

CHAPTER

4

I T WAS, JULIA told herself, her own fault.

Not twenty-four hours earlier she'd exulted in the startlingly rosy turn her life had taken. The last time she'd felt that way—happily married with a brand-new law career and a baby on the way—two frozen-faced Marines in dress blues had paced up the walk to her door and blown it all to hell.

The insults heaped upon her in the past day would never exceed the magnitude of that body blow, but in terms of sheer volume, they were impressive.

She ticked them off as she stomped back along the long hall from Decker's office into the warren of glorified closets that housed the assistant public defenders.

The murder charge against Ray.

Adonis brought in on the case.

A likely end to family outings with Dom, under the circumstances.

And the sound of voices coming from her office, which reminded her of the final indignity: the intern.

Goddammit.

She paused and summoned resolve. Marie St. Clair wasn't going to further spoil her day. She stood outside the door, taking a breath, holding it and blowing it out, a calming technique advised by the useless long-ago grief counselor assigned to her after Michael's death. It hadn't worked then and it didn't work now.

Was that laughter? Not something she'd expected from her first encounter with the dour Marie. A man's laugh boomed louder still.

She opened the door to see Deputy Sheriff Wayne Peterson perched atop her desk, legs swinging, and Marie at the desk once occupied by Claudette. Julia would be damned if she thought of it as belonging to anyone else.

Marie's pasty cheeks flushed pink at the sight of her.

"Hey, Julia." Wayne lifted a hand. "Ree and I were just catching up."

Ree?

"Catching up?"

"She was one of our high school cadets." The cadet program immersed high school students in the sheriff's department, taking them on ride-alongs or field trips to the training academy or even the state prison, with an eye toward enticing them into careers in law enforcement. A move that had failed when it came to Marie, Wayne said now.

"We thought sure we'd see her back with us when she finished college. But no, she opted for the dark side. Not just law, but the Public Defender's Division." He mock-frowned.

The glower that had greeted Julia the previous day was back. "This was the only place that would take an intern early."

Which made a cockeyed sort of sense. The public defenders defined overworked and underpaid. Someone had probably thought an extra body would lessen the load, without taking into account the distraction that training and mentoring an intern would involve. Or, Julia thought, more likely she'd offended Deb in some way and this was Deb's revenge.

"Be careful not to piss her off," Wayne warned Julia now. He made his thumb and forefinger into a gun and aimed it at the wall. "Nine times out of ten, she outshot me on the range. Bang."

He lifted his forefinger to his mouth and blew.

Marie's blush deepened. "I haven't been to the range in weeks. Law school gets in the way of everything fun."

"Added to your collection lately?"

"Picked up a Beretta Bobcat last week as a reward for how well I did on my fall semester finals."

Wayne whistled. "That's a decent little pocket gun. More accurate than most."

Great, thought Julia. Bad enough she was stuck with an intern, but it looked as though Marie was one of those cop-loving, tough-on-crime law students who ended up in the prosecutor's office and made her life hell until they settled down and realized compromise was in everyone's best interest.

And she was a gun nut too. Julia didn't have a problem with guns—people in Duck Creek fanned out each fall into the surrounding mountains in search of elk to fill their freezers—but she drew the line at handguns or the excessive firepower of semiautomatic rifles. She eyeballed Marie's utilitarian purse, sitting on the shelf behind her, and wondered what it concealed. Although, given what she was fast learning about Marie, if the young woman carried, the gun was probably on her person, maybe strapped behind her hip, just below her the waistband of her skirt, safely hidden beneath her boxy blazer.

"Anyhow." Wayne held out a stapled sheaf of paper. "I just came by to drop off the affidavit for Ray Belmar. Figured you'd want it first thing."

Marie sat up a little straighter in her chair, her pale eyes darkening with interest. She held out her hand.

"Easy there, Speedy." Julia snatched the affidavit from Wayne.

He raised an eyebrow. "Time for me to get back to work. Ree, come downstairs and find me if she ever gives you time for coffee."

"Mm-hmm." Marie nodded assent but never took her eyes off the pages in Julia's hands.

Julia said good-bye to Wayne, scanned the pages, then made a show of unlocking her file cabinet and slotting the affidavit inside.

"I was hoping to get a look at that. Maybe start doing research into the perp and the vic."

"*Alleged* perpetrator. *Alleged* victim." Julia wondered if her use of the full words even registered. She turned the tiny key in the file drawer's lock and dropped it into her pocket. "You can just print out the affidavit, you know."

"I don't have a login to the computer system yet."

"You should call IT. Deb can give you the number."

"I already asked her. I called. They said it could take two or three days."

"Sounds about right." She retrieved the files on her day's cases from her in-box and zipped up the parka she'd never removed. "I'm off to jail to interview today's clients before the funeral. See you later."

"Can I go with you?" Marie half rose from her chair. But she addressed a closed door.

Julia was gone.

5

THE LOW CONCRETE building housing the Peak County Jail crouched on the outskirts of town, a badly needed upgrade from the dank cells in the courthouse basement that now served as a repository for one-armed office chairs, three-legged desks, and dented file cabinets that would have adequately served Marie if only there'd been space in the office.

The present jail had been state-of-the-art when it was built thirty years earlier. Now, in an expression favored by Julia's image-conscious mother-in-law, it looked "tired," likely due to the fact that it had been filled to capacity the minute it was built and overcrowded ever since, something that attracted the occasional ACLU lawsuit, with a series of reliably inadequate improvements as a result.

Throughout the week the public defenders took turns meeting at the jail with the clients they'd represent later in the day at the initial court appearances that followed their arrests. During those brief court proceedings, held assembly-line fashion, their clients entered pleas—nearly always "not guilty"—and then saw their bail set, or were released on their own recognizance.

Most of the people Julia represented had been picked up on drunken driving or minor drug charges. Mondays brought a handful of assault cases stemming from Saturday-night barroom brawls, and holidays bore out the truism that domestic violence always worsened then.

Truly serious crimes—rape, felony assault, and the like—were rare, and Julia hadn't seen a homicide case in the five years she'd worked in the Public Defender's Division. She'd lost count of how many times she'd represented Ray Belmar over the years, but each time he'd been the same—funny, sarcastic, and defiantly unrepentant, an attitude unaffected by his recent sobriety. They'd fallen into an easy, companiable banter, Julia gently chiding him, Ray's responses teasing and almost—but respectfully not quite—flirtatious, a welcome alternative to the outright grotesqueries voiced by some of her male clients.

But today he slumped at the table in the interview room, arms folded across his thin chest, eyes dull. The goose egg on his forehead seemed larger and more violently hued, purple shading into a greenish yellow. He didn't look up as she came into the room; didn't respond to her hello.

"Ray. What the hell happened?"

"Nothing."

His voice was so soft she leaned across the table to hear him.

"Not nothing. I just read the affidavit. They've got people saying they saw you down by the river Sunday night into Monday morning when that guy was killed."

"Probably because I was down by the river."

It was one of his haunts. Members of Duck Creek's homeless and transient communities congregated there, the tangled willow shrubs along the bank shielding their drinking and other unsightly behavior from the town's solid citizens. Every so often, the police and sheriff's department joined forces to clear out their makeshift camps, donning face masks and neon-blue rubber gloves as they tossed rotting tarps and foul-smelling sleeping bags into heavy-duty trash bags and taking it all away to be burned, while the camp's inhabitants cursed them from a safe distance.

Julia, fearful for Ray's fragile sobriety, had hoped he'd abandon his old companions, but he'd passed every breath and pee test mandated by his program. Until his arrest in the courthouse rotunda.

"Your blood test showed a point-three-oh blood-alcohol level. That's got to be a typo. I'll get it fixed. But still, Ray. What'd you do, chug a whole bottle of vodka?"

He finally looked up, meeting her eyes with his own, which were still spider-webbed with red.

"I haven't had a drink since I went into rehab."

She turned her hands up. "Blood tests don't lie, Ray."

He rubbed his arms, thin and brown and pimpled with gooseflesh, his short-sleeved orange jumpsuit an inadequate defense against the interview room's default thermostat setting several degrees shy of comfort. Julia assumed it was intentional, complained intermittently, and always brought a sweater, even on the most sweltering August days.

She noted Ray's swollen fingers, the scratches and bruises mapping the backs of his hands. "Those Rotary folks did a number on me when I landed on their float," he'd told her, and she'd believed him.

"Stupid," she muttered now, castigating herself for falling for it. "Hold your hands out." As though she'd know the difference between injuries inflicted by elderly feet in orthopedic shoes and those incurred during a deadly fistfight.

He complied, showing her first the backs of his hands and then his palms, pink and unmarred. Something caught her eye, a shadow on the soft flesh inside his elbow, as though someone had pressed a thumb deep into his skin.

"Jesus, Ray."

She'd never known him to use hard drugs. When he'd fallen off the wagon, he'd fallen hard. Too late to get into that now.

"Jesus, what?"

"Stop the innocent shit. Do you realize what you're looking at here? Just be glad Claudette's not hitting you with deliberate homicide. Otherwise you could end up in the single-wide."

The state's execution chamber was enough of an embarrassment to make even the most zealous prosecutor glad it was so rarely used. It lived within a house trailer in a weedy lot on the prison grounds, in sight of the exercise yard. Occasionally someone in the legislature submitted a bill for something more dignified, a macabre version of a steel-and-tile operating room, but given the cost, lawmakers inevitably decided the single-wide was good enough for the rare and brief procedure involved in lethal injection.

Julia tried to soften her tone. "Even with mitigated deliberate homicide, you could end up with forty years."

The orange jumpsuit shifted with a shrug. He crossed his arms again.

Julia pushed her chair back from the table. "I suppose we'll be entering a not-guilty plea today."

"Yeah." Finally, a bit of life to Ray's voice. "Because I didn't do it."

"Then help me out here."

"I tried. You wouldn't listen,"

It took her a moment. Right. He'd reminded her in court yesterday that he wanted to talk. Had blown up her phone with voice mails earlier, calls she'd ignored.

"Let's just get through today. I'll do my best, but there's probably no getting you out on your own recognizance. You know that, right?"

He didn't bother to respond, just stood and waited for her to leave.

6

A LINE OF DARK-CLAD people moved slowly up the sidewalk toward Duck Creek's community center, site of Leslie Harper's memorial.

Julia, who hadn't been to such an event since her husband's funeral, tamped down twin urges to run away and throw up on the spot. She motioned so many people ahead—legislators and lawyers, cops and social workers, curious strangers and even the county medical examiner—as she wrestled her memories into submission that the program had already started by the time she slipped through the door and found one of the few seats left in the back row.

As usual, she couldn't see over the heads of everyone in front of her. But in this case, a wide screen on either side of the room broadcasted the proceedings, which launched with a brief laudatory speech by the governor.

Julia, so agitated moments earlier, very nearly smiled at the sight of his pinched features, the sourness curdling his tone as he delivered the mandatory praise of the woman who'd publicly termed him "the sort of man who would snatch a crust of bread from a starving orphan and feed it instead to his dog."

The governor was a far-right Republican who'd succeeded years of Democrats in the job, and he'd promptly set to work vetoing the few bills that Harper had managed to get passed, along with any others that hinted at increases in social services in a state that routinely ranked near the bottom for such. "If he'd been the Tin Man and the

Wizard had given him a heart, he'd have eaten it raw," Harper had once said of him. Again, on the record.

Now he stood at a podium, his bald head and tiny twitching mustache glistening with sweat as he mouthed begrudging platitudes about Harper's years of service and the deep regard she inspired among her fellow lawmakers—neglecting, of course, to mention that this affection had emanated only from Democrats. The Republicans, even the formerly moderate among them now marching in cowed lockstep with the governor, thought her the Antichrist—a favor she'd returned by calling them "the party that once had a spine."

"Naturally, Representative Harper and I disagreed on a few things," the governor said with his huckster's grin, to chortles from some of those present and stone silence from the rest. He yielded the podium with an obvious mixture of relief and resentment to the previous governor, who spoke with such genuine warmth that the packets of Kleenex placed thoughtfully on each chair rustled as people extracted their contents.

"She knew what needed fixing in this state and was unafraid to call out those who stood in the way of our citizens' needs," he said, his glance flicking the man who'd defeated him in the last election. Rumors ran rampant that the two would face off again, this time with a U.S. Senate seat as a prize, and Julia took his remarks to be a warm-up of sorts for his pending stump speech.

Likewise with Li'l Pecker, who rose to tout Harper's accomplishments and point out that the justice system reforms she sought would actually reduce crime—exactly the sort of thing a man planning to run for judge would say.

So it went as speaker after speaker rose, somber-faced legislators slyly scoring political points over a body not a week cold. Julia imagined Harper would arrive in her grave already spinning.

People began to fidget. Julia guessed she wasn't the only one who found the predictable posturing tedious. A couple of sheriff's deputies in the row in front of her stifled yawns. Another, the department's lone woman, sat apart from them, blinking repeatedly as though trying to force back tears. Julie hoped she'd be successful. Being the only woman was bad enough, but crying would set the timetable for hiring the next woman back a good five years.

She shifted from side to side until she found an angle that gave her a view of Claudette, several rows ahead. She could tell by the set of Claudette's jaw and the barely concealed quiver of her ramrod posture that she seethed with fury at the deepening pool of political pablum.

Julia wondered whether Claudette, too, would succumb to the opportunity to subtly remind people of the advantages of having a prosecutor who hewed to Leslie Harper's vision. Or would she let loose with the tongue-lashing so clearly seeking release?

But Claudette sat still as carved marble when the legislative aide tasked with keeping things on track asked if anyone else wanted to speak, and people had begun to stir in their seats when a woman in the front row rose and spun on a pointy-toed pump to face the packed room.

Her ash-blond hair—the color that women of means adopted when they went gray—was pulled back in a true chignon, not the messy bun that Julia sometimes attempted, and she wore a black suit dress cut so expertly it managed to look both dignified and chic.

Julia assessed the hair, the clothing, the understated gold at her earlobes and wrists, and sized her up as Not From Around Here. Informality reigned in the mountain West, even in courtrooms, where lawyers got away with blazers rather than full suits and the best restaurants saw jeans as acceptable attire. The suits many people wore today had the hastily steamed appearance of being retrieved from the backs of closets. A faint odor of mothballs hung in the air.

"Ma'am." The aide gestured toward the podium. She waved him off.

"I'm Leslie Harper's sister," she said, her voice cracking, but nonetheless strong enough that even Julia, squirreled away in the rear of the vast room, could hear. Julia half rose from her seat, trying to find a resemblance between this woman, so sleek and polished, and Harper, who'd settled into the aging hippie look favored by so many women in Duck Creek, her silver hair as long and flowing as her swirling skirts.

The woman lifted her chin and fixed a severe eye on those before her, and finally Julia saw the resemblance: just as Harper herself, this woman was accustomed to commanding attention.

"My sister hated injustice, as many of you have so boldly noted."

Ouch. Even some of the Republicans had trotted out that line, although only the Democrats had continued with details.

"So let's talk about the elephant in the room."

Several people looked around, as though expecting to see an actual elephant, trunk high, testing the trepidation in the air. The aide cleared his throat and made a vague gesture, one that someone else might have interpreted as a hint to dial it down. Leslie Harper's sister ramped it up.

"Let's talk about the real injustice: the fact that my sister's death is being portrayed as some kind of tragic accident. Let me be clear. My sister was focused on the future, *her* future, the people's future. There have been suggestions—oh, yes, I've heard them—that she was discouraged by the change in administration, in this state's priorities."

The look she shot at the governor would have shriveled even a stronger man in his shorts.

"Nothing could be further from the truth. Leslie relished nothing so much as a good fight, and she saw this as the fight of her life. So why would she walk away from it? I leave you with that question. I hope to have an answer. Soon."

And with that, she strode up the center aisle and through the double doors, letting them bang shut behind her.

The room buzzed with equal parts shock and outrage, along with a tinge of admiration. Julia wondered if everyone else had correctly interpreted the message that—to her ears—Harper's sister had delivered as clearly as a clanging cathedral bell.

If Leslie Harper hadn't died of an accidental overdose of pills and alcohol, if she hadn't killed herself, then that left only one explanation:

She'd been murdered.

J ULIA COULDN'T BRING herself to go back to the office after the
funeral and confront Marie's moon-faced stare, the tinge of dis-
dain in the young woman's voice.

Instead—in the interest of researching the case, she told herself—
she headed for the scene of the crime.

The creek that gave the town its name ran just two blocks from
the courthouse, dividing the town's business district from its residen-
tial streets. Paved paths lined either bank, populated during Duck
Creek's achingly brief and beautiful summers with runners, cyclists,
walkers, and the town's ubiquitous Labrador retrievers bounding
sopping and ecstatic from path to creek and back again.

In winter, though, the creek froze in varying degrees of thickness, icy water running fast and black just below its treacherous surface, waiting to grab the foolhardy and pull them to their mercifully
quick deaths. The creek's high banks also formed a sort of wind
tunnel, and winter gales screamed out of the mountains and along its
surface, chivying the runners and cyclists into more sheltered areas.

The now-deserted path ran between the creek and the high
school, and Julia had been in the habit, since she'd started seeing
Dom, of waving toward his office window whenever she passed. If he
saw her and he had a break in the myriad tasks that made up a principal's day, he'd duck out and join her for a few minutes along the path.

They'd rarely speak during those brief walks, preferring to take
in the beauty of the creek, which attracted great blue herons, ospreys

swooping away with fish in their talons, chattering mallards, and fat beavers who attempted to dam the creek no matter how many times wildlife officers live-trapped them and moved them to the next county. An occasional bald eagle soared arrogantly above it all, hovering for long moments as though to invite admiration.

Today she didn't wave—too soon, far too soon, to be able to face Dom again—but he must have glimpsed her through a window, because a moment later she glanced up to see him heading her way at a dead run.

"Julia!"

She waited, staring at her feet. The last time she'd seen him, he'd been clutching a sheet around his body, stumbling over the trailing fabric as he followed Elena back down the hallway, shouting his daughter's name, much as he was calling now for Julia. At least this time he was dressed, albeit coatless in the biting chill.

He stood before her, gasping, a hand pressed to his side.

"Dom, I—" She stopped. What in the world did one say under these circumstances? *So sorry your daughter saw us fucking like bunnies and is probably scarred for life as a result*? As though it were Julia's fault. As though it were anyone's fault.

But what Dom said next was very much someone's fault.

"Susan just called."

Susan Parrish was Peak County's former lead prosecutor, who'd resigned after Julia had humiliated her by providing proof without a doubt that Susan had bungled a big case. She was also Dom's ex-wife.

Susan had moved to the university town in the next county, which as far as Julia was concerned was entirely too close, given her sworn enmity.

"Oh no. Please tell me she doesn't know about this."

He didn't, glossing over the obvious and going straight to something even worse: that Susan had swooped into Duck Creek at nearly midnight after a tearful phone call from his daughter.

"She's keeping Elena there. She's already enrolled her in school, or at least started the process. And Julia." His breath came ragged. His eyes shone with moisture, possibly due to the bitter wind, but his next words made the cold and wind seem inconsequential.

"She's suing me for full custody. Said Elena wants it and that she's of an age to choose."

Julia moved toward him at last, her arms wide, wanting to fold him in them, lend him her strength, whatever comfort she could.

But he backed away, shaking his head.

"No. I'm going to fight this. And if I'm to have any chance of winning, we can't see each other, at least not until it's over. I'm sorry, Julia. But for now, we're done."

8

JULIA STUMBLED DOWN the path toward the crime scene, barely able to focus on her original purpose.

Done?

Her mind seized on the words "for now," clung to them, massaged them, inflated them to outsize importance. He was upset, as well he should be. She tried to imagine anyone attempting to take her son Calvin away from her, and even that farfetched scenario made her heart race, her breath come short.

If staying apart—for now—would foil Susan's little revenge plot, then so be it.

Newly resolute, she turned her thoughts to the creekside death that had somehow been pinned on Ray. The walking path petered out toward the edge of town, the creek turning wilder there, running faster, its banks thick with brush. Duck Creek's small year-round homeless population lived there, in everything from tarps strung between bushes to semipermanent structures banged together from construction pallets.

But only the hardiest exercise enthusiasts used the walking paths in the winter, and the camp's denizens crept closer then, preferring to be near downtown with its abundance of bars, steam vents, and sheltered doorways. At night they built fires in oil drums along the creek, and as Julia walked home from the courthouse each evening, she saw their wavering light like hopeful beacons amid the darkness.

She knew better than to visit their hangouts at night. By then, many would have been drinking for hours and turned surly. Or, if they used, they might be coming down and looking for easy money for their next hit and not shy about what they had to do to get it. Even in the middle of the day, in the middle of town, the creek banks bore hints of desperate lives—a torn and stained sleeping bag stowed deep beneath a winter-bare bush, a crushed Styrofoam fast-food container, a scrap of toilet paper fluttering in the wind—just a few feet from the path.

The spot where Ray's supposed victim had met his demise was easy enough to find, a large trampled patch in the snow a few yards from one of the blackened oil drums, in a thicket of willows. The curious had already been and gone. A supermarket bouquet lay frozen in the snow, along with a couple of hand-lettered signs on torn pieces of cardboard. *We love you, Billy. RIP.*

Duck Creek's transient population swelled in the summer months, but in winters it shrank to a core group, one whose frequent squabbles led to the court appearances that crammed Julia's schedule but who remained fiercely protective of their own when confronted by outsiders.

A bit of blood, preserved bright red rather than drying black as it would have in summer, splashed the snow—an irresistible image already displayed in the morning paper and used as B-roll in the television stories about the slaying.

Julia closed her eyes against Duck Creek's cut-glass winter brilliance and tried to imagine the scene. The crackling fire, never quite warm enough. Mingled scents of woodsmoke and cheap booze and unwashed bodies. Booted feet shuffling in the snow, gloved hands pounded together, ungloved ones pulled up into sleeves. Laughter, maybe; curses, certainly. An argument—something stupid. An accidental jostling, booze spilled. An insult, a jeer. Somehow escalating into a beat-down that killed a man.

She couldn't see it. She opened her eyes.

A deputy sheriff stood a few feet away.

Julia jumped. "Jesus. You scared the crap out of me. How'd you sneak up on me like that?"

"I stuck to the path." The vehicle and foot traffic associated with the investigation had cleared the walking trail of snow, which squeaked underfoot in Duck Creek's dry cold.

Julia crunched her way back across the trampled snow to the trail, yanked off a glove, and extended a hand.

"Julia Geary. I don't think we've ever formally met."

"Cheryl Hayes. I know who you are."

Julia knew who she was too. She'd just seen her at the funeral, the department's lone woman deputy, something trumpeted with great fanfare when she'd been hired a couple of years earlier. Her handshake was perfunctory, and Julia sized her up as another law enforcement official who considered public defenders an unnecessary speed bump on the road to justice.

Hayes pulled her own glove back on and nodded toward the signs. "Did you know Billy?"

Julia didn't want to admit that she didn't even remember Billy's last name from the affidavit. She shook her head. "You?"

Hayes surprised her by saying yes. "Nice guy. Big guy. Takes a lot to kill someone that size. He must have died hard."

"How'd you know him?"

Julia expected Hayes to say that she knew Billy the same way Julia knew Ray—a series of arrests for petty crimes. But Hayes surprised her again.

"I know most of these guys—the locals, anyway. I make the rounds, bring them coffee, hang out a while." A wry smile. "My own version of community policing. Last I checked, the community was more than the downtown and your neighborhood."

So the woman knew where she lived. Or maybe she'd just made an educated guess. Julia's clothes—the Sorels, the hooded down parka, the windproof mittens with the fleece glove liners, all combining to make Duck Creek's arctic winters almost bearable—were nobody's idea of stylish, but their total cost would have fed the camp's denizens for weeks.

Something in the woman's demeanor reminded Julia of her new intern. Maybe it was the implied judgment when Marie learned Julia had never handled a murder trial, and now this woman flaunting her knowledge about the victim.

Julia knew that no matter what kind of man Billy had been—simply a stumbling drunk, or a raging child molester—Claudette would confer a sort of sainthood upon him, the better to turn a jury's head.

She'd have to do the same for Ray. And, conversely, demonize Billy, whoever the hell he was. Time for her to find out—and she was pretty sure Deputy Cheryl Hayes would be disinclined to help.

"Nice meeting you." She edged away.

A few yards down the trail, she glanced back just in time to see Hayes drop to her knees beside the blotch of blood and place a hand gently on the snowbank beside it.

*   *   *

Hayes's colleague Wayne Peterson fell in beside Julia as she pushed through the back door of the courthouse. The sheriff's office was in the rear of the building, as was a coffee cart to which Julia sometimes resorted when she didn't have time to make a run to Colombia.

The coffee wasn't nearly as good as Colombia's roasted-on-premises blends, but it was several steps above the pale brew concocted every morning by Deb, who resisted even the most tactful suggestions aimed at improvement.

"Hey, Wayne. Quad-shot vanilla cappuccino as usual? I'm buying."

"Can't turn that down. How is it out there?"

"Sun's nice. If we're lucky, we'll get out of single digits today. But I'll take the cold over the inversions any day."

The hills surrounding Duck Creek had a way of trapping impenetrable warm layers of cloud above cold air, resulting in endless days of gray that saw irritability climb and in turn overloaded Julia's schedule with people booked for domestic disputes, bar brawls, and all-around bad behavior.

"I'll drink to that."

He lounged against the counter, his dark-brown pants and khaki shirt freshly pressed, the gold threads in the seven-pointed star on his shirt sleeve patch glinting in the overhead fluorescent lights.

Julia ordered his syrupy concoction as well as her own oat-milk latte. "Not on patrol today?"

The territory under the sheriff's office included the county's far reaches, deep into the canyons that sheltered those who sought solitude for reasons both benign and scarily malignant. When it was Wayne's turn to patrol there, he suited up as though for an arctic expedition in snowpack boots, a hooded parka that reached nearly to his knees, a fleece neck gaiter that could be pulled up beneath his eyes, and clumsy snowmobilers' mittens. Even the sheriff's department's most rugged SUV—where he stowed snowshoes and an avalanche shovel—was no match for some of the places where the scattered residents managed to find enough of a cell signal to make the occasional 911 call. If the SUV broke down—or, more likely, slid off the road despite studded snow tires and sometimes even chains— in the middle of the night in the middle of winter, he was in for a long, cold wait before help arrived. People froze to death every winter in and around Duck Creek. Wayne wasn't going to be one of them.

"Paperwork day," he said. "Unless, God forbid, something happens." He knocked the faux-wooden counter just in case.

Julia handed him his drink and waited until he'd taken an appreciative sip before launching.

"What the hell, Wayne? How'd this end up getting pinned on Ray? The guy's a world-class screw-up, but he wouldn't hurt a fly."

The foamed-milk mustache on Wayne's upper lip undercut the intended effect of his glare. "Should've known you were bribing me with the coffee. You know I can't talk about an ongoing case."

"Please. Half the courthouse is talking about this case."

"Not as much as they're talking about Leslie Harper."

Fair enough.

Even though Harper's death was largely considered an unfortunate accident, she had the benefit of social prominence and thus public fascination, especially after her sister's broadside at the funeral. By comparison, a fatal fight between a couple of Duck Creek's "gentlemen of leisure," as Wayne referred to the denizens of the creek-side camps, hardly had the same sizzle.

"My guess on Ray's case?" Wayne licked his lip and took another drink. A snowy new mustache appeared.

Julia looked away, fighting a smile.

"It's just what it looks like. Both of them drunk. Maybe Ray hit our vic just right. Lucky—well, unlucky—accident."

"*Vic.* You sound like my new intern. What's the deal with her, anyway?"

Wayne took a sudden interest in the contents of his cup, removing the lid and peering into it. "Aw." He shook the cup and addressed the dregs within. "She's a sweet kid. Smart. She'd have made a great cop but for some reason decided on law school." He hacked up a laugh.

Julia peered at him, but he refused to meet her gaze. A flush pinked his ears.

"Wayne? Oh no. Tell me you didn't."

Wayne, like a lot of guys on the force, had more than one divorce under his belt and grabbed overtime shifts whenever possible to keep up with his alimony and child-support payments. Julia imagined the ride-alongs with Marie, miles alone in his patrol car together, the impressionable young woman, the whole man-in-uniform thing.

"Jesus, Julia! Of course not. What do you think I am?"

Julia finished her own coffee, crumpled the cup, and aced a rim shot off a hallway trash can.

"I think you're a normal testosterone-addled guy is what I think." Maybe nothing had happened, but she'd bet her measly public defender salary that Wayne had entertained the notion.

"About Ray," he said.

Under the circumstances, Julia granted him the change of subject.

"I know he's been sort of a pet project of yours."

Julia started to object, then stopped. He was right.

"Everybody's got that client," Claudette had warned her when they first started working together. "They look at you with the big goo-goo eyes and tell you they're innocent, or they've been abused—which they probably were—and that they're going to change, which they actually mean when they say it. We're usually too smart to fall for it. Because let's face it, most of our clients are guilty. Our job is to see them treated fairly by the courts, which is a lot tougher than it ought to be.

"But when you find yourself falling for someone's bullshit, watch out. Time to kick the case over to someone else. Because when that happens, when you start turning yourself into a pretzel, going way overboard in terms of a defense, good prosecutors will tear you apart and smile while they're doing it. You don't do your clients any favors when you get too close to them. Don't be that idiot."

Julia had sworn she wouldn't. But now here was Wayne, accusing her of being exactly that idiot. Her turn to change the subject.

"I met one of the new deputies down at the scene. Cheryl Hayes."

Wayne's affable demeanor vanished. Cops, Julia thought. They all had that ability. Your best buddy one minute and *Just the facts, ma'am, and you have the right to remain silent* the next. She supposed it was necessary in their line of work.

"Sorry to hear that."

"What do you mean?"

His lips tightened. He shook his head. "Talk to her long?"

"Just a couple of minutes. Why?"

"No reason." He started to walk away.

She grabbed his arm. He spun and faced her with a *Don't fuck with me* look that she supposed was another of those second-nature skills.

"Whoa." She let go and held up her hands. "Sorry. It's just— you wouldn't believe the crap that's rained down on me in the last twenty-four hours. If there's something I need to know about Hayes, tell me."

"Can't talk about the case."

"Goddammit, Wayne."

It was their familiar push-pull dynamic, her coming at him from various angles, trying to find out more about whatever case she was working, knowing from the start it was hopeless but trying anyway.

Usually he strung her along, feeding her useless tidbits before turning away with a *Gotcha* grin.

But this time, the grim lines in his face only deepened.

"If you're on this case, you'll find out soon enough. Just don't say you weren't warned."

9

JULIA KEPT FORGETTING about Marie.

But when she pushed open her office door, there was her new intern, hunched over a mess of papers on her desk that destroyed the military precision of its original arrangement.

"Hey." Marie held up a legal pad covered with scrawled notes. "I pulled the jackets on both the perp and the vic."

Julia took her time removing her coat, stuffing the mittens in a sleeve, and stepping out of her boots and into the clogs she kept for working indoors. The files that Marie had taken from Julia's cabinet remained untouched on Julia's desk. Marie's own files appeared to be stuffed into a couple of cardboard bankers boxes resting precariously on the shelf that had once contained Claudette's law books.

Julia took a breath of very warm air. The ancient and unreliable heating system in the courthouse periodically kicked into overdrive, pushing the temperature toward eighty and tormenting people still bundled in winter clothing. This was one of those days.

"For God's sake, drop the cop talk. For starters, you just convicted Mr. Belmar." She emphasized the *mister*, then decided subtlety was probably lost on Marie. "We refer to all of our clients by honorific, as we do anyone else involved in the proceedings. Respect matters. Mr. Belmar is not a perp—no one is, unless and until they're convicted—he's the accused. And Mr. . . . . ah, Billy . . . if this were a regular assault case, we'd refer to him as the accuser, not the victim, so as not to build sympathy for him with a jury. But since he's dead, we'll just call him by name every time. Respectfully."

Marie made a note on her pad and for good measure read it aloud. "Always refer to victim as Mr. Williams."

Julia forgot she didn't want anyone to know that she'd never even learned Billy's last name. "His name was William Williams?"

Marie smirked. Busted. "Appears so. And Mr. Belmar was really wasted. Point three oh."

Julia shed her blazer. Her blouse stuck to her skin. She was glad she'd worn black, so at least the damp patches wouldn't show.

"Pretty sure that's a typo."

Marie shook her head. "It's not. I called to make sure."

Julia sat down hard. "You're kidding. That must have been one mighty tumble off the wagon. And that blood test wouldn't have been done until after they arrested him at the courthouse. It would have been a lot higher earlier. It's a wonder he's not dead."

The corners of Marie's pale lips twitched.

"It's a wonder," she echoed, "that someone so blind drunk could manage to get in a single punch, let alone beat somebody to death."

Their eyes met.

So there, said Marie's.

Julia jerked her head toward the boxes on the bookshelf, then pointed to a corner of the room.

"Claudette used to keep a birdcage there. She had a canary, name of Pavarotti. Never mind about him. There's just enough room there for a file cabinet. I'll show you the stash in the basement. If you try to requisition one from Deb, you'll be out of law school and on to your third job before she comes through. You'll have to move it up here yourself after hours. It won't be pretty—you'll be lucky if the drawers work—but it's a step up from a cardboard box."

*   *   *

Tim Saunders, aka Adonis, strode through the halls of the Peak County Courthouse like a conquering hero.

Which he was, given his success rate in defending the wealthy among Duck Creek's drunk drivers, bar brawlers, wife beaters and—by far the most common among his particular clientele—tax cheats and swindlers.

Also, if Deb's always annoying but usually reliable gossip were to be believed, he'd conquered half the women who worked in the courthouse, all of them envied by the other half. Or the other 49.9 percent. Julia counted herself among the vanishing minority of those who remained unswayed by the abundance of chestnut hair that fell in a curl over his forehead (a dab of mousse would have kept it in place, albeit ruining the winsome effect, she thought whenever she saw him), the Kennedyesque dentition (really, he'd gone overboard on the whitening), the shoulders that strained at his Italian-cut blazers (how'd a soon-to-be partner manage to spend that much time in the gym?), and oh, that ass. At which even Julia had sneaked the occasional admiring glance.

But her icy heart refused to melt when he stood in her doorway and threw his most disarming grin her way. All those damn teeth. If she'd had sunglasses at the ready, she'd have put them on.

"So you're the famous Julia Geary."

Not working, pal. She granted him a frosty nod.

He waited a beat and flashed his teeth at Marie.

"And you must be . . ."

Somewhere, Marie had scrounged up a nameplate for her desk. Julia suspected she'd gone to the local office supply store and had it made up herself. Now she simply pointed to it, no more vocal than Julia had been. Julia resisted the impulse to raise her opinion of Marie a millimeter.

"I didn't realize Bill had hired a new public defender. Good for him. You guys are way too overworked."

"Marie's an intern." Julia wondered why the statement felt so defensive.

"Oh, good. Because I was wondering where I'd work, given the size of this office. But Marie can relocate for the length of this case. Don't worry, Marie. It shouldn't take long. I'll get him to plead to negligent homicide, and you two can go back to the necessary and noble work of defending the indigent."

He said it with a straight face, looking each of them in turn in the eye, his voice oozing sincerity. So why did Julia feel as though she'd just been slapped?

I'LL get him to plead . . .

That's why.

"You're right." Julia spoke through lips gone stiff. "There's barely enough room in this office for two people to work. Talk to Deb. Our receptionist."

"Oh, I know Deb," Tim interrupted.

Dear God. Had he slept with her too? Julia would have a very, very hard time erasing that particular image from her mind. She wondered what tidbits of gossip Deb had gleaned during their pillow talk. She shook her head, hard. "I'm sure Deb knows of a vacant office somewhere in this place. She'll set you up."

"Fine. But." He turned to Marie and cranked the charm up to high, positioning one superb ass cheek on her desk and leaning toward her. "I'll want you to work closely with me on this. I can't imagine a better learning experience. As soon as I get settled, I'll let you know where I am."

And then, but for a trace of woodsy aftershave, he was gone.

Marie breathed a single word, and Julia experienced another split-second thaw toward her unsought intern.

"Dick."

"What did you just say?"

But Marie turned to her with cold eyes—"Nothing"—and Julia decided she must have been mistaken.

10

PROBLEM WAS, TIM was right.

The best-case scenario, and the traditional route in such a case, would be for Ray to plead guilty to an amended charge, in this case negligent homicide, which carried a maximum twenty-year sentence as opposed to the possibility of life in prison or even death that would accompany a deliberate homicide conviction.

Claudette had been smart enough not to slap Ray with the most serious charge. That would have required premeditation, which would have been more difficult to prove and also would have carried the possibility of the death penalty, an administrative nightmare reserved only for the cases likely to provoke the most outrage. Instead, she'd gone for a mitigated homicide charge, which still allowed for the wiggle room of accepting a plea agreement to negligent homicide.

Until St. Patrick's Day, Julia told Marie in response to the intern's relentless probing the day after Adonis was added to the team she'd never sought, Ray's saving grace was that nobody gave a shit about him.

"We'd have been even better off if he hadn't pulled that little stunt at the parade. Now everybody knows who he is. He sure didn't count on the Rotarians stomping him the way they did. But people will forget about that part. All they'll imagine is some big scary naked dude—nearly naked dude—cavorting among a bunch of community leaders."

Marie picked up a pen and bit the end of it. "What about a change of venue?"

"We'll ask. In fact, why don't you draw up the request? I'll review it when you're done."

Throwing her a bone, one that had no chance of success. Julia couldn't remember the last change of venue in Duck Creek, even in cases that had raised the community blood pressure far more than one involving a couple of transients slugging it out by the creek. But at least it would keep Marie busy and off her back for a little while.

Fat chance.

Marie chomped down on her pen again, so hard Julia feared she'd end up with a mouthful of ink. "Another thing. Is the medical examiner's report back yet? Because what if it shows the vic—uh, Mr. Williams—just slipped on the ice and hit his head?"

Checking with the medical examiner was on Julia's list. She just hadn't gotten around to it yet. "I've already got a call in to her office." She rose and reached for her coat. "In fact—" She started to declare her intention to visit the medical examiner in person but realized Marie would probably just invite herself along. "I'll check back after I make a coffee run."

She edged out the door, ignoring Marie's pointed look at the half-full cup from the coffee cart sitting on her desk.

When she and Claudette had shared the office, they'd had an understanding that whoever made a coffee run would always bring back a cup for the other.

She didn't ask whether Marie wanted some.

*　*　*

The crime lab shared space in an office complex located conveniently near the jail. Its nondescript beige buildings also housed bail bondsmen, a title search business, a mediocre takeout restaurant catering to the office workers, and the county Motor Vehicle Division, whose long-suffering clients, Julia often thought, were only slightly less miserable than the inhabitants of the medical examiner's cold-storage compartments.

"I've got the report on William Williams right here," Dr. Amanda Pinkham said in response to Julia's query. She tapped a few computer keys, and a printer whirred into action. "You want to see him?"

Despite her cheery, pastel-hued name, Pinkham dressed the part of someone who spent her day digging around in dead bodies, her white lab coat thrown over an all-black wardrobe.

Julia wondered if Pinkham had adopted the look that had earned her the nickname Morticia as a defense against the inevitable. She suspected the hair piled high on Pinkham's head owed its raven sheen to a bottle and wondered how Pinkham managed to don her surgical gloves without tearing through them with her long, ebony-painted nails. She took what felt to Julia like an unseemly enjoyment in showing police and the occasional attorney the actual basis for her reports, leading them into the morgue and pointing out proof of, say, suicide versus homicide.

"He didn't leave a note, but nobody pushed this gentleman from the top of the Orpheum Theatre," she'd explained once as Julia looked queasily away from the broken body on the table. The Orpheum's owner had been in a long-running and very public dispute with the owner of the neighboring property, a tech entrepreneur who'd wanted to buy the old theater and tear it down in order to put up the sort of high-end condos his high-paid employees could afford.

The two men had had such a violent street-corner quarrel the day before the theater owner took his midnight swan dive from the roof that the neighbor had been arrested in connection with his death, only to be released when Pinkham rendered her report.

"Look." She'd shown Julia a pair of wire-frame glasses, their ear-pieces neatly folded, on a nearby table. "The cops found those on the roof. Murderers don't bother to remove someone's glasses."

Julia apparently had passed some sort of test that day, because Pinkham didn't make her usual offer of showing her a fresh cadaver. Julia couldn't really fault the medical examiner for trying. Pinkham was justifiably proud of her work—her results had stood up to the most determined court challenges—and like any other professional at the top of her game, she liked to show off from time to time.

"Here." Pinkham paper-clipped the report and handed it to Julia.

"Any chance it was accidental? Ray Belmar was really, really drunk. I can't imagine he could even connect a punch, let alone hit someone hard enough to kill him."

"I read the arrest report. And I had the same thought. But if you could see the injury to Mr. Williams' head . . ." She left it at that, inviting Julia to say that yes, she'd very much like to see it.

Julia would not.

"What kind of injury?"

Julia tried to tune out Pinkham's recap, but her mind caught on words and phrases like "shattered" and "deep" and "maceration of the brain."

"My guess? Something heavy and metal. A tire iron, maybe, given that the wound was elongated rather than smaller, as it would have been if caused by a hammer."

Julia held up her hand. "Enough. But two things: Nothing like that was found at the scene."

"Correct."

"Whatever it was is probably sitting at the bottom of the creek, and the hole in the ice is already frozen over."

Pinkham didn't bother to respond. Speculation was not part of her makeup.

"Anyway, my initial qualm remains. Ray's a little guy. A little, very drunk guy. I can't imagine him wielding a tire iron any more effectively than swinging a fist."

Pinkham finally weighed in. "If he'd been coked out, or flying on meth, the superhuman-strength theory would apply. But there's a reason they call it stumbling drunk."

"Pretty sure he was on something." Julia thought again of the tiny bruise on Ray's inner arm. "The affidavit didn't mention anything other than booze in the blood draw. Know if they checked for anything else?"

"Not my area of expertise."

Pinkham grinned at Julia's startled look. "Land of the living," she said. "I don't check that stuff until they're cold."

"Of course. But speaking of the dead, I saw you at Leslie Harper's memorial service. What's the deal with her?" Maybe she could ferret out a scrap of information from Pinkham and pass it along to Wayne Peterson, trade it for something that might help Ray.

"You want to know if it was suicide. So does everyone else. That reporter, Chance Larsen, he's called me every day. I'll tell you the same thing I've told him. I'm checking a couple of things. If there's any update, you and the rest of the world will know at the same time, when I release my report."

To her credit, Pinkham was known for not playing favorites in terms of doling out information, something Julia usually respected—unless she was the one seeking the information.

"She just didn't seem the type to kill herself." Harper frequently breezed into the courthouse to pick the public defenders' brains before drawing up legislation. She knew everyone, down to the bailiffs and custodial staff, and her booming voice preceded her as she called greetings along her route. Unlike the courthouse regulars who tended toward dark blazers or the starched uniforms of law enforcement, Harper favored flowing dresses in neon colors accessorized with fringed scarves and jangly bracelets that crowded her arm nearly to the elbow. She called everybody "darling," even and especially those with whom she was at odds—usually the prosecutors—and rarely showed up without tins of still-warm oatmeal cookies. She'd been one of the few people from whom Julia welcomed a hug.

"She was so full of life. Suicide just doesn't make sense."

"You'd be surprised." Pinkham loved proving people wrong. "I sometimes think of these sorts of deaths as unintentional suicide. She lived alone. Never married, no kids. Sometimes, no matter what kind of public face they put on things, people who live alone get too sad. Men, they eat a gun. Women sit around at night and cry into too many glasses of wine and then take pills when they can't sleep. Sometimes it goes south. They fall asleep in the tub and drown, or in bed and don't wake up. Or, they slip and hit their head. In this case, there was blood on the kitchen counter."

She arched a severely drawn eyebrow. "And she'd really been putting it away. Her alcohol level was off the charts. Well, nearly," added Pinkham, a stickler for precision.

"She was a large woman. Stands to reason she drank the way she ate."

Pinkham looked around and lowered her voice, as though even the corpses had ears. "Did you ever know her to partake in something stronger?"

"Like weed? She strikes me as one of those old potheads who probably still fired up. But then, you could say that about half the county."

"No." Pinkham's voice went lower still. Julia had to lean in. "The hard stuff."

Julia wasn't quite sure what the hard stuff was, but she doubted Harper had been a druggie and said so. Harper had managed to wrangle the conservatives who dominated Peak County's legislative delegation into supporting some of her more liberal bills. "She'd never have been so effective if she was any kind of a user. Why? Was there more in her system than booze?"

Pinkham pursed her lips and shook her head. "No. Just wondered. Something I heard, maybe." Which might have been true or might just be a diversionary tactic on Pinkham's part.

"I never heard anything to that effect, and God knows, in that courthouse you eventually hear everything about everyone."

Pinkham cast a look over her shoulder, clearly longing to get back to her beloved cadavers.

Julia took the hint. "Thanks for this." She spindled the report and saluted Pinkham with it.

Pinkham tucked a stray strand behind her ear and gave her a tight smile.

"Good luck with this case. You're going to need it. Oh, as to the official cause of Harper's death?"

Julia stopped. Was Pinkham really about to give her some inside information?

But no.

"Make sure you're not busy at around four PM. I expect to send over my report then."

11

Julia lurked outside the entrance to the public defenders' office until she saw Deb take a call.

Moving fast, head down, she hurried through the reception area and toward the hallway leading to her own office.

But Deb was a pro. She put her hand over the phone and snapped her fingers a la the rudest of customers summoning a hapless server. "Julia!"

Julia assembled a smile before she turned.

"George just went home," Deb said of one of the other assistant public defenders. "Sick kid."

Spoken with the same disapproval so often directed Julia's way for the audacity to have a child, the biggest disadvantage to anyone serious about her (George notwithstanding, it was usually a *her*) career. Kids distracted from the Almighty Job, with their annoying tendencies to fall ill, have demanding school schedules, and call at all hours with all manner of emergencies demanding immediate attention.

"You'll have to do his initial appearances. He's done the interviews and left you his notes. I put the files on your desk."

Because no one else in the office could take his cases? Julia had given up wondering how she'd gotten on Deb's bad side. She'd whiled away more than one insomniac night on elaborate revenge fantasies, all of which ended with Deb being replaced by someone who knew how to make something stronger than dirty dishwater in the office coffeepot.

She looked at the clock. The initial court appearances, held for people who'd been arrested the day before, would start in five minutes. She ran down the hall, grabbed the files without looking at them, and made it into the courtroom just as the justice of the peace stepped up to the bench.

The prosecutor for the day, a new hire, looked Julia's way as she rose in response to the judge's appearance. "Where's George?" she mouthed.

"Sick," Julia whispered. For all her displeasure at the extra work forced upon her, she took small satisfaction in the concern flitting across the young woman's face. Julia had a newly formidable reputation as a result of her earlier success, something that had yet to translate to a raise even though Decker reassured her, as he had for months, that one was in the works.

The judge rapped her gavel. "Be seated."

Julia looked over her shoulder into the gallery and did a double take at the sight of Deputy Sheriff Cheryl Hayes. It was not unusual to see law enforcement officers in the courtroom during trials, either after they'd testified or in support of a fellow officer called as a witness. But initial appearances were quick, pro forma events. Maybe Hayes was just refreshing her memory on court procedure. Julia shrugged and scanned the rest of the room.

Chance Larsen lounged in the back row, tapping away at his laptop. The newspaper's offices were several blocks away, and sometimes, rather than going back to the office to write his stories, he simply co-opted a spot in a courtroom where little of interest was expected.

Chance looked up, met her gaze, and nodded a greeting, then looked beyond her. His eyes widened.

Julia followed his gaze to the first inmate being led through the door.

"Oh, *shit*," she breathed.

Mack Coates, a sinewy figure cloaked in jailhouse orange, fell into the chair beside her with a wide grin, the tip of his tongue massaging a scar that pulled a corner of his upper lip south.

"Hey, Thumbelina."

*   *   *

It was her nickname among the frequent fliers, an allusion to her diminutive size and also her seemingly magical abilities to wangle lower bail amounts or even to get defendants released on their own recognizance.

Mack, though, was one defendant she'd have been happy to let languish in jail forever.

It wasn't just his appearance, which at first glance was deceiving. Mack had the golden curls, soft cheeks, and plump lips of a cherub, and that face, along with his slender body, too often led people to near-fatal mistaken assumptions.

Julia, along with everyone else in the courthouse, knew the story about Mack's first stint in the Peak County Jail, when an Aryan Nations contingent awaiting sentencing for stomping a Hispanic tourist who'd walked into the wrong bar took one look and called first dibs. But when three of them cornered him in the shower, he spun quick and catlike toward them and, with a winsome smile and a shiv fashioned from a chicken bone, sliced their leader's face to the bone, molars showing between the flaps of bloody flesh.

The would-be assailants had failed to properly respect what was tantalizingly on display in the shower—the corded biceps, the enviable six-pack, the thighs and calves toned from years of martial arts. Given the ever-shifting jail population, new inmates could be forgiven their ignorance when Mack waltzed in for one of his many short stays, and similar scenes in varying degrees of severity played themselves out again and again, usually ending with Mack ambling away from a whimpering hot mess. Somewhere along the line, someone had inflicted a blow serious enough to cause the scar. It inevitably focused attention on his pillowy lips and distracted from his coiled, menacing quality, the elegant hands in permanent clench, the nearly lashless baby blues fixed in an unblinking stare.

He gave Julia the creeps in a way her more violent clients never had. During court appearances, she usually made sure to stand close to her clients, to touch their arm, lay a hand on their shoulder, demonstrating to all their worthiness. But she'd never once touched Mack and fought hard to keep from leaning away from him as he stood beside her.

Rumor had it he pimped a string of girls that he trucked over to the university town in the next county on football weekends to service the aging stalwarts in the booster club, but no one had been able to pin that on him.

His file rivaled Ray's in thickness, though it easily surpassed Ray's in terms of serious charges. But he always skated, never spending more than a few days in jail before witnesses shut up, evidence got misplaced, and the unseen hand of Satan intervened. That last being the only reason Julia could imagine that Mack hadn't ended up in the state prison long ago.

What was it this time?

She grabbed his file and checked. Surprise, surprise—promoting prostitution. She peeled a sticky note in George's crabbed, back-sloping handwriting from the page and deciphered it. No surprise there, either. The woman who'd reported Mack for pimping her out had told George she'd made the accusation in a fit of anger, she was withdrawing her complaint, and if he insisted upon pursuing the case, no way, no how would she testify against Mack.

"Your Honor," Julia sighed, and explained the situation, moving to drop the charge. She didn't have much choice, even though it meant she'd soon see Mack strolling through town like a solid citizen, turning that lopsided grin her way.

She heard the courtroom door open and close. She turned. Cheryl Hayes was gone. The bailiff approached to usher Mack away to fill out the necessary release paperwork. Give her Ray any day, she thought, smiling at the bailiff in relief. But Mack waved him off and bent to whisper in her ear. It was everything she could do not to flinch.

"This thing with Ray? Let him take the fall now before things get even worse for him. It's best for everyone."

His tongue emerged and flicked the scar.

Julia looked away. But his words stayed with her.

"For you most of all."

12

THE INITIAL HEARINGS dragged on until almost four. Julia's phone, off while she was in court, vibrated with a message as soon as she turned it on again.

Acting Peak County prosecutor Claudette Greene, along with the mayor and chief of police, had called a news conference for four PM sharp.

Julia slumped. Pinkham had promised her updated report on Leslie Harper's cause of death then, and she'd wanted to pore over it. But whatever Claudette was up to sounded important.

At least, thanks to the weather—the calendar finally said spring, but snow squalls made a mockery of that—the news conference would be held indoors, in the courthouse's vast and echoing rotunda.

Julia trudged down the grand curving staircase and joined the crowd already gathering. An elbow dug into her ribs.

"Do you know what this is about?"

Somehow Marie had gotten wind of the news conference. She bounced on the balls of her feet, betraying her excitement despite her habitual studied indifference.

"No idea. But if she's including the mayor and Chief McNulty, it's going to be quite the dog and pony show. We're about to find out. Here they come."

Claudette strode to the lectern that had been set up in the middle of the rotunda, the mayor and police chief scurrying like minions behind her. Julia looked up. The rotunda rose three stories, capped by the courthouse dome. A few curiosity seekers leaned against the polished brass second- and third-floor balustrades. They jumped when Claudette's voice boomed through the microphone, running through the de rigueur *Thank you for being here* remarks.

"I've asked our mayor and police chief to join me because of the seriousness of this matter and the importance to our community. I've just received an updated report from the medical examiner's office about the death of state representative Leslie Harper."

"Goddammit."

Marie turned to Julia in surprise. "Is that a bad thing?"

"No. It's just that . . . oh, never mind." Claudette had probably leaned hard on Pinkham to break her usual practice of not playing favorites, and when Claudette leaned, people tended to comply. Quickly. "Shhh. Whatever it is, here it comes."

"Representative Harper was found dead in the kitchen of her home on March fifteenth after failing to report to work. There were no signs of forced entry, and her death initially was thought to result from a tragic accident. The preliminary cause of death was listed as a head wound attributed to striking her head against the granite counter as she fell, causing a fatal hemorrhage."

Claudette tactfully omitted the alcohol and prescription sleep medication noted in the original report, something that could have contributed both to the original fall and to Harper's inability to rouse herself and call for help before she bled to death.

"But a subsequent examination by the medical examiner of the kitchen itself, made at my request"—nifty bit of grandstanding there, Julia thought—"revealed her discomfort with that initial assessment."

Julia cut her eyes to the police chief, who seemed to fold a bit farther into himself with every word Claudette spoke. The initial accidental death determination had come from the police.

"Dr. Pinkham remains unconvinced that Representative Harper could have fallen with such force against the counter to have caused the blow that killed her."

Claudette paused, her face set in grim lines.

"Because of this possibility, our law enforcement agencies will continue to pursue the possibility that Representative Harper's death may have been a homicide."

Even though her previous words had made it clear, a gasp ran through the crowd.

"The police will intensify their investigation—Chief McNulty will speak to that—and I want to assure this community that if this possibility is borne out, in order to bring justice to the family of Representative Harper and to ensure everyone's safety, my office will prosecute the perpetrator or perpetrators to the fullest extent of the law. Mr. Mayor?"

Julia ignored the mayor's blathering, which merely expanded upon Claudette's remarks about community safety. "Our police force has our utmost confidence . . ." That sort of thing.

But she perked up when Chief McNulty stepped to the mic, vowing to interview anyone recently convicted or even accused of a violent crime in Duck Creek, adding that the Peak County Sheriff's Office would assist in the investigation. "And," he said, "we'll be looking at associates of Representative Harper. To her credit, she worked on behalf of people many of us would consider unsavory."

By which, Julia assumed, he meant that *he* found them unsavory.

"Who knows how one of them might have taken offense at something she said or did? We intend to find out."

He was talking about people like Ray, Julia thought. Anyone other than a solid citizen would now become a suspect—even though people were usually killed by those close to them, which meant more than even odds one of those same solid citizens had killed Harper. Her heart dropped at the thought of the pending harassment of Duck Creek's less reputable citizens, many of them her clients.

And one of those clients, though now sitting in jail in connection with one of those deaths, had been a free man when Harper was killed. She pushed the thought away as soon as it arose.

But Chance Larsen had had the same thought. His hand shot up.

"Chief McNulty? Duck Creek hasn't seen a homicide in five years. Now we have two in the space of a week, with both victims—while vastly dissimilar in all other respects—suffering head injuries. Is it possible the same person killed them both?"

No, Julia thought. It was not.

"Of course," McNulty said. "It's a possibility we'll examine very carefully."

At his words, Julia wrapped her arms around herself as though someone had flung up the courthouse's double doors, letting in great gusts of snow and frigid air.

CHAPTER

13

JULIA DRAGGED HERSELF from the courthouse at the dot of five.

Usually she worked late, calculating to the minute the time it would take to race to her son's after-school program before it closed for the day at six. Parents who arrived after that were fined increasing amounts for every fifteen-minute increment of lateness. Julia had enriched the program's coffers considerably.

Her mother-in-law, whose home she shared, was a big help with Calvin, but understandably drew the line at school pickups and drop-offs except in emergencies. The day had dumped a shitstorm of particular pungency upon Julia, but she doubted Beverly Sullivan would see it as a catastrophe deserving of a break in her routine.

Only a few weeks earlier, Julia's workdays had ended in full darkness, the streetlamps casting bright circles onto the snow, the blackness beyond somehow more ominous by contrast. But now stars were only just emerging in a still-blue sky that teased her with the promise of spring, cruelly undercut by the lingering, record-setting cold.

She glanced toward the river. A tiny orange light flashed and wavered, revealing itself after a moment's determined squint as an oil drum fire. She looked back at the courthouse clock tower. She had nearly an hour before the after-school program for Calvin's kindergarten ended.

Halfway down the block, she ducked into the business district's lone liquor store, tolerated by the Chamber of Commerce because it also sold artisan breads and cheeses featured in weekly wine pairings along with a selection of high-end single-malt Scotch that lived behind lock and key.

But the proprietors, cognizant of their proximity to the creekside habitués, also stocked the cheapest rotgut available on a shelf by the cash register to discourage the light-fingered tendencies of that clientele. Julia brushed past an older man surveying the pricey Scotch and brought a pint of Jim Beam to the counter. The clerk looked her over, raised an eyebrow, and rang it up.

"Ms. Geary?"

The man who'd been studying the Scotch selection approached with an outstretched hand.

"Gregory Abbott."

Winter wear in Duck Creek tended toward shapeless parkas or neon ski gear, but Abbott wore a long black double-breasted woolen coat and a homburg that, combined with his snowy hair and neat mustache, made him seem like someone from another, more formal, era. "I run the bookstore."

"Of course." She took his hand. "I believe my mother-in-law has cleaned out your entire children's section. For a while she ran a one-woman preschool for my little boy. His kindergarten teacher said he's bored stiff because he already knows everything in her lesson plan."

"She did keep me busy with regular orders." Had he just winked?

"I'll be sure and give her your regards."

Julia stuffed the pint bottle in her coat pocket, hoping he hadn't registered her selection.

"Good-bye, Ms. Geary. I'll see you soon."

He would? Maybe a subtle reminder that, while Beverly and Calvin apparently were frequent shoppers, it had been months since Julia had been in the bookstore. She couldn't remember the last time she'd read something other than a legal document or the newspaper.

During her few short minutes in the store, the sky had darkened and the temperature dropped. She hurried to the creek, unsure of what to say to whomever she might find there but knowing she wanted to be long gone by true nightfall.

Two men and two women stood close to the oil drum, feeding the fire with copies of that day's paper, which Julia suspected they'd pilfered from honor boxes. Flames raced across Chance Larsen's follow-up story about Ray's arrest, relegated to a single column low on the front page. Julia supposed the coming story about Leslie Harper would likely merit a banner headline.

They stared unsmiling, leaving it up to her to speak first.

"I'm Julia," she said. "Ray Belmar's lawyer."

The older of the two women cocked her head. "You the one he calls Thumbelina? I can see why."

With her knit hat topped with a festive pom-pom, a long down coat that was only a little frayed and dirty around the hem and cuffs, and her brisk, no-nonsense manner, she could have been a school-teacher. She was about—well, Julia couldn't tell how old she was. Her weather-ravaged cheeks and the charcoal-dark skin beneath her eyes—characteristics her companions shared—added decades to Julia's original estimate of about forty.

"He tried to talk to you, you know. Guess you didn't listen."

Julia shrank from the accusation, made worse by the sting of truth. "I was supposed to meet with him. But then he got arrested."

"What do you want?" one of the men said. He had a cadaverous, Ichabod Crane look, although instead of Crane's voluminous cape, an outsize backpack liberally patched with duct tape hung from his shoulders. His companion, nearly as short and slight as Julia herself, shot her a look of pure hatred and turned his back.

"Were you here the night that Mr. Williams—Billy—died?"

The younger woman's high-pitched cackle ended in a wet cough that bent her body double. She straightened and wiped her mouth and aimed a toothless smile Julia's way. "We're here every night."

Julia remembered the contents of her pocket. "Here. I have some-thing that might help that cough."

The woman snatched the bottle from her hands and twisted off the top, the scent of whiskey briefly competing with that of smoke. The small man whipped back around, the hostility in his eyes diminished.

Julia formed her questions carefully, making them vague, open-ended. The last thing she wanted to do was put words in anyone's mouth, something that could—if it came to that—return to haunt her in court.

"Can you tell me what happened that night?"

Toothless wiped her mouth and handed the bottle to Ichabod Crane. The little guy beside him performed an impatient jig, stamping feet shod in filthy Chuck Taylors that might once have been red.

"Billy and Ray, they had words. Fighting words."

"What did they say?"

"Couldn't hear. They went off a ways and never did come back."

"Then how did you know they were mad?"

Little Guy finally got his hands on the bottle and tilted it high.

"Ahhh!" He smacked his lips in appreciation. Gratitude loosened his tongue. "Same way you can tell anyone's mad. Ray was waving his arms all around, pacing back and forth." He demonstrated, kicking through the crusted snow, arms windmilling, endangering the bottle's contents. "And Billy, he just stood there shaking his head."

"Did they fight a lot?"

It was the older woman's turn for the bottle. "No," she said as she lowered it, more than half-empty now. Julia wondered if she should have bought a fifth instead. "Ray got into the occasional scrap, but mostly he was just a goof-off, always going for a laugh. And Billy." She looked to her companions. "How would you describe him?"

"Slow, like."

Little Guy nodded confirmation of Ichabod's assessment.

"Was he . . ." Julia sought the right phrase. "Was he mentally disabled?"

"You mean, was he a—"

Ichabod broke in before his compatriot could launch the insult.

"No, just slow. Walked slow, talked slow. You asked him a question, he'd turn it over forever in his mind before he answered. But he was all right in the head. Gentle, just like Ray, but in a different way. A quiet way. Just a big, slow-moving guy."

Maybe, Julia thought, the kind of guy who couldn't duck a punch.

"Was he drunk? Was Ray?"

Little Guy had gone positively garrulous. "You mean like us? Half-lit before the sun goes down. Before noon on a good day!"

Toothless emitted another racking laugh.

Again, Ichabod furnished the answer. "Naw. Billy, he'd had maybe a beer or two. But not drunk, not even close. And Ray stopped drinking some time back. Regular Boy Scout these days."

"Hey!" The older woman elbowed him. "Maybe that's why he jumped up on that parade float. A Boy Scout looking for a Girl Scout to claim as his own."

Toothless glared. "Knock it off. Ray had all the woman he could handle."

Julia felt the conversation veering off track.

"Not even the slightest idea what they were fighting about?"

Both men turned to the older woman. "Miss Mae?"

Her face went blank. "No idea."

Just like that, Julia was back where she started. It was almost dark. Time for her to get away from the creek and pick up Calvin. But she had one more question.

"I know Ray wasn't drinking anymore, but did you ever know him to use? Heroin, maybe?" Many of her clients used every manner of drug that existed, in combinations she'd not have imagined possible.

A soft smile played at the corners of the toothless woman's mouth. "Ray? Never. He was a rummy, just like us. Until he wasn't."

"Thanks."

Julia turned to go, then swung back, trying to sound casual.

"Turns out Billy wasn't the only one murdered. Someone else was killed last week. A legislator."

Miss Mae's sage nod set her hat's pom-pom bobbing. "The lady, right? Thought she killed herself."

"Turns out she might not have."

"Shame." All four nodded and bowed their heads, as though they'd known Harper personally.

"They don't know for sure. But the police will be questioning anyone ever arrested on a violent crime."

She didn't need to say more. They grasped the implications right away. "Shit. Just when things were dying down. Now they'll be hassling all of us again."

Julia waited for a round of curses to die down. She couldn't feign casual any longer.

"Anybody know where Ray was a couple of weekends ago?"

Their previous curses had been general, directed at the universe. This round took direct aim at her.

"Fuck you, bitch. What are you saying?" Toothless shoved the others aside, her face inches from Julia's, words riding on spittle.

"Angie. Angie. Take it easy." The others tugged at her, though it seemed to Julia their efforts were halfhearted.

Julia wiped her face. "I'm only asking the same thing the cops will. They found Leslie Harper last Tuesday. She'd been dead a couple of days. So . . ."

A fresh spray bathed Julia's face. "He works on weekends. That goddamn job, washing those goddamn dishes. And then he's with us. Tell that to the fucking cops."

"Tell them yourselves," Julia said, backing away. "Because for sure they'll be asking."

14

THE HOUSE BLAZED with light when Julia and Calvin—retrieved from a scowling after-school program worker at 5:59 PM—approached.

Calvin cocked his head. "Mom?"

"I know, buddy. It's weird." Beverly, at constant war with profligacy, relentlessly patrolled light switches throughout the rambling Victorian, flipping them down in unoccupied rooms with a loud "Aha!" followed by muttered, meant-to-be-overheard comments about the electric bill.

But the lights appeared to be on in nearly every room, and even more astonishing, warmth wrapped them when they shed their coats.

"Mom?" Again, Calvin turned wide eyes on Julia. "It's hot in here."

"No, it's not," Julia said. "It's just not cold." A heavy sweater hung on the hallway coatrack. Julia usually donned it upon entering the house. She left it hanging. "Beverly?"

She and Calvin left their shoes beneath the coatrack and padded down the hallway into the kitchen, where something smelled very good indeed. A bottle of wine stood open on the counter. Beverly lifted a near-empty glass at their approach.

"Oh, good! You're just in time. This boeuf bourguignon will be ready soon. Calvin, give Gamma a kiss." She bent her cheek, rosy from either the heat or the wine or both, to his pursed lips. "Julia, a glass of wine?"

"Um, sure? Calvin, honey, go wash your hands."

When the powder room door closed behind him, Julia took the glass Beverly offered and raised it warily. "What's the occasion?"

Beverly's flush deepened. "Let's wait until we're seated. Could you please set the table? Use the good china. And the silver. Here's a cloth."

She handed Julia a tea towel soft with age.

Julia ran it across the china's translucent surface, her frown deepening with each plate she pulled from the sideboard.

Beverly had already set out glasses and lighted the candles, which were now dripping wax onto the linen tablecloth, their flames glittering in the Waterford's faceted surfaces. And . . . Beverly had set out glassware for four.

What the hell was going on?

Julia headed back into the kitchen with a fistful of silverware.

"Are we expecting company?" she asked, just as the doorbell rang.

"I'll get it!" Beverly whisked off her apron, patted at her hair, and rushed for the door.

Julia hurried to place the flatware in its designated settings, turning just as Beverly walked into the room with Gregory Abbott in tow, a bottle of champagne tucked beneath one arm.

"You remember Mr. Abbott from the bookstore, don't you?"

Julia had to make a conscious effort to close her gaping mouth.

"Please." Abbott may have winked again. "Call me Gregory. And I'm pretty sure Julia remembers me. After all, it hasn't been that long."

"We saw each other—" Julia started to explain but stopped before she got to the part about their encounter in the liquor store. Beverly would wonder why she'd come home empty-handed. "Downtown today," she finished.

Calvin emerged from the bathroom, face and hands shining pink and damp, and there was a bustle of introductions and food being served, Julia and Gregory trying to be helpful and only succeeding in getting in Beverly's way as Calvin watched bright-eyed and curious, his mouth working at the questions he couldn't quite form.

Finally, the main dish arrived at the table in a tureen and a salad appeared, along with a wrapped basket from which the scent of warm bread emanated. They all sat. Julia wondered if there'd be a prayer.

Instead Gregory rose, wrapped the champagne bottle in a napkin, and deftly freed the cork with a satisfactory pop and hiss.

He poured, even splashing a teaspoonful into Calvin's glass, and then raised his own. Julia followed suit, and with a child's unerring gift for mimicry, so did Calvin after a moment's uncertainty. Beverly's glass trembled in her hand.

Gregory cleared his throat. Once. Twice.

Julia lost patience. "What are we toasting?"

Gregory held his glass higher still.

"To our beautiful, accomplished, brilliant chef . . ."

Of course. "To the chef," Julia echoed.

But Gregory wasn't finished.

"Who earlier today did me the immense honor of agreeing to be my bride."

* * *

Only the thickness of the Persian rug beneath the dining room table preserved the Waterford glass that tumbled from Julia's hand upon Gregory's announcement.

"I'm so sorry," she gasped, and was sorrier still a moment later as she and Gregory cracked heads when each bent to throw a napkin atop the spilled champagne. Calvin crowed in delight, rescuing the moment.

"Let's start again," Beverly suggested. She brought Julia a clean glass. Gregory filled it and they all drank, Calvin sneezing after his single sip.

Julia waited until the food was served—"Beef stew," she told Calvin—before asking the obvious.

"When did all of this happen?"

Several months earlier, Beverly had claimed to have resumed her affiliation with the local bridge club, which as far as Julia knew comprised the entirety of her social life. She hadn't known much, apparently.

"As you noted earlier today," Gregory reminded Julia as he dipped a piece of bread into the stew, "she spent a lot of time in the bookstore trying to choose exactly the right learning materials for this young man."

He bowed in Calvin's direction. Calvin grinned and bowed back.

"At some point, we started meeting outside the bookstore. I believe"—he cast a mock-stern glance in Beverly's direction—"she may have overstated her bridge commitments."

Holy hell. Was it possible that even as Julia herself had been enjoying surreptitious romps with Dom, Beverly and Gregory had been luxuriating in trysts of their own? Julia drained her champagne in an effort to erase the image from her head. Certainly Beverly was entitled. She'd been widowed for nearly a decade.

"When's the big day?"

"As soon as possible," Gregory said, just as Beverly added, "We haven't decided."

Their laughter carried an edge of giddiness.

Julia, herself a widow having recently rediscovered romance, couldn't help but smile, remembering the heady rush that she'd once thought would never be part of her life again. She held up her glass.

"To the happy couple!"

The Waterford rang like bells as they touched glasses. "Maybe, when you decide on a date, Calvin can be a ring bearer. It's a very important job," she assured him.

"There's so much to do before we get to that stage," Beverly said. "Gregory's going to live here. He offered to share his apartment over the bookstore, but we thought this would be more comfortable."

They laughed fondly together at a joke clearly already grown familiar. Beverly reached across the table and lay a hand atop Gregory's. He stroked it and gazed into her eyes.

Really, Julia thought, they were adorable.

"We'll have to find space in this house for all of Gregory's books. I thought maybe"—Beverly bit her lip before continuing—"we could turn your room into a second-floor sitting room and library."

"Of course," said Julia, suppressing a flash of resentment. She liked her room with its bay window whose seat was piled with pillows, a perfect place for her to huddle beneath a blanket and go through her files on weekends with a thermos of coffee at hand. It was, after all, Beverly's house, one that she shared rent-free, allowing her to finish paying off her law school loans. Julia supposed she'd move into Calvin's room, and maybe Calvin would take over the small guest room that Beverly used as a sewing room.

"After all," Beverly said, "I know how long you've wanted a place of your own, especially now that Calvin's started kindergarten. Gregory and I didn't plan it this way—we didn't plan any of this—but the timing couldn't be more fortuitous."

Which was how Julia found out that in addition to her favorite client being charged with murder, a smug and supercilious intern being foisted upon her, the unwanted intrusion of Adonis into a case that should rightfully be hers alone, and the abrupt withdrawal of Dom from her life, she was about to become homeless.

15

"Homeless. Please." Claudette blew ripples across the top of her coffee. "You know who's homeless? Those poor people down along the creek."

After so many years of friendship with Claudette, Julia should have known better than to seek sympathy.

They faced each other across a table in Colombia, a weekly get-together that had started after Claudia moved out of their shared office and into the job as top prosecutor, imposing an unspoken rule of never discussing each other's cases, although they commented long and loud on others moving through Peak County's court system.

But today was for the personal stuff they rarely discussed.

"I'm happy for her."

Claudette eyebrows climbed high.

"Really, I am. You should see them together. They're like a couple of teenagers."

Claudette shoved the piece of pie they were sharing toward Julia. "I remember somebody else acting like a teenager not so long ago."

"Oh." Julia mumbled around a piece of triple-berry gone to cardboard in her mouth. "That." She swallowed. "It's off."

Claudette dropped her fork. She'd been an early proponent of Julia's relationship with Dom, often reminding her, "You're too young to be the sad widow forever."

Julia looked around, ascertaining the necessary distance for earshot, and lowered her voice. "His daughter walked in on us."

Both fork and pie lay forgotten, a measure of Claudette's shock. Colombia's pies were legendary.

"As in . . . ?"

"As in into the bedroom. Her shift at the refugee center was canceled. She wasn't supposed to be home for another couple of hours."

"Any chance you were just getting going? Still dressed, even? Or maybe afterward, just cuddling under the covers?" Claudette ran through all the best bad-case scenarios, Julia shaking her head at each one.

"You mean . . ."

"No clothes, no cuddling. Full howl, if I remember correctly. Which I wish I didn't."

Claudia's long, low whistle turned heads. "Damn. His daughter's a teenager, right?"

"Sixteen."

Claudia winced. "Years of therapy, guaranteed. But as awful as that is, why the breakup? Can't you two just see each other on the sly until the embarrassment for all concerned eases up?"

"You mean in a century or so?" Julia pushed the pie back to Claudia. The single bite she'd forced down threatened intestinal mayhem. "That was my thought. But Susan had other ideas. She's sued for full custody."

"Bullshit." Claudette was herself again, in control and ready to fight. She dispatched the pie in a few efficient bites. "If the girl is sixteen, it's not up to the courts. She gets to choose."

"Looks like she's already chosen. She's staying over in the next county with her mother. Already transferred to the school there. Dom looks like—well, you can just imagine."

"Oh, I can," said Claudette. Just the thought of losing a child injected steel into Claudette's spine. Her eyes blazed. Her fingers curled into fists.

Dom, on the other hand, had seemed diminished, gray, receding into himself. Why couldn't he have been more like Claudette? He'd been so quick to give up on Julia that she wondered if she'd missed some sign that their still-new relationship was already faltering.

Claudette uncurled one fist and drummed her fingers on the table, thinking it through. "As a legal maneuver, I suppose it's smart. Saying he's not seeing you anymore. It gives his daughter time to calm down and rethink things, and it's probably the right thing to say to a mediator or a judge, even if it's utter crap. Speaking of which."

She stood and shrugged into her coat. Julia followed suit. Their weekly meetings were by necessity brief, with Claudia increasingly focused on her campaign and Julia on her always-crushing workload, complicated by the addition of Ray's case.

"What?"

"Given that I'm going to be prosecuting the case against Ray Belmar and you're going to be defending him, we probably should put these kaffeeklatsches on hold for a while. You understand, right? The optics—they're terrible."

Julia had never known anyone less concerned about optics than Claudette and said as much.

"The campaign . . ." Claudette's voice trailed off. She blew a breath. "Wayne Peterson paid me a visit today. Said if I wanted an endorsement from law enforcement, I'd better cool it on backing all those reforms Leslie Harper proposed."

Julia stepped through the door and stood to one side, her back to the icy wind. "But those are key to what you want to do with the prosecutor's office! Focus on serious crime and quit filling up the jail with people who can't pay their fines and fees."

Claudette faced the wind full on, as though welcoming its bracing slap. "No shit. But I need to get elected before I can push for them. Wayne's no fool. He knows we'll all be better off if we can get those changes through the legislature. But not every cop agrees with Wayne. Anyway, he has his own agenda. He doesn't want to be Deputy Dawg forever. He wants to be the Big Dawg. If I can get past this interim shit and get elected and Wayne can get elected as sheriff, between the two of us, we can get stuff done. But first . . ."

"You've got to get elected." Julia finished the sentence for her. She wondered at the toll the campaign was taking on her friend. Claudette's idea of gamesmanship relied not on elaborate bob-and-weaves but on clobbering her opponent into oblivion with the sheer force of her facts. Defense attorneys who found themselves facing Claudette begged their clients to go for the plea agreement rather than go up against her in a trial.

Now Claudette found herself in a situation that called for accommodations, dissembling, smiling to mask the impatience within.

"Of course we shouldn't see each other." Julia gave a wan smile. "I understand completely."

She waved her friend ahead of her so that Claudette would not see the moisture in her eyes, her unavoidable reaction to the loss of her friend—the sour cherry on top of the shit sundae of the last few days.

*   *   *

She didn't see Claudette again until Monday, when they confronted one another at a bail reduction hearing that Julia had requested for Ray. He'd been slapped with $100,000 bail at his initial appearance, standard for a homicide case—but not for one with such flimsy evidence, Julia argued to the judge.

The case had moved into the higher court that was the next step after initial appearances. The judge, who'd held the seat for decades, had a well-deserved reputation for unpredictability and lived up to it on this particular day.

Maybe Claudette was a little too sure of herself.

Maybe Julia, mad at the world over the bad luck burying her up to her chin, argued more forcefully than usual.

Maybe the sight of Ray, slumped and dispirited within his jailhouse jumpsuit, worked on the judge's hard heart.

Julia thought the most likely explanation was that the judge was just feeling mischievous, wanting to shake things up, put Claudette on her back foot to even up the odds.

At any event, when he tapped his gavel with more force than usual, Ray was declared a free man, to the extent that anyone about to have a hard plastic electronic monitoring device fitted to his ankle was free.

"Your Honor," Claudette protested, even as the gavel landed.

The judge swept from the room without a backward glance.

Julia turned to Ray with a surprised smile and suppressed an urge to hug him.

"Congratulations. Now all you have to do is keep your nose clean."

Ray's tone could have cut glass.

"That's what I was doing before. Look where it got me." He glared down at the table, refusing to meet her eyes.

"Before all this happened, you wanted to talk to me."

"Yeah, but you didn't want to."

Julia pushed away the memory of all the calls from Ray she'd ignored. "I did. But you got arrested first. Let's try again. Now?"

The sheriff's deputy who escorted the jail inmates to and from their court appearances cleared his throat. He jerked his head toward the door they used.

Ray's lips twitched in a bitter smile. "Gotta go back to jail. Get my things, get this electronic ball and chain fitted on my ankle." He rose.

"Tomorrow, then," Julia said. "Same time, same place as we'd planned before? I'll see you there."

But Ray followed the deputy without a word.

16

J ULIA SCROLLED THROUGH apartment listings on her phone while
she waited for Ray at the Starbucks the next day.

The last time she'd lived in an apartment, she'd been struggling
through law school and an unplanned pregnancy as her husband,
Michael, focused on the nascent newspaper career he'd later abandon
in favor of the comparable low salary and infinitely better benefits of
the military.

At the time, she'd paid scant attention to the apartment's worn
carpeting, its windows whose loose frames readily admitted the savage winter gusts howling out of the mountains, the stovetop with
only three functioning burners, and the balky freezer that produced
ice cubes with defiantly liquid interiors. But she'd shared it with
Michael, falling exhausted—but never too exhausted—into bed
with him after hours of studying, waking barely less exhausted but
at least well loved and smiling because of it.

Until recently that apartment was the last place she'd thought
herself happy. She'd moved into Beverly's spacious Victorian when
Michael was deployed and had lived there since, gradually becoming
accustomed to a level of comfort well beyond what she could afford
on her own, a fact that became painfully apparent as she looked at
the offerings in her price range.

She'd had hazy images of finding a place in one of the older,
refurbished homes near the center of town, a house like Beverly's
that had been divided into two or three units with high ceilings, tall

windows, and maybe even a fireplace. Lots of charm with the added advantage that she could continue to walk to work and to Calvin's school.

She found those listings quickly, and almost as quickly abandoned them. The most she could afford was a studio or one-bedroom, and of course, with Calvin, that wouldn't do. She widened her search, and widened it again, ending up with listings on the far edges of town in buildings not much of an improvement over that long-ago apartment she'd shared with Michael. She'd have to get up half an hour earlier than her already zero-dark-thirty rising time in order to get Calvin to kindergarten, and they'd get home even later each evening—and there wouldn't be a home-cooked meal courtesy of Beverly awaiting them.

She'd also lose the twice-weekly free evening babysitting that had allowed her semisurreptitious encounters with Dom while Elena worked her volunteer shift at the refugee center. Then she remembered that she and Dom were through and remembered why. Even in the anonymity of Starbucks, she ducked her head in embarrassment, as though the people waiting in line for their overpriced drinks had a way of divining her thoughts.

She looked at the time. Ray was late. Typical. She texted his Tracfone, using the familiar tone they'd adopted over the years. *Dude. Where are you?*

She went back to the rental website and looked again at the apartments closer to town, the ones with loads of character and little closet space, and recalculated her budget. If she cut out her daily coffee runs to Colombia—but no. She shuddered at the thought. Anyway, even the obscene annual amount she spent at the coffee shop wouldn't give her the necessary budgetary breathing room.

"Christ." A half hour had passed. She had to get back to work. She texted Ray again. *One of us takes their commitments seriously. I'm going back to work.*

She returned downtown, heading for the side street several blocks from the courthouse that offered free parking. It was enough out of the way that other downtown workers had either not discovered it or viewed it as not worth the extra effort. Claudette had tipped her off to it, so Julia wasn't surprised to see her friend emerging from her own car as she drove up. She wondered what task had been sufficiently urgent to demand the attention of Claudette, a militant practitioner of working through lunch hour.

Claudette approached with quick, firm steps, her face set, tugging at Julia's car door before Julia had even freed herself from her seat belt.

Julia lowered her window. "Didn't your fancy new job come with a free parking space at the courthouse? And aren't you the boss? Can't you do something about that?"

Claudette just looked at her.

Julia glanced at the sky, checking to see if a cloud had just veiled the sun, something that would explain the chill icing her veins.

"I wanted you to hear it from me first."

"Oh God. Is Calvin—?" Julia couldn't even form the question. She scrambled from the car. If anything had happened to her son . . . but the school would have called. Or Beverly. This had to be something to do with work.

She relaxed.

Too soon.

"It's Ray." Claudia grasped her by the elbow, as though bracing her against imminent collapse. "He's been arrested again."

Julia shook herself free. "Jesus, now what?" She tried to think of the dumbest thing Ray could have done—which, given Ray, would be monumentally foolish indeed. No matter what, he'd find himself back in jail, his freedom, albeit supervised, yanked away within twenty-four hours of being granted. How stupid could one man be?

"Did he go after, oh, let's say the Girl Scouts? Maybe steal some boxes of cookies from their setup outside the supermarket? Please tell me he was at least dressed this time."

Claudette didn't crack a smile.

"He went back down to the creek last night."

Okay, that was ill advised. He had no business going back to the scene of the crime, no matter who had committed it. This would play havoc with her defense. Maybe she'd kick the case to Tim Saunders after all.

She pressed her key fob. The car locks clicked. "Thanks for letting me know. I wonder how long it'll be before the judge grants a release on recognizance for anyone again. So what did Ray do—allegedly—down there, anyway?"

Claudette's hand was back on her elbow, her fingertips digging in through Julia's heavy coat.

"What?"

"The woman known as Miss Mae. You know who I mean?"

"I met her the other day. See her on the street, you'd think she was a solid citizen."

Claudette gave a grim chuckle. "That solid citizen has a helluva reputation. She rode the rails for years. Still did until fairly recently. Way I hear it, she was handy with a switchblade. Women out there alone don't have an easy time of it, but word on the street was that nobody messed with Miss Mae."

Julia tried to put her finger on something bothering her about Claudette's biographical sketch. That was it. The past tense.

"*Was* handy?"

Claudette clutched her tighter still.

"They found her this morning. Bashed in the head, just like Billy Williams, only worse. Whoever attacked her left her naked in the snow. Maybe sexually assaulted her. You think Ray was in trouble before? That's nothing compared to what he's up against now."

17

Somehow Julia made it back to her office, brushing aside Claudette's offer to walk with her.

She sprinted up the courthouse steps, veering away from the clerks and others who approached her with *Have you heard?*s, practically shoving Chance Larsen out of the way when he came at her with his reporter's notebook held high and snapping at Deb as she leapt from her desk in an attempt to get the news firsthand.

"I'm not discussing it with anyone other than our defense team," Julia said, her words awarding Marie a promotion and including Tim Saunders in the fold. "No calls, no interruptions."

She felt Deb's glare all the way down the hall. Marie waited at her desk, not even pretending to work.

She took one look at Julia's face. "It's true?"

"Afraid so. Claudette told me herself."

"I guess that's that, then," Marie said with the dead-eyed stare and pursed lips of eternal skepticism she affected in what Julia could only assume was an effort to give herself the appearance of a full-fledged lawyer.

Julia suppressed an urge to slap it away and tried to channel the physical compulsion into a verbal one.

"What was the very first lesson you learned in law school? Surely you haven't already forgotten."

"What part of it?"

"Occam's razor."

Marie delivered the answer in an aggrieved singsong. "Entities should not be multiplied unnecessarily."

"Looks like you forgot the second rule too. It's similar to the first."

Marie didn't even bother to ask. She folded her arms across her chest and waited.

"KISS. Keep it simple, stupid. As in *English, please*. Use lawyer-speak in front of a jury and they'll fall asleep right before your eyes."

"Occam's razor: the simplest explanation is the best," Marie mumbled.

"With that in mind, answer me this." Julia hated her professorial tone but couldn't help herself. "Why would someone whose lawyer had just pulled off a miracle in getting him released on his own recognizance in a homicide case do something like that? He had to know they'd be watching him. That he'd get caught."

She hung up her coat and paced the room, which given the small space involved three steps in one direction, then three in the other until her toes bumped up against the beat-up file cabinet that Marie had scrounged from the basement and wedged into the space once occupied by Pavarotti's cage.

She missed Pavarotti, missed his inquisitive, tilt-headed stare, the way he'd lean his head against the bars for a scratch, then let loose with an operatic trill, lightening the inevitable tension of their days.

"We don't know that he got caught doing anything. We don't know why they decided to take him into custody. Last time, it was pretty circumstantial. I don't know what they have on him this time, but they'll have to release him after forty-eight hours if they don't come up with probable cause. Maybe there's a crazy person out there picking on homeless people. You see it from time to time. There was a case in Colorado back in the late nineties, early aughts, where a whole gang of street kids was preying on them, beating them to death. People don't like them. They're unsightly. They smell bad. They make people uncomfortable. Every so often somebody takes it into his head to get rid of them. Because God forbid anybody should help them."

She stopped, surprising herself with the bitterness that had crept into her voice. She took a breath and forced herself to sit, to log in to her computer, tap at its keys, stare into the screen whose blankness mirrored her own defeated gaze. An old tactic: act the way you want to feel, and at some point you *will* feel that way. She took another breath and awaited the calm she sought.

"Knock-knock."

Julia hated people who announced themselves with the faux-cheery greeting rather than just actually knocking. Even if the door was open, as she'd left hers, the jamb offered a perfectly acceptable alternative.

But there was nothing cheery about Tim Saunders's expression.

He stepped inside without being invited. "Guess you've heard."

"Seems like half of Duck Creek has heard."

"Hi, Mr. Saunders. How do we handle this one?"

He awarded Marie a tight-lipped smile.

"Here's the thing. With just one case and only circumstantial evidence, we might have had a chance. Two killings, things get dicey."

He punctuated his delivery with a sober shake of his head.

Julia had heard enough. "We don't know that Ray killed one person, let alone two." Shit. She shouldn't have called Ray by his first name. Too late.

Saunders's eyebrows crawled toward the low-hanging curl on his forehead. "No matter your personal relationship with the defendant," he began.

"Jesus! You make it sound like a love affair."

The eyebrows inched higher still. "Was it?"

Marie gasped.

Julia looked around her desk for a weapon. Her old-style metal Swingline stapler, if launched correctly, would put quite a swerve in that beautifully straight nose. She slid her hands beneath her thighs on the off chance that she might give in to the impulse.

"I'm not even going to dignify that."

"I had to ask."

"No. You did not."

Saunders held out his hands in a gesture she supposed was meant to be conciliatory. She stared at them, momentarily distracted by the manicure.

"All I'm trying to say is that now more than ever, it becomes incumbent upon us to keep him from going to trial. That first case, a fight between vagrants—the public doesn't really care how long the punishment is, as long as it's something. But if they charge him with a second, especially with this one being a woman and the added insult of possible sexual assault, a trial would be beyond ugly. Even if he pleads guilty, he's looking at decades. But at least if he pleads— especially if it turns out he had help and he can implicate anyone else—there's a chance he won't get life."

Julia stood and flattened her hands on her desk. She leaned across it and spoke very slowly and clearly.

"He's not going to plead guilty. And he's not going to get life. He's not going to get any time at all, because I'm going to get him acquitted."

* * *

As soon as the door closed behind Saunders, Marie turned to Julia.

She didn't have to ask.

"I don't know how I'm going to do it," Julia admitted. "That's why we've got to get as much information as possible."

"We?"

Before now, Julia had never given much thought to the notion of swallowing one's pride. Now it felt literal, her own a choking lump in her throat, making it nearly impossible to speak. But she didn't have a choice. She couldn't do this alone, and she'd be damned if she'd seek help from Adonis.

She looked pointedly at Marie's feet, tucked into lady-lawyer low-heeled pumps. "Got boots? Real, functional boots, not the look-good kind?"

"Yes. They're in the bottom drawer of my file cabinet." Her voice caressed the words as she cast a glance at her unlovely new acquisition.

"Hat? Gloves?"

Marie nodded twice.

"Shame you wore a skirt today. You'll be sorry."

"Why?"

"Because you and I are going to walk up and down the creek and interview every single homeless person we encounter about what they might have seen on the nights when Billy Williams and Miss Mae were killed. And if they didn't see anything—I don't expect we'll find many who did, if any at all—ask what they've heard through the grapevine."

"I have a long coat." But Marie's voice had lost some of its brief assurance. She looked toward the coatrack, her wool herringbone number—the sort of thing that screamed Student's First Grownup Coat—appearing thin and inadequate next to Julia's sturdy, puffy parka. She knew as well as Julia how the wind would skate up from the icy creek and creep beneath the hem, wrapping itself lovingly around her calves and knees, turning them into reddened, frozen things.

"That's good. Now. What about pencils? Do you have any?"

Marie slid open the shallow drawer in the center of her desk and withdrew two freshly sharpened Dixon Ticonderoga No. 2s, clacking them together like chopsticks. "Right here. Why?"

"Because you're going to take notes on what people tell you and, to the extent possible, get names and contact information."

Marie regained a bit of her old, supercilious expression.

"Why not just record them on my phone?"

"Come here." Julia beckoned her to the window. The bank across the street had a lighted thermometer, at the moment registering fourteen degrees.

"Hold your phone out in this cold for more than a few minutes and it'll shut down. Use a pen and the ink will freeze. Bring as many pencils as you've got. The points will either break of wear down, but at least until that happens, they'll work.

"Oh, and one more thing." Julia was feeling better by the moment, focusing on the small tasks at hand as a distraction from the overwhelming, insoluble issue of proving Ray's innocence. Because no matter what the law said about innocent until proven guilty, the minute someone was arrested, human nature held otherwise.

"You're going to have to get in the habit of ditching terms like *homeless* and *vagrant* and, God forbid, *bums*. Not even *gentlemen of leisure*, which Wayne seems to think is funny."

Marie subjected her lower lip to the same savage chewing she inflicted upon her pens.

"What about just—people? You know, in English. Like you just told me."

Julia let the jab pass. "Not bad. Let's go one better, though. At least in court, or when talking to the press—which only I will do, understood?—let's call them citizens. Because they are. Just like us."

Thus armed with nomenclature, if nothing else, they donned the necessary extra layers and set out on their mission.

18

AT MARIE'S INSISTENCE, they split up.

"It only makes sense. We don't want to be out here any longer than we have to," she said as they walked together toward the creek.

"Point taken." Julia cast a glance toward the liquor store, wondering if she should buy another couple of pints, but decided against it. Now more than ever, they couldn't afford the slightest appearance of trying to influence people.

"You go east. I'll go west."

She headed down the creekside trail without another word, placing her feet carefully, wary of the sheets of ice that lurked beneath fresh snow, waiting to send the unwary skidding into a bone-shattering fall. Given the cold, she doubted they'd find anyone at all. Duck Creek's homeless *citizens* had likely scattered to their day-time haunts—the large public rooms in the library, a coffee shop known to dispense free java to those who had the good sense to keep quiet and not disturb the paying customers, a day shelter run by a nonprofit group. But the last, much like the town's official homeless shelter, refused admittance to anyone drunk or high, which left a significant portion of Duck Creek's transient population literally out in the cold.

She passed a few blackened oil drums, cold and unused, and even a fire ring deep within the inadequate shelter of the willows, along with a couple of makeshift lean-tos. Once she started looking, signs of habitation—a bedroll here, a couple of empty pint bottles there—abounded everywhere that offered the slightest protection from the wind and snow. She approached one of the bridges that arced over the creek. And there, huddled against the abutment, a veritable solid, dry palace compared to the pathetic spots she'd seen, three people surrounded the barest flicker of orange.

They turned as one, wary, defensive. A tall, skeletal man spoke up.

"It's okay. She's not a cop. This here's Ray's lawyer. Remember?"

Julia nodded confirmation to Ichabod Crane and his little red-sneakered sidekick, along with a woman wearing a man's Stormy Kromer cap pulled so low on her forehead that the bill shaded her features. Julia wondered if she'd snatched it from the head of a solid citizen. The unlovely but gratifyingly warm wool baseball-style caps, named for a long-ago ballplayer, had earflaps that could be fastened under the chin and were ubiquitous in this part of the world. But they weren't cheap.

Julia looked at the flames, which offered only a suggestion of heat. "That's not much of a fire."

"We don't dare do more," the woman said. "Cops'll come. Or the sheriff. That one deputy, he's a real bastard. Most of them, when it gets this cold, they give us a break. But not that asshole."

Miss Mae had looked like a schoolmarm. This woman looked like exactly what she was, someone who lived hard and had been used even harder by life. Julia, slight as she was, felt fat and soft by comparison. The woman's deeply grooved cheeks were sunken, her eyes hollow, her teeth nonexistent.

"Angie, right?"

"That's right."

"Which deputy?"

"That big guy."

That could be any of them. Duck Creek's firefighters, an impressively lean and fit crew who bragged about their feats in the region's marathons and triathlons, poked fun at the noticeably pudgier cops and sheriff's deputies, who in return disparaged the firefighters for having jobs that gave them plenty of time to work out.

A gust of wind found its way around the abutment, threatening to vanquish the feeble blaze. The group drew close, protecting it. Julia didn't want to be out there a moment longer than she had to.

"I'm here about Ray again. He's really in trouble now."

"No shit, Sherlock." The little guy. For someone who looked like such an easy target, he had a mouth on him.

"I heard he came back down here as soon as they let him out."

"Like a bee to honey."

Julia winced at the woman's gummy grin. Had Ray come to see her? She considered Ray's options when it came to female companionship and thought—maybe. Probably.

"Who'd he talk to? What'd he say? Was Miss Mae here?"

"Whoa, whoa, whoa." Ichabod looked at her empty hands, clearly hoping for a repeat showing of a bottle.

Julia shook her head. "I wish I could. But all I need is a prosecutor coming at me, saying I bribed you all to tell me what I need to hear to protect Ray."

The woman nodded. "Good on you. Ray needs all the protecting he can get. Because he ain't killed nobody."

"You don't know that." The troublemaker again, Little Guy.

"It's what I'm trying to find out," Julia said, stepping between them as the woman's face darkened. "You told me he and Billy had fought the night Billy was killed. What about Miss Mae? Was she here the night he got out of jail? Were you here too?"

"We all were." The others nodded agreement. "It was a party, Ray being out of jail again and all. But he wasn't in a party mood."

"What do you mean?" Julia's fingers, despite her thin glove liners encased in unwieldy mittens, began to ache. She dreaded the thought of freeing them in order to take notes.

"He was like you were, asking all those questions about Billy," Ichabod said. "Wanted to know where Billy went after they got crosswise. Like, did Billy talk to anyone else?"

"Wait." Cold be damned, Julia shed her gloves and mittens and pulled out her notebook and pencil. "You mean Billy left after they argued?"

Heads bobbed. "Stomped off calling Ray all kinds of names. That was the last any of us saw him."

Julia's pencil paused in midair. "Did you tell the cops that?"

"Told that lady sheriff."

"Then why did they charge him?"

As though they would know.

They tossed the question right back to her.

"You tell us. You're the smart lawyer."

"I have no idea, but I aim to find out." She held her fingers to her lips and breathed inadequate warmth on them. "Did you tell the police all of this?"

"Oh, I told 'em," Angie said. "Didn't matter a damn. Once they make up their minds about things, that's that."

"What about the other night, after he got out of jail again? Did he and Miss Mae get into a fight too?"

Ichabod pulled a crumpled fast-food bag from a pocket and fed it to the fire, which flared without an appreciable increase in heat. "Naw. Kind of the deal as before. He and Miss Mae went off a ways and talked, sure, but it wasn't any kind of a fight. He went with Angie right after that."

Angie ducked her head. Julia could have sworn she blushed, a girlishness that softened her features. When she looked up, her eyes were wet. "And Miss Mae left right after they talked."

"Where'd she go?"

The three exchanged glances, shrugging. "Miss Mae, she goes her own way. Kind of a loner. Stays with us long enough to have a few beers and then splits. Says she's got secret places all over town where nobody can bother her."

"Did you tell the cops that too?"

Curses littered their affirmatives.

"Thing is," said Angie, "nobody can prove it. Ray and I broke into a car like we always do when it gets this cold and spent the night there. It's warmer than you'd think. I've scored some primo sleeping bags." Julia, glancing again at her primo hat, didn't ask how. "But nobody else saw us. I mean, that was the whole idea. Last thing we wanted was to get caught, so now it's just my word and Ray's, and guess how much they believe anything we say?"

Julia could no longer feel her fingers. "I'd like to get your names, please. And, uh, any contact information, in case I need to call any of you as witnesses."

She had little hope of the latter, but to her surprise, they all had Tracfones.

"To check in with family," said Ichabod, who'd given his name as Johnny Harrow. He registered her look of surprise. "Think we don't have anybody out there who cares about us?"

Little Guy—Craig Thompson—stepped forward, taking up the challenge.

"You think you're so different than us. What if you lost your job tomorrow? Had a taste for drink, or pills? Used up all your family's patience? It happens like that." He snapped his fingers.

She jumped.

"Of course, of course," she mumbled. "Thank you for talking with me."

She fled, shoving her hands deep in her pockets in a futile attempt at restoring something approximating warmth, nearly running into Marie as she barreled head down along the path.

"Hey." Marie fell in beside her, both of them quick-stepping back toward the office, a route that seemed to have lengthened during the time in the cold.

Julia grabbed Marie's arm and pulled her down a side street. "This way." A sign beckoned: Colombia, her favorite coffee shop. "In here."

She pushed open a door, into a space so warm and redolent of coffee and baked goods that she nearly wept.

She spotted a single empty table. "Why don't you go ahead and take that before someone else comes in out of the cold. I'll order. What do you usually drink? Cappuccino? Just black?"

"I don't." Marie's glasses had fogged up, underscoring her blank expression. "I can't afford things like fancy coffee."

But you can afford a fancy gun, Julia thought.

"You can today," she said. "It's on me." After all, Marie had spent just as much time in the cold as she, in a skirt, no less.

"In that case." Marie took off her fogged glasses, rubbed her gloved fingers across them, and put them back on, revealing a mischievous glint. "I'll take whatever's most expensive."

Julia returned with her own latte, along with a mug of hot chocolate heaped high with whipped cream and dusted with sparkly green mint sprinkles. "I took a guess."

Marie wrapped her fingers eagerly around the mug. "I actually don't care what it is, as long as it's hot."

"Same. But drink it anyway. You'll warm up even faster."

They sat in silence for a few moments, wincing as sensation returned to frozen digits.

"I can't even get to the hot chocolate through all this whipped cream," Marie managed, slurping through it with great concentration. "Ahh," she said a second later. "I think I can feel my feet again."

So could Julia, and it was agony. "Those people. Out there all the time."

She didn't have to explain.

"I know." Marie ran her finger around the inside of her mug, capturing a lingering smear of whipped cream. "How long were we out there? A half hour? Forty-five minutes?"

Julia watched with interest. Their prolonged—albeit relatively brief—sojourn in the cold had wreaked havoc on Marie's cultivated smugness. Confusion crept across her features, and something else. Doubt?

Julia remembered the first time a case had knocked her sideways, forcing her to readjust long-held certainties. In the long run, it had made her a better, more compassionate lawyer. In the short run, she'd been a mess.

"How'd it go?"

Marie shook her head. "I don't know."

"Didn't you find anyone?"

Marie held up her mug. "May I have another one of these?" Her voice was small.

The expense would be worth it, Julia thought, as she handed the barista her debit card, if the second cocoa loosened Marie's tongue. She brought it back to the table, along with another latte for herself, and waited while Marie worked her way again through the whipped cream.

"I found people," Marie said finally. "Only a couple. And they didn't see anything directly, so for our purposes they're basically useless."

She looked up at Julia, who nodded confirmation and nudged Marie for more. "Sometimes what they say can point us in the right direction."

"Right. Well." Marie held the warm mug against her cheek. "Oh, that feels nice. They said they'd heard stuff."

"What sort of stuff?"

"They said . . ." Marie swallowed. "They said that Ray stormed off after he and Billy argued. That the other times they saw him, he was running with some woman, not Miss Mae."

"Angie."

"That's it. I got their names, anyway."

"Good. You earned those hot chocolates, Marie."

Julia's words were as grudging as the half smile Marie offered in return.

"But." The young woman's features were in motion, the doubt returning stronger than ever despite her obvious attempts to vanquish it. "I don't understand."

Julia thought she knew what Marie was getting at but wanted to be sure. "What don't you understand?"

"The affidavit in Mr. Williams' case. It didn't say anything about that. About Ray leaving."

Julia played devil's advocate. "Maybe he came back."

"But." Marie pushed her mug away with a sudden, sharp motion, nearly upending it. "What if he didn't?"

"Exactly." Julia smiled grimly. "That's what you and I are going to figure out."

19

"PROBABLE CAUSE, MY ASS."

The affidavit accompanying the formal complaint against Ray in Miss Mae's death had been filed with five minutes to spare before the forty-eight-hour deadline, based on the fact that he was the last person seen talking with Miss Mae before her death.

Julia looked at the clock, its hands pointing to five PM. She'd have to wait until morning to call the jail and set up an interview with Ray. Better yet, she'd go in person.

But when the doors to the jailhouse lobby were unlocked at eight the next morning, the deputy sitting in the bulletproof-glass-enclosed admission booth had a message for her.

"Geary, right? Got something for you from Ray Belmar."

Hope nudged her for the first time in days.

The deputy hit a few keys and brought up something on his screen. "Says he's not seeing anyone. Especially you."

"Now what do we do?" Marie asked after Julia had calmed down upon her return to the office.

Julia wondered if she'd been too quick to use *we* with Marie, creating the illusion of a true partnership. But it couldn't be helped. She couldn't handle all of it alone, and the alternative was to turn to Adonis.

"You're friends with Wayne Peterson." So was she, but she wanted Marie to stick with the basics. "Can you please give him a call, sound him out about the report on Mr. Williams' and Miss Mae's deaths?

Find out why they were so quick to pin both of them on Ray? I mean, Ray and Mr. Williams at least had an argument, but we haven't heard anything like that with Miss Mae. Here."

She handed Marie her credit card. "Take him to coffee, and not at the downstairs cart. Go to Colombia and get the good stuff. Maybe even some pie." That would put them both in a good mood, she reasoned. "Expense it. Be sure to get a receipt."

Her phone rang. She waved good-bye to Marie and grabbed it.

"Julia? This is Sasha Berman."

It took Julia a moment to place the name. Right. A real estate agent, a friend of her mother-in-law's. Beverly had suggested she contact the woman, even as Julia protested that, as Beverly knew full well, she wasn't in the market for a house.

"She can help you with a rental. She owes me a favor. We've been carpooling to bridge for more than a year now, and guess who never, ever drives? I've heard every excuse in the book, with apologies to match. I've begun to wonder if she doesn't know how to drive, which seems a liability in her line of work."

Julia suspected Beverly just wanted her out of the house as soon as possible so that she and Gregory Abbott could set up their own little love nest. It didn't matter. The sooner she moved, the better, before she got too deep in the weeds of Ray's case. *Cases, plural*, she reminded herself, even as she listened to Sasha's excited announcement.

"I've got a line on a rental house, one near downtown, not too far from Beverly's. It's a wonderful location and just perfect for you and your little boy. Three bedrooms, along with one full and one half bath, finished basement, fenced yard. You could get a dog if you wanted."

Julia did not want. She could barely take care of herself and Calvin.

But even the few apartments in that area whose listings she'd scanned had been beyond her reach. "That doesn't sound like something I can afford."

"You can. It's not online yet. Can you come look at it right now? I wanted to give you first crack."

Julia looked at the clock. The day was already getting away from her. She'd have to bring a stack of work home in order to catch up—which she did most nights anyway.

"What's the address?"

*   *   *

It turned out that Sasha Berman did know how to drive. At least, she alighted from the driver's side of a gleaming maroon Lexus. She made a sweeping gesture toward a neat frame bungalow surrounded by an actual white picket fence. Trees—bare now, but whose spreading branches promised ample summertime shade—flanked either side of a deep porch. Julia could see more behind the house, hinting at an oversized yard.

Sasha confirmed her assessment as she held the gate open. "It's a double lot. If the owner had subdivided, she could have retired on the proceeds, but . . ." She bit her lip. "Here. Let me get the door. We don't even have a lockbox on it yet." She fumbled with a key, talking fast.

"I'm sorry it's unfurnished. Places always show better when you can see how people live in them. But the cleaning crew just finished up yesterday. It's spotless now. You could move in tomorrow if you wanted."

Julia's mind snagged on "cleaning crew" and "spotless *now.*" What had it looked like before? Had it been one of those hoarder houses, something that necessitated an entire crew? But no, she told herself. Half the women in Beverly's neighborhood used a cleaning service that saw battered cars disgorging pairs of exhausted-looking women lugging buckets of cleaning products and what Julia assumed were industrial-strength vacuums.

She forgot her misgivings as soon as she stepped into the house. The hardwood floor, immaculate as promised, caught the light streaming in through large windows flanked by built-in shelves.

She kicked off her boots, not wanting to mar the floor's fresh polish. A short hallway, with the half bath, led to a sunny kitchen that ran the width of the house. Julia ran her hand across granite countertops, peered into the depths of a subzero refrigerator, and looked doubtfully at a restaurant range. Whoever had lived here before obviously liked to cook. This kitchen would be wasted on her own efforts, which made heavy use of the microwave.

"The owner had just remodeled," Sasha said. "Just look at these cabinets." She flung open doors, revealing shelves that slid on silent runners and lazy Susans that rotated for easy display. Julia's things wouldn't fill a quarter of the space. "These windows face east, so you'll have morning sun when you come down for breakfast. And just look at the size of that yard! Plenty of room for a swing set. I'm sure the property manager wouldn't mind. Oh, and there's a dog door in the back door, so you wouldn't have to get up in the middle of the night to let the dog out."

"I don't have a dog. My mother-in-law has a cat, but it will stay with her."

Sasha bustled past her, beckoning her upstairs. "You won't believe this. There's a laundry chute in the hallway, so you don't have to lug heavy baskets of laundry down to the basement. Aren't these old houses charming?"

"Yes. Until you see the closets."

The house was so perfect—the sort of place she and Michael had dreamed of having one day—that Julia felt obligated to find a drawback. Sasha glanced back with a sly smile and flung open the door to a surprisingly large bedroom with two deep dormer windows. Sliding doors ran the length of one wall. "Go ahead," she urged.

Julia slid one open. The closet was bigger than the one in her room at Beverly's, with one end given over to shelves for sweaters and racks for shoes. She offered Sasha a rueful smile, admitting defeat.

"The other two are a little smaller, but with the same sort of closet space. You could use one for a home office. But I've saved the best for last."

A bathroom stood between the bedrooms, with a shower and a separate claw-foot tub the approximate length and depth of a tiny swimming pool. In her pre-Calvin life, Julia had been an aficionado of long, near-scalding baths, preferably with a book in hand and a glass of wine on the rim of the tub. Then she'd moved in with Beverly, who prided herself on thrift and set the water heater at the lowest possible temperature, ensuring quick showers.

Julia stood motionless before the tub, entertaining a brief, bliss-ful fantasy before mentally slapping herself back to sanity.

"You'll want to check out the basement. The house comes with washer and dryer—rare in a rental. And the rest would make a per-fect playroom for your little boy. And a puppy, of course."

What in the world was her fixation with a dog? Julia took a breath.

"It's beautiful. And whoever gets this house will be lucky. But you know what I can afford, and we both know this isn't it."

"Oh, but it is." Sasha lowered her voice, even though they were alone. "The, uh, the property manager is eager to see it rented. She's from out of state and wants to get back home as soon as possible. And of course, she wants someone reliable. If you're ready, we could sign the lease today."

All of Julia's antennae quivered, a sensation nearly as strong as her yearning for a house like this one. That old saying: If something looks too good to be true . . .

She heard the front door open. "Sasha? Is that you? I saw your car outside," a woman called.

"Oh no," Sasha breathed. "She's early."

Now, thought Julia. This is where I find out what the deal is.

She turned to Sasha.

"So, what's the problem? Mold? Termites? Did someone get mur-dered here?"

A woman ascended the stairs, preceded by a bounding, half-grown floppy-eared dog that leapt at Julia until she stooped to pet it. Its silky white hair, generously splashed with patches of orange, was so soft that she automatically scooped it up, giving it an opportunity to cover her chin with enthusiastic swipes of its little pink tongue.

"Sorry." The woman took the dog from Julia and put him down, whereupon he immediately began running circles around them.

"Jake, enough," the woman said hoarsely, with no discernible effect. She removed a wool cap, revealing hair that looked as though it hadn't been washed in days. Her eyes were red and wet, her skin mottled as though she'd just been crying; not the tears whipped from one's eyes by Duck Creek's cruel wind but racking, body-curling sobs.

"Is this the renter?" she asked Sasha.

Sasha looked at Julia. "We hope so." But her voice sounded anything but hopeful.

"Oh, thank God. I can't wait to get away from here." The woman visibly steeled herself. "I'm sorry. I've been rude. I keep forgetting myself these days. I'm Caroline Harper."

Julia stared, mentally twisting the lank hair into a chignon, replacing the yoga pants and oversize shirt with a severe black dress.

Harper. As in Leslie Harper? Found dead in this very house?

She looked to Sasha, who nodded confirmation.

"Caroline is Leslie's sister."

*   *   *

Their state didn't require sellers or landlords to reveal that a death, even a murder, had occurred on a property. So why drop the rent so low?

Even if the killing was revealed, it might discourage a few potential renters, but the house was a jewel and the rental market was tight. If Julia didn't take it, someone else would.

"Of course I love it," she began. An understatement. She wanted to rip Sasha's designer leather tote from her shoulder, root around in it until she found the lease agreement, and sign on the spot. The logical side of her brain—which was it, right or left? She could never remember—drummed insistence. *Too good to be true, too good to be true, too good to be true.*

"But why rent it? Why not just sell it?"

"It's going to take a while to get my sister's affairs in order. I want someone in here who will take care of it in the meantime. And of course"—Caroline's voice took on a pleading look—"I'd look favorably on the renter when it came time to sell."

As if she could ever afford a house like this. Julia's fingers twitched, anticipating the feel of the pen in her hand, scrawling her name across the lease.

Caroline and Sasha exchanged a very long look, then started to speak at the same time.

"Just one thing . . ."

"There's an unusual clause . . ."

Ah. Here it comes. Julia thought of the cookie-cutter apartment buildings on the edge of town, forcing herself to get reacquainted with reality. That would be her future—the sound of her neighbors' televisions, their cooking smells, their weekend revelries, their fights and their makeup sex. She was so intent on her internal talking-to—for God's sake, she'd lived a life of unearned privilege for so long—that she had to ask Caroline what she'd just said.

The woman lifted the puppy and held it out toward Julia.

"He's part of the deal."

What the ever-loving fuck?

Had Julia spoken aloud?

It didn't matter. They'd probably anticipated her reaction.

"We should go," Sasha said, with a real estate agent's rehearsed practicality. When a deal falls through, move on to the next one.

But Caroline was an amateur, acting as though there were still hope. She stepped closer, practically forcing Julia to take him. He wriggled in glee for a moment before settling in her arms like an infant.

"My sister loved this little guy. Loved him! Every day, she'd text me photos. I'd take him if I could, but we live in an apartment in Manhattan and the kids are about to go off to college and I work about a million hours a week at a job that's ready to fire me because I've been gone so long dealing with all of this."

The puppy turned over, finding a more comfortable position. It was warm against Julia's chest. No, she thought. No.

"Can't you just adopt it out?"

Caroline flinched as though Julia had slapped her. "Send it to the pound? Are you out of your mind?"

"But it's a puppy. Or at least, it was one fairly recently. It's still a long way from being grown. Everyone wants puppies." She peered at the creature in her arms. It was cute—of course it was; it was a goddamned puppy—but if possible even more winsome than most. She touched a finger to a floppy ear and once again marveled at its softness. Its large eyes flew open, gave her a long soulful look, and closed again.

"No. He's already been through enough upheaval. He was here alone with her after . . . after . . ." Caroline's voice broke. She turned away. Her shoulders heaved. The puppy in Julia's arms whimpered.

The woman faced them again and the puppy relaxed. "Getting here from New York took three flights. A whole day of travel. A neighbor took care of him until I arrived. Can you imagine what those few days must have been like for him? He's lost his person. I can't stand for him to lose his home. I'm willing to drop the rent into the basement for someone who will take him and truly care for him."

The plea in Caroline's eyes stabbed Julia.

Behind her, Sasha shrugged. *I know it's crazy*, her face said. *So sorry.*

Julia looked at the puppy, its butterball stomach, its legs limp in sleep. The outsize paws at their end. How big would it get?

They were still in the upstairs hallway, outside the bathroom. The door stood open. The tub awaited. The lease would probably only be for a year. But for that one year, she and Calvin could live in the sort of home she'd always imagined. Calvin was five, going on six, more helpful around the house every day.

"What's his name again?" she said. "My little boy will want to know."

CHAPTER

20

JULIA HADN'T COUNTED on taking the puppy immediately.

Seemingly within moments, she'd signed a lease and found herself in possession of a tote bag containing a leash, a small dog bed, a bag of puppy kibble and a couple of bowls, and a collection of squeaky toys that filled it to the brim.

Loath to leave him in the house—her new home!—and not knowing else what to do, she took him back to Beverly's, nudging the front door open with her foot as she clasped him to her, fearful he might leap from her arms and run into the street, straight into the path of a passing car. No chance of that, though. Maybe it was merely the warmth of her body, but Jake seemed perfectly comfortable where he was, blinking brief adoring gazes her way before returning to sleep.

Julia tiptoed down the hallway toward the kitchen, wary of waking him. Beverly stood at the counter, rolling out a crust for chicken pot pie. She turned, and Julia watched in amazement as her indomitable mother-in-law's composure cracked, her gaping mouth snapping shut as she fought for control.

Calvin streaked past her.

"A puppy!"

Jake, so sound asleep moments earlier, wriggled free from Julia's arms and leapt directly into her son's.

Calvin fell backward onto the floor and squealed as the puppy gamboled around him, yapping. Lyle the cat shot from a hiding place and scrambled halfway up the stairs, where he turned and yowled outrage.

Beverly's floury hands flew to her ears.

"What in the world? Julia, what have you done? This house cannot possibly abide a dog."

Which was how Julia found herself, a mere two days later, ensconced in the echoey new house, hastily furnished with the few pieces she and Michael had owned, along with some rejects from Beverly's home.

That first night, Calvin fell asleep early, worn out from the day's excitement, puppy Jake slumbering beside him, his chubby body vibrating with soft snores.

Julia walked through the rooms, trying to imprint this new strange layout on her memory. She'd lived in Beverly's house for years and could have negotiated it blindfolded. Its very size had afforded her the illusion of privacy, albeit always with the prickling awareness of another adult in the household.

Before that, she'd shared the apartment with Michael. There'd been roommates in college and law school and in those first years as a public defender, before she'd met Michael. And of course, before that she'd lived with her parents.

How had she reached her thirties without ever having been truly on her own?

"Oh, Michael," she breathed. Her husband would have so loved this house. But a sneaking realization wormed its way into the nostalgia that had finally supplanted the raw pain that for so long had accompanied any thought of Michael: she loved this house, too, and possibly loved it even more because she wouldn't have to share it with another adult, just her son and this canine invader into their lives.

Jake, she reminded herself. A Brittany, Caroline had briefly informed Julia, tossing only a few details her way in her rush to get away from the tragedy that had befallen her family. A kind of spaniel, a bird dog, with auburn and white patches and soft feathery fur on its legs.

"It won't get that big. Maybe forty-fifty pounds."

Which to Julia sounded pretty big. But Calvin had assured her he'd take care of the dog, and given the fact that the two were already inseparable, Julia decided to focus her energy elsewhere. Specifically, on a bath.

The first thing she'd done after she'd locked the door behind the movers Beverly had generously found and hired on short notice was to set the temperature on the water heater as high as she safely dared. When she twisted the faucet, the resounding gush was satisfyingly just short of scalding.

She'd carved out a few minutes in the rush of the previous days to duck into one of the boutiques increasingly lining Main Street, emerging with an assortment of bath salts and candles. Over the last few years, she'd seen increasing references to something called "self-care" and snorted each time. Who were these women who had the time and money for massages, exercise classes, elaborate skin care regimens?

But now she was going to join their ranks, to the best of her limited ability, sinking into lavender-scented water up to her chin, the candles' tiny flames twinkling on the windowsill, the radio turned low to a classic jazz station.

She closed her eyes and let her mind drift. How did this work? She was supposed to think of peaceful, pleasant things—a sunny beach, a flower-strewn meadow. Her mind apparently didn't work that way. She conjured images of a childhood trip to California, only to bring back memories of itchy sand and a fierce sun that had left her redhead's fair skin blistered and peeling. And the postcard-perfect mountain meadows north of Duck Creek were home to grizzly bears that, though rarely glimpsed, imposed a nerve-jangling awareness that tempered even the most enthusiastic appreciation of the abundant wildflowers.

She sank deeper in the tub, tilting her head back, letting the water lift her hair. She had to stretch her legs to touch the tub's far end with her toes. Leslie Harper had been a big woman. Julia supposed she'd ordered a custom tub to comfortably accommodate her dimensions.

Her enjoyment of a dead woman's tub should have been discomfiting, but she couldn't help it. She'd barely known Leslie, as she'd explained to her sister as she signed the lease. "She and a friend of mine were close, though."

Her phone buzzed. Julia sat up, water sloshing from her shoulders. Caroline Harper's number, as though summoned by her thoughts, flashed on the screen.

What could Caroline possibly want at this hour? Especially given that it was nearly midnight back in New York? Had Caroline finally come to her senses and realized how profitably she could cash out on the house if she put it on the market? Were wannabe buyers already clamoring? Given the area's hot housing market, Julia had heard, some people scanned the obituaries, sniffing opportunity. But she had a lease!

The phone stilled.

She sank back into the water, all the way under this time, hair twisting in auburn corkscrews above her. But even underwater, the phone's insistent buzz sounded again.

"Goddammit!" She splashed to a crouch, grabbing it from its perch on the sink, half hoping it would slip from her soapy hand into the tub and kill the bad news that surely awaited.

Caroline voiced an apology, her words tentative, even pleading, exactly the way one would sound when about to screw somebody over.

"Julia? I hope I'm not calling too late."

"It's ten o'clock here." Fuck her. Julia wasn't going to make it easy.

"You're a lawyer, right?"

She'd remembered. Which meant she'd probably hired some fancy-ass New York lawyer to wiggle out of the lease.

"A public defender." As though that made any difference,

"Then I suppose you know the cops in this town."

Was she going to marshal the police to her efforts? Maybe have them bodily throw Julia out if she resisted? Julia had treated herself to a second glass of wine with dinner and now wished she hadn't. Although the muddled quality of Caroline's voice made her wonder if they'd shared that particular indulgence.

"Pretty well, actually." Trying to imply they'd be on her side. Take that, Ms. Evil Landlady.

"Why are they so incompetent?"

Julia pressed the phone's speaker button and set it very carefully back on the sink. Just seconds ago, it had been her enemy, one she'd seriously contemplated drowning. Now, she wanted no harm to befall it.

"What do you mean?"

"I talked with them today. Well, I talk with them every day, asking if there's any progress on her case. And you know what they told me?"

Julia couldn't imagine. But she guiltily suppressed a moment's envy for Caroline's right, as a victim's survivor, to have access to the kind of information unavailable to her.

"What?"

"That they think the medical examiner got it wrong. They went right back to that business of my sister drinking too much. But Leslie had been sober for years. As I told them right away. So why do they keep coming back to that?"

Sober people fell off the wagon all the time, Julia thought. Ray being exhibit A. That said, she was surprised to hear there was any doubt about Pinkham's findings and said as much.

"I'm just telling you what they told me."

"You know I'm not on the case. I mean, I might be if they arrest someone," she began cautiously.

"*If* they arrest someone. Great. Just great. You're just like everyone else in that fucking town."

Which left Julia sitting in water gone cold, looking at a call gone dead, and wondering what had gone sideways in the investigation into a case that—she reminded herself as she climbed from the tub and wrapped her shivering body in a towel—was not hers to wonder about.

21

S HE PUT IN a call to Amanda Pinkham as soon as she dropped Calvin off at school Monday morning.

"Hi, Julia. You'd better be calling about Mary Brannigan."

"Who?"

"She went by Miss Mae."

"Um, yes. Of course I am." A call she should have made a day earlier. It would take her a week of scrambling to make up the time she'd lost during the move into her new home.

"I can help you cut to the chase. Same manner of death as William Williams. Deep, crushing blows to the head. Something like a tire iron again. Maybe a pipe or piece of rebar. It's what killed her, but if it hadn't, the exposure would have. Whoever did it stripped her bare. Which nobody did to Mr. Williams."

"So I heard." Julia braced herself, and practically collapsed across her desk in relief at Pinkham's next words.

"No sign of sexual assault. No semen in or on her body, or—as best as anyone could tell—at the scene. Of course, that doesn't mean anything. Your serial offenders these days, a lot of them use condoms. But there were no other injuries that would indicate it."

"Oh, thank God." At least they couldn't pin that on Ray.

"Weird, though. What kind of pervert gets off on taking the time in the freezing cold to strip someone? You'd think this weather would kill anyone's libido."

"You said it yourself. A deviant. But while I've got you on the phone, I just wanted to check something you said about Leslie Harper."

"You too?" Sudden frost rimed Pinkham's words. Julia rubbed at her ear as though the chill had made its way through her phone. Pinkham knew full well Julia had no official reason for asking and had often complained about questions both gossipy and ghoulish that wasted her time.

"She was dead for at least a couple of days before they found her. But I thought alcohol went out of a person's system within hours."

A bit of information picked up quickly by anyone working in the criminal justice system. Usually cops arrested a drunk driver on the spot, but occasionally one sideswiped a block's worth of parked cars or, far worse, hit a child and then drove away in a panic, managing to avoid arrest until a day or two or even more later, by which time the alcohol would have been absorbed by his body, undetectable by standard tests and thus removing a drunken driving charge from a prosecutor's arsenal. Which was good for Julia but bad for the world at large.

Julia couldn't figure out how to ask her question without it sounding like a challenge. On the other hand, Pinkham was no fan of obfuscation. "So how did you know she was drunk?"

But Pinkham seemed unperturbed. "Hair sample. It stays in the hair for up to three months. We take them in homicide cases. We don't know she was drunk, though."

Even through the phone, Julia could sense Pinkham's waspish enjoyment of her befuddlement. "Okay, I give up."

"She'd been drinking. Last I checked, though, drinkers got killed too. Case—cases—in point: William Williams and Mary Brannigan."

Julia detected the slightest of thaws. They were back in Pinkham's bailiwick now, talking numbers on a scale. She pressed her advantage.

"How much had she had?"

"No clue."

So much for an advantage.

"What do you mean?"

"Hair just shows that somebody's been drinking, not how much."

Julia thought back to that anguished, late-night phone call from Harper's sister, the one that had ruined her first bath in her new tub. "I heard she'd been sober for years."

"A lot of people have heard a lot of things about Leslie Harper. And they all want me to confirm them. For what reason is anyone's guess."

"Like whom?"

"That reporter."

Duh. Of course Chance was asking. It was his job. "C'mon. Tell me something I don't already know. Who else besides Chance?"

"And some cops."

"What cops?"

"That new deputy, for one. The woman."

Julia was glad they were talking by phone so that Pinkham couldn't see her silent *ohhh* of surprise. She swerved away from dangerous territory. "You asked me if Harper had ever been into the hard stuff. Why?"

"Just wondered. I got the tox screens back, though. Nothing."

Caroline Harper's face swam before Julia. Those haunted eyes, fury at war with grief and puzzlement over her sister's death.

"How strong are the chances that this was anything other than an accident?"

A faint tapping came through the phone. Julia smiled. She'd seen Pinkham a few times on the witness stand, giving expert testimony as to cause of death, and knew her habit of tapping the stand with one of those long, shiny black fingernails as she collected her thoughts.

"There was blood on the kitchen counter. I collected that sample myself. The blood was hers," Pinkham said finally. "There wasn't anyone else's blood in the house, and the crime lab folks didn't find any fingerprints. But Harper was a busy woman, always holding meetings in her house."

A few more taps.

"Which doesn't necessarily mean anything. She obviously didn't invite anybody into her house after she died. And maybe she went on some sort of cleaning frenzy before she died. Or—" She waited for Julia to figure it out on her own.

"Or somebody wiped it down. Jesus, Amanda. That's TV crime-of-the-week-special stuff right there." She hoped her light tone belied the chill zinging through her at the thought of someone methodically walking through Harper's home, erasing invisible marks from doorknobs, drawer pulls, faucets, and even toilet handles.

"Not to be cynical, but if you ask me, they're having a hard time tracking down whoever might have done this, and they just want a tough case to go away. It'd be a shame if they're wrong and they don't find the person who did it."

Julia followed the thought to its logical conclusion. "Because then a killer will have gotten away with it."

"That too."

"What else?"

"Because then I won't be able to take the stand and prove exactly how right I was to be skeptical."

* * *

Her next call was to the clerk at the sheriff's office, where she put in a request for the original report on the unattended death of one Leslie Harper.

"You too?" the clerk said. "Poor woman. Whatever happened to letting the dead rest in peace?"

"Who else?" Julia started to ask.

But the clerk's other line rang. "I'll email it over."

The report, when it blinked its arrival in her in-box, was several degrees short of helpful. It was, however, written by Deputy Sheriff Wayne Peterson, a stroke of luck as far as Julia was concerned, though it was strange that a sheriff had handled the case rather than the town police. The two agencies cooperated closely, though. If the cops had been busy that day, they might have kicked the call over to the sheriff's office. Julia printed the report out and reread it.

Leslie Harper had lived alone and had never married or had children. Her absence went unnoticed all through Monday and well into Tuesday, at which point she failed to show up for one of the legislature's interim committee hearings. *Subject was noted for her punctuality*, the report read.

Her absence occasioned a desultory round of telephone calls. Several more hours went by before a legislative aide was dispatched to knock on her door, but he heard only the faint yips and whines of a puppy. The police were then contacted to do a welfare check.

Entry obtained by forcing door. Subject found prone on kitchen floor fully clothed, but for shoes.

Nothing unusual about that. People in Duck Creek routinely took off their shoes as soon as they came indoors, especially in winter, so as not to track snow inside.

Subject appeared to have been deceased for some time—accompanied by the queasy-making indications of same.

Gash on back of head, attributed to possibly striking on kitchen counter during fall. Blood found on counter edge. No signs of a struggle. Open bottle of wine, partially consumed, noted on counter, as well as prescription sleeping medication in medicine cabinet, nearly gone. No note was observed.

Wayne hadn't come right out and called it an accidental overdose—he wasn't qualified to make that determination—but his unofficial conclusion was clear.

Julia read the report a third time, then reached for her phone and scrolled back through her calls until she came to Caroline Harper's number. She braced herself and tapped it.

"Caroline? It's Julia Geary, your new tenant. I'm terribly sorry to bother you."

"Oh God. Is something already wrong with the house? I meant to line up a property manager in town—I'm not cut out to do it myself—but I haven't gotten around to it yet. There's just so much to deal with."

Caroline's words came in a ragged rush. Julia wondered if she'd had a single full night's sleep since her sister's death. On the other hand, Wayne's terse report had referenced sleeping pills. Maybe insomnia ran in the family.

"Caroline, the house is fine. It's wonderful. My son is thrilled."

"And Jake? Is he all right?"

In their short time in the house, the puppy had chewed through one of Calvin's brand-new sneakers, had half eaten a bra that fell from the armful of clothing Julia had dumped down the laundry chute, and had somehow hoisted himself onto a kitchen chair and then the table, after which all that remained of the contents of the butter dish was a glistening slick around his furry muzzle.

"He's fine. He's . . . adorable." Which wasn't what Julia had called him after the butter dish incident. "Caroline, I don't want to cause you any more pain, but who, uh, cleaned out the house after your sister's death?"

A short, sharp exhale. "I did."

Her sister had lain dead for days. At least it was winter. Julia hoped Leslie Harper was one of those people who went around bragging about their low thermostat settings.

"I'm so sorry."

"I had help. There's a company that specializes in such things. Can you imagine? But thank God for them."

"Oh." Julia's heart sank. "Did they move the furniture and all the household goods too?"

"That was another company. But I had to sort through things first. Why?"

"This is going to sound crazy. But was there any wine or liquor or even beer anywhere in the house? Or in the trash or recycling?"

Julia knew the police would have taken the bottle on the counter as evidence, just in case. But others might provide a different sort of evidence.

"I already told you. She'd been sober for years."

Julia apparently didn't chime in fast enough this time. Caroline ended the silence first.

"You think she fell off the wagon. And police said there was an open bottle of wine. But my guess would be she'd had company and was being polite by offering someone a glass. She was so many years into her recovery she was comfortable doing that. I know my sister. I talked to her the Friday before that weekend, and she was sober as a judge. She was planning to come visit me once the legislative session was over. She had some big bill she was sponsoring and something else, some sort of panel she was leading. So she didn't commit suicide either."

By now, Julia knew her role. Agree fast and, with luck, Caroline would keep talking. "It doesn't sound like it. Especially since there wasn't a note."

It was Caroline's turn to agree. "There wasn't. Believe me, I looked. Probably in more places than the police did."

Julia cleared her throat. "The report said something about sleeping medication."

Caroline gave an unambiguous snort. "Ambien. She kept it for when she had to fly, mostly when she visited me. My guess is, the prescription label on that bottle was years old. She was scared to death of flying, and her way of coping was just to conk out during a flight. I take it too, for insomnia. She knew that and she was forever warning me to be careful with it."

In the course of her job, Julia came into contact with her share of addicts and knew well their tendency to deflect; to accuse others of worse behavior than their own. She was a long way from being convinced of Caroline's theory.

"Wait a minute." Caroline ended another lengthening silence. "Why are you asking? Aren't you a public defender? That means you protect the bad guys, right? Are you involved in my sister's case? Do they have a suspect? Have they arrested someone?"

The rising hope in her voice knifed through Julia. She felt like a murderer herself when she stumbled through an apology, telling Caroline that no, she was just curious.

But when she hung up, even though she spent long moments lecturing herself about the foolishness of Caroline's protestations—that the half-bottle of wine seemed at odds with Leslie Harper's long-standing sobriety; that she rarely resorted to Ambien; that the lack of a note was proof positive the woman hadn't killed herself—Julia had to admit those same things stuck her, too, as odd.

At which point, she gave herself a final lecture. Whatever had happened to Leslie Harper was none of her business. At least it wasn't until Marie returned from wherever she'd been, cheeks reddened with cold or excitement or both, practically bursting in her phlegmatic way.

"How's your day going, Julia?"

"Fine." Julia knew she was supposed to ask in return but didn't feel like opening herself to another conversation that would give Marie a chance to flaunt her supposed superiority. She pulled Ray's file toward her and flipped through it, scanning the court dates she already knew by heart and making a pretense of checking whether she'd entered them into her phone.

Marie logged on to her computer, sneaking frequent glances at Julia.

"For God's sake," Julia said finally. "Whatever it is, out with it."

"I just had coffee with a law enforcement source." Her eyes glittered.

Apparently she'd forgotten that Julia had suggested she talk with Wayne. Julia wondered if she herself should have a different sort of talk with Wayne. Attention from a starstruck young woman was probably flattering, but the last thing any of them needed was an interoffice entanglement. Those occurred with depressing regularity in the hothouse atmosphere of the courthouse—see Adonis—but they rarely ended well, resulting in whole divisions barely speaking to one another for weeks on end as people chose sides.

Julia formed cautionary phrases in her head, but just as she was ready to start lobbing them, Marie spoke again.

"Looks like they're thinking about starting some sort of internal investigation."

Another pause.

"Okay, Marie. I'll bite."

"He talked in circles"—for sure, that sounded like Wayne—"but as best I can tell, it's about that woman deputy. I got the feeling he thinks she's sitting on some evidence in Ray's case."

Marie had Julia's full attention now. "Such as?"

"Maybe it's something that can help us, although I got the sense from him that it might firm up the case against Ray. Either way, it's best we know what it is, right? Hey, where are you going?"

Julia had her coat half on and one foot out the door.

"To find Cheryl Hayes and talk to her."

The minute a formal investigation was launched, Hayes wouldn't be able to talk to anyone about it. Julia aimed to get to her first.

22

THE PROBLEM WAS, she couldn't exactly barge into the sheriff's office and demand to speak to Deputy Hayes.

She could lurk outside the sheriff's department entrance to the courthouse and hope that Hayes would appear, but the cold snap lingered. Most of the cops and deputies took their breaks at a nearby café, but Julia had never seen Hayes with them. It was lunchtime, though, and just in case, she sauntered past the café, trying not to peer too ostentatiously in the window. Sure enough, Wayne was there, along with a couple of the other deputies. But no Cheryl Hayes.

She couldn't have gone far. It was too cold, and besides, her break was too short. Julia stuck her head into a bagel place. Nothing. Same with a pizzeria. She almost walked past a tea shop, something new for Duck Creek and entirely too precious for Julia's tastes, tending toward crocheted doilies and delicate china pots with pastel flowers. But she caught a glimpse of brown uniform through the lace curtains and backtracked just in case.

The door opened as she approached.

"Hello, doll. Fancy meeting you here. I didn't take you for the tea-and-crumpets type."

Julia looked into the lopsided grin of Mack Coates.

He let the door close behind him.

Her "I guess I could say the same about you" came a beat too late.

"There's a lot you don't know about me," Coates said with the arch, flirtatious tone he used with nearly everyone. Julia thought of him as a particularly beautiful snake, all bright colors and sinuous hypnotic charm, one so seductive you barely detected the flashing strike, the poison seeping through your system.

He chucked her beneath the chin with a leather-gloved forefinger, then strutted away, a laugh trailing behind him.

Julia's chin burned. She rubbed it, trying to erase his touch, and pushed her way through the door. A bell tinkled daintily. Julia ignored the woman at the counter and looked toward the back corner where Cheryl Hayes sat in her brown uniform, nose deep in a book.

Julia glanced back toward the door. Hayes had attended Coates's initial court appearance.

Had she been meeting with him here? If so, she'd recovered quickly. Or maybe she was just made of stronger stuff than Julia, whose nerves jangled so after every encounter with the man that she couldn't have concentrated on a book if she'd tried. But Hayes didn't even look up.

The woman at the counter cleared her throat.

"A perfect day for a nice cup of tea to warm you through and through. What will you have?"

"What do you suggest?" Julia parried. She really wanted coffee.

"Green? Black? Herbal?"

"Um."

"Smoky notes or flowery?"

"Um."

The woman's lips crimped. "Let's start with some basics. Caffeinated or non?"

Thank heavens. She was finally speaking Julia's language. "Caffeinated, definitely. The strongest you've got."

"If it's caffeine you're after, you might want to try yerba mate. It's Argentinian."

The price would have purchased Julia a perfectly good latte. She glanced back at Hayes, who was still reading, then at her watch. She had, at most, fifteen minutes.

The woman fiddled with something at the other end of the long counter. How long did it take to boil enough water for a single cup of tea, for God's sake?

She finally returned with a tray, which she handed to Julia with the air of bestowing something precious.

Julia eyeballed a small round pot with a metal straw protruding from it.

"Enjoy!" the woman said brightly.

Doubtful, Julia thought.

She'd thought to fake surprise at seeing Hayes, but at this point, the direct approach was best.

She carried the tray carefully over to Hayes's table and joined her without asking permission.

"Deputy Hayes. We meet again."

Hayes put her book aside with obvious reluctance, leaving it open to the page she'd been reading. Julia glanced at it, expecting maybe a procedural manual or a crime novel. Instead—"Dostoyevsky?"

Which, she supposed, was the ultimate crime novel.

"You thought it might be something with a lot of pictures?" Hayes looked tired, and in no mood to entertain company.

"I don't know what I thought," Julia said honestly. She put her lips to the metal straw and sipped a mouthful of what tasted like liquid grass cuttings. "Gah! That's awful."

Hayes lifted her own cup. It wobbled in her trembling hand, and she set it back down quickly. "There's nothing wrong with a cup of Earl Grey."

"If I'd been able to come up with the name, that's what I would have ordered. I don't usually drink tea."

"Then why are you here today?"

The woman was certainly direct, her question brisk and saturated with irritation, at odds with the tremor Julia had seen. Julia looked again, but she'd tucked her hands beneath the table.

"I thought I might find you here. Not here, necessarily. But somewhere downtown during lunchtime." She'd thought to ask the woman straightaway about Ray's case. But—Coates in a tea shop? "Were you meeting with Mack Coates?"

Hayes ignored her question about Coates and responded with one of her own.

"And you wanted to find me because . . . ?"

"Because you're working the case—the cases—of Billy Williams and Miss Mae. I've heard some things that don't add up and wanted to run them by you."

Hayes picked up her book and snapped it shut.

"You've come to the wrong place. And definitely the wrong person. I'm not working those cases."

"But I saw you at the crime scene. The first one. You were . . ." She didn't finish the sentence. *Kneeling by the spot where Billy died.* It seemed too personal.

"I saw you there too. Should I make something of that?" Hayes rose and thrust an arm into her parka.

"Wait. Please. Could we have an off-the-record conversation? I just want to know whether I'm crazy to think this case is bogus. Or, if not bogus, whether they charged Ray with way too little evidence. Is there something I'm missing? Something that might help him?" Grasping at straws, even though Wayne had implied to Marie that whatever Hayes was withholding might convict Ray.

Hayes chugged the last of the tea from her pretty little cup and set it down so hard Julia feared the delicate china would shatter.

"Oh, there's plenty missing. But maybe you didn't hear me when I said I'm the wrong person. Wayne Peterson is your man. You guys are friends anyway, right? So you should have your *off-the-record* conversation with him," she said, giving the term a twist of disgust. "But you probably already know that nothing in this goddamn town is ever off the record, so good luck with that."

Hayes zipped her parka to her chin. "You're right about one thing. This case is about as bogus as it gets."

She wrapped Julia's forearm in a mittened hand, squeezing so hard Julia nearly yelped.

"Never mind what I said about nothing being off the record in this town. That thing I just told you? About it being bogus? Repeat it and you'll find yourself in shit so deep your eyeballs will turn brown."

A comment that left Julia so shaken she finished her yerba mate without even noticing the taste.

* * *

At least she knew where to find Wayne. She trailed the group of deputies from the café to the courthouse and called to him just as they were about the enter the building.

"Wayne. A word?"

"Darrell, start my car for me? Otherwise I'll be halfway up the mountain before my ass thaws. I'll be there in a few." He tossed a set of keys to one of the other deputies and turned to Julia. "Child abuse case. When it's this cold for this long, people cooped up together— you know how it goes." She did, and she hated those cases, the way it took everything she had to dredge up empathy for the defendants.

"Just wanted to pick your brain again about Cheryl Hayes." No need to mention that she'd just hunted the woman down, especially not after Hayes's warning. "Is there something she knows about Ray's case? Any idea what it is?"

"What's this? You and Ree double-teaming me now?"

He jammed his hands in his pockets and stood hatless in the wind, grinning.

"C'mon, Wayne. It's too cold out here to screw around."

The grin vanished. "Thought I warned you about Hayes."

"You did. But I don't know why."

Wayne started in the direction of the parking lot beside the courthouse. Julia hustled to keep up with his long strides.

"Listen, Julia. I can't talk about an ongoing investigation, but that woman is trouble. Everything she touches turns to fuck."

"What ongoing investigation? Into the killings? Also—*turns to fuck*? What does that even mean?"

Wayne stopped so fast she nearly ran into him.

"Spend much time around Hayes and you'll know exactly what it means. Take anything she says with a whole shakerful of salt."

Hayes had said she wasn't on the case. Julia had just asked Wayne flat out if she was. A simple no would have sufficed. He hadn't offered one.

* * *

"And . . ." He was off again, nearly jogging now, heading toward a black SUV whose tailpipe belched a stream of exhaust.

Julia sprinted to catch up. "And?"

They were at the car. He opened the door, releasing a blast of warm air, and scooped the keys from the seat. Julia took a step toward the heat.

"Can't talk about an ongoing investigation. Whether it's the homicides or . . ." Another long pause, in case she didn't already get that he was messing with her. "Internal."

He waved as the car slid away. His grin was back, wider than before.

23

J ULIA STOOD IN her new kitchen that night, using two of the six burners on the restaurant-style range.

Bubbles nudged the surface of the water in one pot, signaling that it was almost ready for pasta. In the other, meatballs from the frozen food section bobbed in sauce from a jar. Their meal would be neither creative nor fancy, merely fast and filling, which met her—and more important, Calvin's—requirements.

He waited impatiently at the table, picking the croutons from his salad and crunching them audibly between his teeth.

"You have to eat the lettuce too," she reminded him. "And you should wait until we're both at the table, and—hey! Stop feeding the dog!"

Jake danced at his feet, awaiting another crouton. A few slices of mushroom lay untouched beside him on the floor.

"He's like me," Calvin said, unperturbed. "He doesn't like mushrooms either."

It was a flagrant violation of a newly established rule, but Julia wasn't paying attention. She stared at the expanse of tiled floor, wondering exactly where Leslie Harper had been found.

But if her death had been accidental—the deadly mixture of booze and pills that killed far too many people—wouldn't it make sense that she'd have been in bed, or sprawled on a sofa in front of a television? Sure, people drank all the time while cooking. Julia herself had a glass of Chianti at her elbow.

But who guzzled wine, popped pills, and then wandered around the kitchen? Besides, the pills had been in the upstairs medicine cabinet. Harper would have had to wander back downstairs before face-planting on the kitchen floor.

"It doesn't make sense," she murmured.

"Mom. *Mom*."

Jake barked. Julia looked up.

"Your water. It's boiling." Calvin pointed to the water, which was boiling so furiously it splashed onto the stovetop.

"Right. Sorry." She dumped in the pasta and gave it a quick stir.

Her phone rang. No ID on the number, but she answered it anyway, just in case, hoping it was one of the people from the creek calling on a Tracfone.

"Hello?"

"Julia." Something familiar in the voice, speaking in low, confidential tones. "How are you tonight?"

"Who's this?" She tucked the phone between chin and shoulder and put a couple of bowls in the microwave to warm them. She picked up the wooden spoon again and gave the pasta another quick stir.

"A friend. Someone who cares about you."

Julia dropped the spoon. She left the kitchen quickly, moving down the hall until she was sure she was out of earshot from Calvin, Jake close at her heels.

"Who are you? What do you want?"

"You ask a lot of questions." That same silky, confiding tone, pitched low, neither discernibly male nor female. "So did Leslie Harper. And now you're in her house. In her kitchen. The very spot where she died. Do you believe in coincidence, Julia?"

She gasped and fumbled for the phone's off button, her hands shaking. By the time she found it, her caller had already hung up.

* * *

Deputy Wayne Peterson was at her door within fifteen minutes.

"Oh God, thank you." Julia held it together until she opened the door to the reassuring sight of someone who would Handle It. Her voice cracked damnably. "I didn't want to call 911 over just a phone call, but . . ."

He held up a hand. "Stop. A, you should have called 911, and B, since you didn't, I'm glad you called me. Stay here for a few minutes. I'm going to check around the outside of the house."

She closed the door and locked it behind him, then watched the sweep of his flashlight as he made a circuit of the house and yard.

"Mom? I'm hungry."

She'd yanked Calvin from his chair and fled into the hall as soon as she'd hung up with Wayne. She'd had the presence of mind to turn off the flames under the pots on the stove, but the pasta had probably turned to mush anyway.

"Just wait a few more minutes. We'll eat as soon as Deputy Peterson goes home."

"But why are we in the hallway? Why can't we go back into the kitchen?"

Why? Because of the darkness beyond that rear wall of windows where someone lurked, watching her as she moved about the kitchen preparing a dinner for her child.

She jumped as Wayne rapped on the door. She ran to unlock it, Jake at her heels, yapping fiercely.

"Well?"

"No sign of anyone. Not that I expected anything, but you never know. Sometimes somebody gets careless, drops something. It happens."

Calvin clutched Bear-Bear, the stuffed toy that now shared top billing with Jake as his favorite companion, Julia herself a distant third. He pressed himself against her legs and peeped around her.

"Who's this big fellow?" Wayne stooped and offered a hand. "And who's his furry friend?"

Calvin hung back.

"Smart boy. You shouldn't talk to strangers unless your mom says it's okay."

She nodded to Calvin. "It's fine."

He took Wayne's hand. "I'm Calvin," he whispered. "This is Bear-Bear."

"And what about this very scary guard dog?"

Calvin managed a smile. "Jake."

"Does Jake have a favorite toy?"

"Benny. His turtle."

"A turtle?" He turned to Julia.

"It's stuffed. Sort of. He shreds a little more of it every day. Benny's down to two legs. It's a constant battle to keep Bear-Bear from meeting the same fate."

"If that's what he does to Benny, just think what he'd do to a bad guy."

Calvin rewarded him with a giggle. Julia, though, imagined Jake—still mostly fluff and lingering puppy fat—up against some shadowy figure bent on harm. Her hands, which had finally stopped shaking, began to dance anew. She knotted her fingers behind her back.

"Tell you what. Why don't you and Jake play with his turtle for a minute while I talk to your mom?"

Julia nodded permission, waiting until Calvin and Jake descended toward the basement playroom. When she turned back to Wayne, his face was grim.

"Couple of things. You got any whiskey in this place?"

Julia rushed for the cupboard and found a glass. "I'm sorry. I'm so rattled I didn't even offer."

"Not for me. For you."

She pointed to a cabinet over the refrigerator. He retrieved a bottle, poured a healthy splash into the glass, added a little more, and handed it to her.

She sipped, coughed, and drank again.

He waited until she put the glass down.

"First things first. Get some curtains for these goddamn windows. All of them. And get your locks changed. Here." He pulled a business card from his pocket and wrote a number on the back. "Here's a guy I've used. He's good. Tell him I told you to call and that I said to put you in front of all his other customers."

"A locksmith! Really? After all, it's not like he threatened me." *No,* Julia thought, *he just scared the shit out of me.* "You don't think he'll try to break in, do you?" She drained the glass.

"Probably not. And new locks probably aren't necessary, but you'll sleep better. He's probably just some guy who walked by, saw you through the window, and decided to have some fun. An opportunist. You'd be surprised how many serial peepers we've got in this town."

"No, I wouldn't. I defend them, remember? Anyway, it wasn't that kind of call."

"I don't guess you recorded it."

"It's illegal without permission in our state. You know that."

He gave her a pitying look. "If he calls again, hit record and worry about the legalities later. I'm a cop, and I'm telling you that."

She tried to smile. "And I'm a lawyer and I'm telling you I absolutely will."

"Good girl." He looked around the kitchen. "I haven't been in this place since . . ." He stopped. "Not just the night we found her. And before too. She hosted meetings for us sometimes. She'd call the city cops, some of us deputy sheriffs, cook up a storm, and pick our brains about reform."

"Sounds lovely." And it did. But her present moment was anything but.

"Wayne, he—I'm just guessing it was a he; I really couldn't tell—knew where her body was found. How would anyone know that?"

He sat down at the table and gestured for her to do the same. "Probably half the town knows by now. You know how things are in Duck Creek. The sister flies in, talks to the neighbor or some of Leslie's friends. She tells them, they tell everyone they know; next thing you know, Chance Larsen's printed it on the front page for the benefit of the three people left who didn't know."

She dug her hands into her hair, then knotted it into a bun at her nape, trying to seem purposeful. "But the person told me to stop asking questions. Wayne, it's like you said—a lot of people in town are talking about this. Asking the same questions I'm asking."

He reached across the table and patted her arm. "Which is exactly why I think it's just some jackoff—I know, not literally in this case, at least probably not—messing with you. I'm sorry to point out the obvious, but it's probably someone who recognized you, maybe one of the frequent fliers, realized that you're living in Leslie's house now, and is trying to turn the whole thing into some B movie haunted-house scenario."

"Do you really think so?"

"I really do. Now, you've got a little boy to feed, and a dog, too, unless you want him to finish eating that turtle. I'm going to head out. If—and truly, Julia, I consider it a big if—anything like this happens again, you either call 911 or me right away. And get those locks changed."

"Thanks, Wayne." It came out small and choked, but Julia was too grateful to be properly mortified.

Only later, after she'd double-checked that the deadbolts were fastened, propped chairs beneath the front and back doors for good measure, and had another whiskey and crawled straight into bed, forgoing the pleasure of a bath, did her mind snag on something Wayne had said.

She reached for her phone and clicked on the *Bulletin*'s website, searching for the names Chance Larsen and Leslie Harper.

Wayne had theorized that her caller had read the details of Leslie's death in one of Chance's stories. But he couldn't have. Because that particular detail had never made its way into print.

CHAPTER

24

THE LOCKSMITH SHOWED up within an hour of her call the next morning.

"Any friend of Wayne's," he said. "He kicks a lot of business my way. You can't imagine how many women in this town have stalker exes."

"I have an idea." She had to defend the men in court, although such cases tended to be slam dunks for the prosecution, given reams of telephone records sometimes showing dozens of calls a day along with lurid texts and voice mails.

But knowing about them was one thing, being on the gut-twisting receiving end quite another. Before she'd finally fallen asleep, just a couple of hours shy of her alarm jolting her into resentful wakefulness, she'd gone online and ordered curtains for the kitchen and draperies for the living and dining rooms, heavy fabric designed to block a prying gaze. The house would feel like a tomb when they were drawn. Or maybe it would seem a shelter from whatever malevolent force lurked outside.

The locksmith handed her the new keys, shiny and sharp edged. She'd considered an electronic lock, but after the shocking damage to her credit card from the curtains and drapes, she'd gone old-school on the locks.

The locksmith bent and gently disentangled himself from Jake, who was doing his best to climb up his leg. "Cute fellow."

"That's one word for him." While Julia had spent the night twisting her sheets into sweaty chaos, Jake had been busy in her closet, silently gnawing her only pair of pumps into drool-slicked oblivion. He tumbled from the locksmith's knee onto the floor and scrambled to his feet, gazing up at her, head cocked, backside shimmying.

"If Calvin didn't love you so much . . ." she said, which was pretty much how all of her conversations with the dog began.

The locksmith handed her the bill. She looked and did a double take. "This can't be right. This counts as an emergency call, right? Isn't there an extra charge for that?"

"Friend of Wayne's," he reminded her.

She should call Wayne, chide him about crossing a line. She couldn't accept favors. But she was already late to work, and besides, Ray Belmar had finally agreed to an interview, and if she left that very minute, she could just make it.

She grabbed her things, turned the key in her new lock, listened for the solid, reassuring click of the new industrial-strength dead-bolt, and headed for the jail.

*   *   *

Ray looked like somebody had shoved a tennis ball into his cheek, skin stretched taut and shiny in rotten-plum hues.

"Good God." Just when Julia thought he'd lost any ability to shock her, he did so by his very appearance. "What happened?"

He started to shake his head, winced, and stopped. "Nothing." He spoke out of the other side of his mouth.

Her hand flew to her own cheek. "That's not nothing, Ray. It looks serious. Who hit you?"

He looked at the ceiling, as though the answer floated some-where among the harsh fluorescent lights.

"Somebody I hit first."

"What?"

Given the amount of time he'd spent locked up, Ray could have taught a master class on jail rules and regulations. Being in a fight was bad enough, but starting one all but guaranteed extra penalties.

"What's going on with you? Starting fights here, getting into that argument with Billy."

He twisted his mouth and forced more words out of the unin-jured side.

"Never mind about me. What's going on with you?"

Their old dance, Ray demanding some tidbit from her before handing over something in exchange. She usually offered up one of Calvin's escapades.

"Let's see. We have a puppy."

"Awww." A smile started but turned into a grimace. "That's sweet."

"Calvin thinks so. That dog eats everything within reach, whether it's food or not. He murdered a pair of my shoes last night. Calvin barely managed to save the remote yesterday."

Ray's shoulders shook in a silent laugh.

"Your turn. What happened?"

Ray folded his arms across his chest. "You're here." He stopped, took a breath, and forced the rest of the words. "To talk about my case."

"Right." She tried to refocus, staring down at the table between them. It was easier than looking at his swollen jaw. She wondered if he'd lost teeth.

"What did you and Billy fight about?"

"Wasn't a fight." He made a fist, punched the air. "Not like that. Just a beef. Verbal, like."

"Fine. But what was it about?"

"Stupid shit. Women."

He could say anything and she had no choice but to believe him. Billy wasn't around to contradict him.

"Angie?"

"Sure."

Which was a lot less definitive than she'd have liked.

He squared his shoulders, twisted his mouth, and forced another sentence from its corner. "What else is going on with you?"

Her head jerked up. One anecdote was all he usually sought before they got down to business. She'd already offered up the puppy.

"Let's see. I have a new house. Here—you'll find this interesting. Leslie Harper lived there."

"Fuck. Are you crazy? Aaaagh." Ray sat up straight, then fell back in his chair, face contorting.

"Why? *Why?*"

"No reason." His response was nearly unintelligible. He cradled his cheek in his hand. The old injuries from his encounter with the Rotarians—seemingly so long ago, almost charmingly mischievous in comparison to the dilemma he now faced—had faded, but new wounds knotted his fingers and purpled the back of his hand. Whomever Ray had hit, he'd hit him *hard*.

"Dammit, Ray, if you know something, you need to tell me. Some asshole called me last night, told me he could see me in the kitchen and that he knew Harper had died there. I just changed the locks today. If there's more to this than just a creeper taking advantage of the fact I hadn't put up curtains yet, I have to know."

Ray rose stiffly to his feet and thumped on the door with his elbow, which at least appeared to be unhurt.

"'Member how I tried to call you? Wanted to meet with you? Before all this?" Blood leaked from a corner of his mouth. "Too bad we never got the chance."

A guard led him away. He didn't look back.

CHAPTER

25

JULIA RETURNED TO the office facing a string of innocuous voice mails that nonetheless demanded attention, and a full afternoon court schedule.

She barely made it to Calvin's after-school program by the six PM pickup deadline, and when she got home, Calvin needed dinner and the puppy demanded kibble in addition to whatever household item he'd managed to destroy that day.

Dinner, of course, meant dishes to be washed; then she had to walk the dog, who viewed his leash as a tug-of-war toy, turning the walk into more of a prolonged drag, which while it delighted Calvin added that many more minutes to an overlong day that still included a bath and bedtime story for Calvin.

Julia couldn't do the research she'd postponed all day until she'd fallen fully clothed into bed, Jake snoring lightly beside her in violation of her futile no-dogs-on-the-furniture rule.

She didn't have the energy to get out her laptop or unearth her tablet from whatever box it had ended up in during the move. Instead she plugged her phone into its charger and tapped her way to the legislature's website, squinting at the dense type on the tiny screen until she found the bills Leslie Harper had been sponsoring before death cut her efforts short. Most of them seemed fairly straightforward for a progressive legislator who knew just how far she could push things in an otherwise conservative state.

Hence a bill to allow the state's popular brewpubs, an outsize number of them located in Duck Creek, to stay open later at night. A bill to create all-day kindergarten. (Julia hoped that one would pass. She paid an obscene amount of money for the afternoon day-care session Calvin attended at the school.)

A handful of proposals that began *Generally revise . . .* followed by some obscure law that needed updating to reflect, say, the fact that people had been driving automobiles for well over a century. Several of Harper's bills, though, had to do with some aspect of the criminal justice system: proposals to compensate wrongfully convicted people for the time they'd languished in prison; one to eliminate the death penalty (which had even less hope of passing than a bill to impose a sales tax); one to eliminate the onerous fees applied to those who found themselves in the court system, fees that mounted extraordinarily quickly and that often saw the Ray Belmars of the world land back in jail, not because they'd committed a new crime but because they hadn't paid their court costs.

Julia hated the fees but knew the good citizens of their state would hate the tax increase necessary to make up the difference even more. Even if Harper had lived, that bill wouldn't have stood a chance.

Julia lay the phone aside, turned off her bedside light, and rolled over, her tumble toward sleep bumping up against a damnable detail. Someone—who?—had mentioned Harper being on a study committee, one of the groups put together by the legislature to delve into pressing issues and fashion bills to address them. She groaned, knowing she'd never sleep with that final question hovering like a mosquito whining at her ear.

She reached again for the phone, blinked a few times to focus, and went back to the legislature's site. It took a while—the legislature hadn't seen fit to spend money making its site user-friendly—but she finally found it. The committee was looking into establishing an oversight board for the state's sheriff's departments, often jealously guarded fiefdoms of patronage, especially in its rural reaches. Until recently, their state hadn't even required sheriffs and deputies to graduate from the state police academy. Maybe Harper had pissed off some small-town sheriff who'd been running some penny-ante protection racket. She'd ask Wayne in the morning.

Which was the last thought Julia had before falling asleep with the phone on her chest and the puppy snuggled tight beneath her chin.

*   *   *

It seemed as though Wayne might prove useless once again.

"Anybody would be a fool to object to a commission like that," he said. "Just makes it seem like you've got something to hide."

She'd found him at the coffee stand, where he'd taken one look at the same sight she'd confronted in the mirror that morning—the crepey flesh beneath her eyes, the blotchy skin, and grooves from mouth to chin—and offered her the cup in his hand, shaking his head and backing away when she refused.

"They got my order wrong," he said. "They gave it to me black. If you don't drink it, I'm just going to toss it."

Julia didn't believe his cockamamy story for a minute but took the coffee anyway, downing it in throat-searing gulps as Wayne talked on.

"Any objection is just as stupid as all the fuss about body cams. People should be happy to have proof they didn't screw up. Same with this study commission. If your department's squeaky-clean, then let 'em study all they want."

Julia tilted her cup, ascertaining that it was truly empty. "But you and I both know some sketchy stuff goes on out in those rural counties. They've got such a hard time finding people to work in the hinterlands for crap pay that they'll take anybody they can get."

He offered a bland smile. "So maybe an oversight board is a good idea. They'll ferret that stuff out and we'll all be the better for it. Glad I work here. Our department's big enough and people are paid well enough that we don't have to worry about it. Although, come to think of it . . ."

He stopped.

Julia had started for the coffee cart for a second cup. She turned back. "Come to think of it, what?"

"Somebody in our department did raise a stink about it. The commission, I mean. But it was probably just on principle. That whole libertarian thing. You know how it is. Did everything work out with the locksmith?"

She gave him a thumbs-up. "Perfect. Nice guy. But Wayne, who?"

He shook his head. "Doesn't matter. You know how people are. Have a good day, Julia. And get some sleep tonight. Hope you don't mind my saying so, but you look like hell."

"Wayne." She had to jog to catch up with his long, loping stride. "Who?"

He stopped at the door of the sheriff's department. "I didn't want to say. I know you think I'm always bad-mouthing her. But I guess this isn't really running her down. Everybody's entitled to their own opinion, right?"

Oh. Cheryl Hayes again.

But when she opened her mouth, he drew his finger across her lips, gently closing them.

"Remember," he said. "I never told you anything."

* * *

"Whole lotta not-talkin' going on," she muttered to his retreating back.

Ray wouldn't talk. Cheryl Hayes wouldn't either. Mack Coates didn't want *her* to talk. Nor did her anonymous caller. The one person who did want to talk with her—Marie the intern, who never quite managed to chase the pleading from her eyes, despite the aloof expression she affected—Julia wanted as little to do with as possible. And she couldn't talk to the two people whose company she most craved, Dom and Claudette.

"Fuck it," she said.

She didn't have the nerve to contact Dom—just thinking about him put her right back in that moment, the sudden splash of light across the bed, Dom still moving beneath her, the glimpse of Elena's horrified face over her shoulder. Why didn't brains come with an erase switch?

But Claudette was a different story.

She headed outside, walking the two blocks to the county prosecutor's office, which for some reason rated its own separate building, fodder for endless snark among the public defenders, who already resented the fact that they were paid less than the prosecutors.

She realized when she pushed through the door that she'd never been to Claudette's new digs; had never been there at all, in fact, even during all the years when Dom's ex was the county prosecutor. So her gasp of appreciation and envy was genuine when a receptionist ushered her into Claudette's lair.

Julia took in the desk sized to impress, the two comfortable chairs—and a sofa!—along with an entire wall of shelves and another of wooden file cabinets topped with a collection of thriving houseplants that would have shriveled for lack of light in the public defenders' office. Pavarotti, Claudette's canary, warbled a greeting from a new, larger cage that swung from the ceiling.

She turned an appreciative circle, arms flung wide. "La-di-freaking-da. How do you even get any work done here? I'd be too busy staring at all the goodies to file a single affidavit."

Claudette leaned back, put her feet up on the desk, and gestured Julia toward one of the chairs.

"I admit to enjoying it. A lot."

Julia stroked the chair's polished arm. "I would too."

"You could." Claudette arched an eyebrow. "If you ever wanted to come over to the dark side, I'd put you at the top of the list."

Julia couldn't deny she'd thought about it. An extra ten grand a year, for starters, just enough to edge her into a category where she wouldn't have had to take a rental deal involving a dog. And a title that people liked—crime fighter!—rather than one that involved sticking up for the criminals. The alleged criminals, she reminded herself.

She imagined herself on the other side of the courtroom, haranguing some poor sap like Ray, always in trouble but never doing real harm to anyone but himself. Trying to persuade a judge to slap him with a bail he'd never manage, leaving him in jail, every day there a day further away from assuming a job, responsibilities, an education, a family. The fact that the odds were against someone like Ray ever doing any of those things anyway was beside the point. At least, out in the world, he'd have a fighting chance.

"Not yet," she said. "But ask me after I'm done with this case."

Claudette opened Pavarotti's cage and offered a finger. He hopped onto it and she withdrew her hand, sitting very still as he clambered up her arm and onto her shoulder, where he proceeded to nibble on an earring.

"You know we can't talk about the case. Unless you're here about a plea agreement."

You had to give Claudette credit. She never stopped pushing, which probably explained her career trajectory.

"Right. But I'm not. I'm here about Leslie Harper. You two were tight, right?"

Claudette's feet hit the floor with a thump. Pavarotti hunched and tucked his head under a wing.

"It wasn't just work. We were in a book group together." Her voice thickened. "We always looked forward to meeting at her house. That woman could cook like nobody's business. The entire kitchen island would be covered with cookies, pastries, you name it."

"Know anything about her work at the Capitol?"

Claudette's fond smile coexisted with the tears in her eyes. "She was *fierce*. You know, criminal justice reform is nobody's idea of popular. But she went after it anyway, even though her bills got shot down year after year. But every so often she'd get something through, maybe just an amendment to another bill. 'It's a long game,' she'd say, and go right back to drafting more bills destined to die in committee."

Pavarotti peeked out from beneath his wing, assessed the change in her mood, and rubbed his head against her cheek. Claudette touched a finger to the corner of her eye. "I hate when we lose our warriors."

A mantel clock—yes, Claudette had a mantel, over a damn fireplace—chimed softly. Julia needed to get back to her own office.

"Know anything about the study commission she was on? The one about an oversight agency for the sheriff's departments?"

Claudette gently removed Pavarotti from her shoulder and returned him to his cage. "Not much," she said with her back to

Julia. "I guess there were some allegations about our department. But they must not have come to anything, or I'd have heard about it."

"That makes sense." Julia stood. "I'm going back to real work in a real office. You have fun here in your luxury suite."

Julia got out of the office as fast as she could, holding her face very still, afraid that Claudette would divine she'd let something slip.

Wayne had expressed relief that the Peak County Sheriff's Office was large enough, its deputies well-enough paid, that it didn't have to worry about the sort of petty corruption that plagued other offices around the state.

But he'd told her that Cheryl Hayes had balked at the idea of oversight. And Claudette had just revealed that whatever problem had snagged the legislature's attention concerned the Peak County department.

Now the person who'd been responsible for gearing up a mechanism to look into it was dead.

CHAPTER

26

No matter how quietly Julia nudged open her office door, Marie's head snapped up and turned her way, her moon face palely aglow with hope that Julia would toss her a new crumb vaguely resembling a meaningful task.

This morning, Julia handed her a whole slice of bread.

"Did you know, or know of, Leslie Harper? The legislator?"

Marie slumped. "The one they think might have been murdered? Even though it looked like she killed herself?"

"We don't know either of those," Julia said. "Listen, before you go any further in this line of work, there's another saying you should memorize. Maybe write it down on a sticky note and put it on your computer."

Marie, who'd taken every opportunity to inform Julia that she already knew everything—at least, that's how Julia saw it—folded her arms across her chest. "What's that?"

"Assume makes an *ass* out of *u* and *me*."

Marie's lower lip crept forward. Her eyebrows pulled together in a single faint line.

"What does she have to do with your case?"

"Nothing."

Marie's expression made Julia think of a saying her mother had employed during her various childhood discontents: *You could perch the whole world on that lip.*

"Maybe something," she amended. "I'm counting on you to find the connection."

She looked away, embarrassed and faintly ashamed at the strength of the gratitude shining in Marie's eyes. She didn't even want to admit to herself, let alone to Marie, that her questions surrounding Leslie Harper's death were probably nothing more than a distraction from the seemingly intractable matter of the charges against Ray.

"I'll get right on it." Marie was all business now, gathering her things, stashing a notebook and a recorder in her briefcase. "I'll talk to the other legislators from Peak County. Unless you were going to?"

Julia was going to do no such thing. But Marie pressed on, even as Julia shook her head.

"Who are you pursuing? I'd hate for us to trip over each other."

No chance of that, Julia thought. "I've already talked to Wayne Peterson."

Marie's shoulders drooped.

"And"—remembering what Wayne had said—"I'll talk again to that other deputy. Cheryl Hayes."

"The one who Wayne said might be sitting on some evidence about Mr. Belmar?"

"That one. He's bad-mouthed her about Ray's case and now Harper's too. What is it about these two cases that's making her monkey around with them? Maybe she's a bad apple who just turns everything she touches to fuck. Wayne's phrase, not mine," she said in response to Marie's startled grimace. "But if it's just these two, maybe there's a relationship."

Marie nodded briskly, all business. "I'll report back to you as soon as I've got something."

As though there were anything to be had.

But at least she was gone, leaving Julia blissfully alone. She picked up a pen and bit down on it. Suppose Wayne was right, that Hayes was one of those people who saw faults and slights everywhere and objected to everything. God knew the Public Defender's Division had its share of malcontents, as did every office.

But three people were dead, all of them either at least a little or a lot drunk, all of them with lethal head wounds. Still, the old Sesame Street tune played in her head: "One of these things is not like the other."

The deaths of Billy Williams and Miss Mae, while tragic, were surprising only in that they'd been murdered. A handful of transients died in Duck Creek every year, with Amanda Pinkham dutifully delivering the results from their autopsies: exposure, longtime illness, drug overdose—"deaths of despair," as would-be reformers, including Harper, labeled them.

She looked at the clock. It was long past time for the deputies' lunch break. She wouldn't be able to track Hayes down again in the tea shop. Which wasn't the worst thing in the world. And she had no appetite for another freezing creekside expedition.

Her best move would be to lurk near the courthouse's back door and try to catch Hayes coming or going. But the seven-to-seven shift changes conflicted with Calvin's kindergarten and after-school-care schedule. She had to pick him up by six and couldn't very well loiter with him outside the courthouse as the last vestiges of daylight leaked from the sky.

As for mornings—maybe she could plead an early meeting and ask Beverly to come by and take him to school; an idea she immediately rejected. She was supposed to be self-sufficient now.

Still gnawing on the pen, she tapped at her keyboard, cyberstalking Hayes, hoping to find a home address, although she knew most of the deputies, along with the town's police officers, were hypercautious about personal information on the web. The town was full of people they'd arrested, people who'd massaged grudges for years, people who tucked handguns into waistbands, coat pockets, purses, in flagrant violation of the state's concealed-carry laws, but what did it matter if they never got caught? Paranoia wasn't crazy when it was justified.

She took the pen from her mouth and glared at its mangled cap. Bad enough she had to share an office with Marie. Now she appeared to be picking up her bad habits. She tossed the pen in the trash and returned to her sleuthing.

Julia wasn't surprised not to find an address. But she found something nearly as good. Hayes was a member of the local running club, which, according to its website, met for group runs on Saturdays—the day Beverly had designated for once-a-week visits with her grandson. The group runs were open-invitation, not just for club members but for anyone interested in running.

While Calvin was helping himself to Beverly's cocoa and cookies, Julia would be going for a run.

* * *

Saturday morning found Julia rooting around in the depths of her new closet, searching for the running shoes she was sure she hadn't given to Goodwill, the puppy snuffling happily beside her, evidently excited about the possibility of more things to chew on.

"Go away," she snapped. Then she saw the shoelace between his teeth. "There they are! You found them! Good boy. Good Jake."

He fell onto his back, legs bicycling in delight.

Julia backed out of the closet and held the shoes up to the light. They were stiff with age, their once-bright colors faded, the laces frayed. She poked doubtfully at the soles, their tread worn nearly smooth.

Her running days preceded Calvin, who was now in kindergarten. The shoes were practically fossils. She didn't even try to find her running clothes, which she remembered as sweats emblazoned with her college logo. The runners she saw around Duck Creek were decked out in sleek, skintight gear, something she'd looked up online at a site she'd quickly closed after gasping at the prices.

She made do with a pair of leggings, a long-sleeved cotton T-shirt and—checking the temperature, which had risen to a comparatively balmy twenty-five degrees—her lightest winter jacket, which meant she was freezing on Saturday morning when she approached the group gathered in a downtown park.

Her first surprise was that there were so many, knots of people who apparently knew each other well spread out around the park, chatting animatedly, clouds of condensation gathering around them. She hovered at the edge of the park, searching the groups for Hayes— a challenge, given that people looked more or less alike in head-hugging beanies, tights whose sheen bespoke a high-tech fabric several levels of cost above her cotton leggings, and formfitting jackets that made her feel bulky and strange in her puffer, light though it was.

After a few minutes, she realized the groups represented a sort of pecking order. The smallest, lean unto stringy men and women in faded, well-worn gear, casually performed stretches and warm-ups while talking.

At the other end of the spectrum were middle-aged and older people, many with actual meat on their bones, seeming no less enthusiastic than the elite runners. Among them was a woman defiantly bareheaded, her cloud of white hair catching the morning sun. A woman jogging late to the gathering came to a stop beside Julia and followed her skeptical gaze.

"That's Sandra. She's in her seventies. I tried to catch her once in a marathon. Never even got close." The woman sighed and wandered toward the slower group, which was where Julia figured she herself belonged.

Except there was Hayes with the other elites, bending as though her back had no bones at all, placing her hands flat on the ground, then stretching them high above her head. The few times Julia had seen her before, Hayes' face had been closed, expressionless. Now she smiled easily, then threw her head back and laughed at something someone had said.

"Let's get this show on the road," she hollered to the group at large. "Just a quick one today—only four miles." She narrated a route that would take them through town and then down along the creek trail. "Everybody got spikes? It's still icy down there. Last thing we need this close to spring is a broken ankle."

Huh?

But a few people lifted their feet to display the spiked ice grippers affixed to their shoes.

Julia did not have spikes. But it didn't matter. She'd started shaking her head the minute she'd heard four miles. No way. Maybe one mile. Half, even.

She hurried toward Hayes's group, grateful they were starting out at a walk. She lengthened her stride and caught up with Hayes.

"Hey."

Hayes turned her head. Her eyes widened.

"Are you a runner? I don't remember seeing you out here before."

"Trying to get back into it." Julia gulped air. They were walking *fast*.

"You've come to the right place. This group is fantastic. There's all levels out here. Some people don't even run, they just walk. But it doesn't matter. The whole idea is to be outside and moving. It's the best thing in the world."

Julia took that as a hint that she should be back with the walkers, something she'd already figured out on her own. Where she should be, she thought, was back at home, maybe indulging in a soak in the tub while Calvin was at his grandmother's house.

"Ready?" the person at the head of the line called.

A shout of assent arose, and suddenly everyone was running—and in the case of Hayes and those at the head of the pack, *really* running, not just jogging. Julia figured she had five minutes at most of enough wind to speak.

No time for conversational warm-ups, easing into what she wanted to ask.

"Harper's study group," she gasped. "What was your problem with it?"

"Problem?"

Hayes loped along. A stitch moved up Julia's side, muscles contracting, commanding her to stop.

"Heard you had some objections."

"I'll bet you did."

Julia forgot about her burning lungs and the pain in her side, so corrosive was the bitterness in Hayes's voice.

"So? What are they?"

"What's your deal with Harper? What about Ray? You should be focused on him."

Were they actually picking up speed? Julia was already moving at a near-sprint even as Hayes pulled away. Who could maintain this pace for four miles?

"I am," she managed.

Hayes stopped so suddenly that Julia nearly crashed into her. Hayes stepped out of the flow of runners and pulled Julia with her.

"Listen." She put both hands on Julia's shoulders and shook her hard. "Ray was fighting. He was *fighting*. Don't you see?"

Julia didn't. But it didn't matter. Hayes let go and galloped away, catching up with her companions, leaving Julia bent double in someone's front yard, sucking in oxygen in long, ragged gasps and cursing herself for the waste of time and energy.

CHAPTER

27

JULIA PUT HER new key into the new lock and opened the front door, only to be confronted with the same sort of surprise she felt whenever she entered her office and found Marie.

In this case, the surprise was Jake, who launched himself as soon as she stepped inside, hitting her knees full force, nearly toppling her. She stepped back but he came at her again, scrabbling at her legs for purchase, whimpering, trembling all over. She picked him up and he pressed himself against her, still keening.

Had he had an accident? Destroyed something so consequential that even he knew he was in trouble?

Her gaze scanned the hardwood floors, already in need of mopping—no matter how often she told Calvin to take off his shoes as soon as he came inside, he inevitably forgot, and yesterday's small boot prints were visible across the polished oak—but saw nothing. She carried Jake into the kitchen, its floor likewise dry.

"What's the matter, boy?"

She'd accepted the puppy as a necessary evil, gladly turning over most of the dog-related chores to Calvin. But something had upset Jake badly, and she couldn't help but feel sorry for him. She stroked him until he relaxed and rewarded her by licking her chin. She put him down and, out of habit, scanned the backyard, checking to see if her anonymous caller was standing there in broad daylight, phone to his ear, readying new harassment.

He wasn't.

But he—or someone—had been there.

A line of footprints crossed the snow from the back gate by the alley to the middle of the yard—where someone had written, in large, crooked letters, *STOP*.

* * *

Wayne Peterson took one look and bent double laughing.

"What's so funny?"

Julia didn't think anything about this situation was amusing and said as much. "Wayne, somebody came into my yard in broad daylight."

"Aw, c'mon." Wayne straightened and wiped his eyes. "You've got to admire the guy's work. That's some pretty impressive pee writing right there."

"Pee writing?" She looked again, noting for the first time the letters' yellow tinge.

"I mean—those letters are big. Guy must've drunk a gallon of water."

Wayne was laughing again. At the look on Julia's face, he stopped.

"I could have been here. With Calvin. As it happened, whoever it was scared Jake half to death."

A grin creased Wayne's face, but he halted another laugh. "Not much of a watchdog, is he?"

Julia surprised herself by coming to the defense of Jake, heretofore viewed as a small, furry enemy of most of her belongings, tolerated only because Calvin adored him. And because of the rent, something she had to remind herself daily.

"He let me know right away something was wrong. Isn't there anything I can do?"

"Whoever did this is guilty of trespassing. Only problem is, you have no way of knowing who did it."

"Can't you tell from footprints or something?"

"Or his—uh—handwriting?"

Julia folded her arms and tapped her foot, playing disapproving schoolmarm to Wayne's recalcitrant student. Even though she couldn't get too angry with him. He had, after all, sped to her house on a

Saturday—the benefit, she supposed, of his most recent divorce, which left him little to do on his weekend days beyond watching an endless series of basketball games and eating takeout in his new apartment.

He swiped a hand across his face as though to physically erase his mirth. "I'm sorry. Really, I am. But very little of what I do involves humor."

"Pretty twisted sense of humor." She heard the forgiveness in her voice. Their jobs had that in common, and had the yellow-snow message not been so personal, she'd probably have laughed too.

"What can I do about it then? What if he comes back when we're here?"

"You're right." Just as she appreciated the dark humor that permeated law enforcement—not to mention the Public Defender's Division—Wayne well knew the tendency of stalkers' behavior to escalate.

But both knew the limits of the law.

"Here's what I've done. I created a file after the first incident. I'll add this to it." He walked to the back door, opened it, pointed his phone at the yard, and took a few photos. "That way, if anything else happens, these things are in an official record. I don't suppose you've got a gun."

"With Calvin in the house? Of course not."

Something else they both knew—the statistics that showed a gun purchased for self-defense was exponentially more likely to injure or kill a family member or friend, sometimes by accident, sometimes on purpose when an argument escalated and, instead of throwing a punch, someone reached for a gun.

Besides, she was an amateur, unlike Wayne, with his years of training and routine practice at the gun range.

He grimaced. "Wouldn't hurt you to get one. You can always take a safety course."

"Not a chance. I couldn't live with myself if anything happened to Calvin."

He looked meaningfully toward the yard, wordlessly emphasizing that a handgun in a drawer wasn't the only threat Calvin might face.

"No, Wayne."

"What about security cameras? The same guy who did your locks? He could install them."

"Christ!" She slammed a hand on the granite counter. "Ow." She shook out her hand and blew on her fingers. "Blackout curtains and drapes. New locks. Security cameras. I don't have the money for all of this. I don't know who this person is or why they're after me, other than that I'm living in Leslie Harper's house."

"What if it's not that?" Wayne fiddled with one of the buttons on his shirt, twisting it until it popped off in his hand. "Damn. That was stupid." He held it out to her. "I don't suppose you sew?"

She backed away. "When have I ever struck you as the domestic type? Not a chance."

He pocketed the button. "Listen, Julia, I'm really sorry I made light of this. The method is funny. The intent clearly isn't. But did you ever stop to think this might not have anything to do with Leslie Harper?"

She shook her head. "What else could it possibly be about?"

"What else are you working on?" He waited for it to come to her.

"Ray Belmar? I don't mean to diminish the case, but the general feeling I get is that the only reason people give two cents for this case is that it raises safety issues about the creek trail. If it was just a couple of transients ending up dead anywhere else in town, nobody would care."

"Solid thinking there, Counselor." But Wayne's smile lacked warmth. "I know you've always considered Ray some sort of lovable goof."

"For God's sake, Wayne. Lovable might be a stretch."

"You know what I mean. Harmless, mostly."

"Maybe not harmless. But not nearly as bad as some," she acknowledged.

"Dude runs with a rough crew. Not just those folks along the river, those sad drunks. I hate to say it, but being sober might not have been the best thing for him. When he was drinking, he was too stupid to get into real trouble. But once his brain started working again, he might have done like a lot of folks—looked at some pissant minimum-wage job with no benefits and decided life as a solid citizen was not for him. That there are other ways to make money. A lot of money. See what I'm saying?"

Julia saw.

She didn't like the picture Wayne was painting, one that went against everything she knew about Ray. But she had to admit it made sense.

She told him good-bye and went online before calling the locksmith to get an idea of just how much security cameras were going to set her back.

28

J ULIA STOOD AT the base of the ladder, watching as the locksmith installed the final security camera.

It pointed at the front door. The house now had cameras by the back and front doors, two-way views on each corner, and motion sensor lights so bright she thought about warning the neighbors in advance.

He climbed down and dusted his hands on his pants. "That should do it. Are you good with the app?" He stood beside her, nodding as she scrolled through the various features. "Looks like you've got it. I'll email you the bill."

"I suppose there's an extra charge for coming out on a Sunday."

He laughed and headed for his truck, calling back over his shoulder, "FOW."

FOW? Oh. Friend of Wayne. She vowed to add something extra when she paid the bill.

She'd spent most of her weekend doing everything she could to turn her charming cottage into a virtual fortress. Even though it wasn't really hers. She hadn't bothered to email Leslie Harper's sister for permission to install the cameras, let alone ask if she could have a break on the month's rent.

"What next?" she asked Jake, who gamboled about her feet, tugging at her shoelaces. "Razor wire atop the picket fence?"

He yipped enthusiastically, which was how he responded to anything she said. One of his positive qualities. Every time she found another object chewed into unrecognizability—her favorite wooden spoon, snatched from the counter, had been his latest victim—she reminded herself of his exuberant good nature, the way he alternated between her bed and Calvin's at night, snuggling close and staring soulfully into her eyes upon waking. At a time when even Calvin's adoration was intermittent, Jake remained unwavering.

She scrolled through the app again, all the various black-and-white views of their home.

"A smart investment," Wayne had assured her. "You won't regret it."

Maybe. But she did regret the fact that she'd have to give up her lattes at Colombia for weeks on end to even out the expense.

"Mom! Can you see me?" Calvin mugged at the back door, sticking out his tongue and contorting his face.

She put her phone away and walked back through the house, throwing the deadbolt behind her even though it was three in the afternoon. Calvin waited for her in the kitchen.

"Can we walk Jake now?"

Jake, whose intelligence was a double-edged sword, went into paroxysms at the word *walk*, scrambling to the wall beside the door where his leash hung on a hook.

"We've already walked him twice today." When she'd agreed to take the dog, she'd hadn't thought his care would entail much beyond feeding him and picking up his messes in the yard, chores immediately delegated to Calvin.

She hadn't reckoned on the need for seemingly constant exercise, something that carved even more time out of her day. On the plus side, her calves, which at first had screamed at the unaccustomed clip and distance demanded by an energetic, half-grown dog, were firming up nicely. At this rate, she thought, she'd soon be able to keep up with the slow people in Cheryl Hayes's running group.

Boy and puppy turned big eyes upon her.

She sighed and reached for the leash. She'd planned to spend at least part of her weekend catching up on work, but installing the cameras had taken longer than expected, and now this. She resigned herself to another late night, files spread across the bed, and told Calvin to get his coat.

At least it was warmer, the temperature climbing into the near-springlike thirties and the occasional shaft of sunlight, so fleeting as to recall childhood tales of mirages, forcing its way through Duck Creek's leaden cloud cover. Every day the snow retreated a little farther, leaving puddles that froze overnight into treacherous early-morning ambushes for the unwary, thawing into mere messiness by afternoon.

Calvin was already pulling on his rubber boots, the bright-green ones with googly yellow frog eyes on the toes. Julia, still thinking about work, tossed out a suggestion that wouldn't have fooled Claudette for a minute. Unfair to foist it on a five-year-old, but at least he'd never know she aimed to co-opt their time together for her own purposes.

"How about we show Jake the creek?"

29

S HE TOLD HIM she wanted to check on the ice, which piled up on the creek each winter in fantastical formations that collapsed theatrically in the spring.

Sure enough, just as they reached the walking path, a sheaf of ice reared up and fell backward into an open patch of rushing black water, breaking into a dozen small floes that chased one another downstream.

"Whoa." Calvin stood transfixed, for once ignoring Jake as the puppy nosed among the willows in wonderment at the unfamiliar scents, his nubby tail a blur.

Julia cast a glance down the trail. A few vagrants huddled at the creek's edge, near the bridge, although this time without the benefit of a fire. Smart, she thought. The cops became increasingly attentive as the weather warmed and runners and cyclists—not to mention young moms with strollers—began to repopulate the trail.

All it took was one solid citizen calling police to complain about panhandlers and Duck Creek's unfortunates would be banished, at least for a while, from one of their favorite places.

Julia tugged at Jake's leash with one hand and Calvin's hand with the other and began strolling along the trail, trying to give every appearance of meandering, even though she wanted to run toward the group. What if someone came along first and scared them off?

But the trio—the woman named Angie and her two friends again—were deep in conversation when Julia finally drew near, breaking off only when they saw Jake.

"Puppy!" Angie crooned. "Oh, the little darling."

"He's not so little," Calvin announced. "He's already six months old."

Angie, who'd stooped to pet Jake, looked up and gave Calvin her toothless grin.

"And who are you?"

Calvin looked to Julia.

"It's all right," she said. "This is Miss Angie."

"I'm Calvin."

"Pleased to meet you, Mr. Calvin." The woman held out a dirty palm for a shake. Julia was embarrassed at the strength of her own relief at Calvin's mittened hands.

Angie stood and looked at Julia. "Oh," she said. "It's you."

Somehow turning *you* into a near-curse.

It got worse.

Angie raised her voice for the benefit of her friends. "Remember? The one who's supposed to be helping Ray." She put a spin on *helping* that made it clear she thought Julia was doing anything but.

They'd moved a few feet out from their sheltered spot beneath the bridge, taking in the sun that cruelly highlighted their dirty, mismatched clothes, the black lines under their fingernails, the bulky tattered backpacks on the ground nearby. Calvin's gaze moved uncertainly among them. His nose wrinkled. This close, he and Julia were well within the funk zone. She reached for his hand and gave it a reassuring sneeze.

Ichabod—Julia had already forgotten his real name—edged Angie aside and reached for Jake. "Give him to me."

Calvin's lip trembled, his face a mirror of Julia's own anxiety.

But Ichabod merely held Jake close, laughing breathily as the puppy sniffed diligently around his face and neck, finally rewarding him with a series of licks that cleared a layer of grime to reveal the reddened skin beneath.

"It's okay," Julia whispered to Calvin. She retrieved a fact from a dog-training book she'd bought in a futile attempt to figure out how to keep Jake from trying to eat every inanimate object in sight. "It's called socializing. He needs not to be afraid of people."

To herself, though, she thought Jake could have been a little more discriminating, even as Little Guy—yet another name she'd forgotten—took Jake in turn, scratching behind his ears until Jake wriggled so enthusiastically in response the man put him down.

Calvin let go of Julia's hand and ran to Jake, hugging him.

"You're a good boy," Little Guy said. "I can tell by the way you love your dog."

Calvin beamed. These strange people liked his dog and that was enough for him.

Julia took Angie by the arm and steered her a few yards down the trail, keeping one eye on Calvin.

"I'm doing my best to help Ray. But it's hard when he won't talk to me."

Angie's gaze slid sideways. She crossed her arms over her chest. "Maybe that's because Ray's finally got some sense in his head."

"But they're looking at him for homicide! Two homicides. Ones that I don't think he did and neither do you. He could end up in prison for decades."

Angie's shoulders lifted and fell. "There are worse things."

Julia gaped. "Seriously? What could be worse? The death penalty? He won't get that—they'd have to show premeditation and all sorts of other things; besides, it's really expensive to pursue." She stopped. The last thing Angie needed was someone going all lawyer on her.

But Angie was nodding agreement.

"You just said it yourself. He could end up dead."

Julia had just said Ray wouldn't get the death penalty. Angie wasn't making sense. Julia inhaled deeply and, she hoped, unobtrusively, trying to detect the scent of alcohol amid that of clothing and a body long unwashed. Nothing. She tried a different tack.

"I heard he was fighting. Not just arguing, like you said." She tried to keep the accusation out of her voice and wasn't sure she succeeded.

But Angie nodded. "Oh, Ray's fighting, all right." She cast a look over her shoulder. "Oh shit." She yelled a warning to the others. "Cop. She told us to stay away from the river. We gotta bounce."

Julia looked. There, far down the trail but approaching fast, was Deputy Sheriff Cheryl Hayes, this time on a solo run.

Angie went one way, Ichabod Crane another, and Little Guy a third. Julia reached Calvin and Jake just as Hayes pulled abreast, slowing to a near-stop, jogging in place.

"Is this child yours?" It didn't matter that she was out of uniform. Her frozen tone, the ice in her eyes, was all cop.

"He's my son, yes."

"And you left him alone with those people?"

"He was in my sight the whole time—"

But Hayes was already off, her shoes crunching on pebbles, shaking her head as she went.

Jake looked after her, ears drooping, seemingly puzzled by the first human who had failed to find him adorable or even pay him any attention at all.

"I know just how you feel," Julia said.

She picked up his leash and took Calvin's hand.

"Come on. Let's get out of here."

* * *

She replayed the nonsensical conversation with Angie in her head all the way back to the house, where she paused before the gate, scanning the street. Nothing.

She closed the gate behind them and unhooked Jake's leash. He bounded across the yard, Calvin in pursuit.

"Stay in the front yard where I can see you," she commanded. The last thing she needed was for Calvin to stumble over another yellow-snow missive. She clicked through her phone, looking at the images from her new security system from the short time they'd been gone.

Also nothing.

She called Calvin and Jake, unlocked the door, let everyone in, and quickly shot the deadbolt behind her. "Shoes," she reminded Calvin, hurrying in her own sock feet to the kitchen, where she raised the heavy shades and scanned the backyard, seeing nothing but melting snow and finally relaxing within the safety of her home.

Something tugged at her, though, hovering just out of reach as she prepared an early dinner of grilled cheese and tomato soup—a new Sunday tradition that weekly made her miss Dom's sauce—after which Calvin would be allowed to watch a movie while she caught up on paperwork.

It floated toward the front of her brain as she slotted the dishes into the dishwasher, skittering away just as she was about to grasp it. It poked her again as she settled Calvin on the sofa with Jake, her no-dogs-on-the-furniture rule having long gone by the wayside. And it jabbed her hard as she dialed up an old favorite, *The Muppet Musicians of Bremen*, with Rover Joe's wailing lament—"I'm old. I'm tired. I'm woooorn away"—that she'd adopted as her own when Calvin made one request too many.

She retreated to the kitchen, checked the back door lock and pulled the shades down a millimeter farther, and spread her paperwork out on the table.

And just then, while she was distracted by the details of a pending bail hearing for another client on Monday, it finally surfaced.

Oh, Ray's fighting, Angie had said.

Present tense.

30

MARIE CONFRONTED HER with a go-cup of coffee Monday morning.

"I stopped at Colombia and asked them what you usually get. I just came from there. You always come in about this time, so this should still be hot."

Julia blinked at the brightness of Marie's smile and accepted the offering in a swirl of wonderment, apprehension, and—at first sip—gratitude. She'd mentally put Colombia off-limits until she was done paying for the security cameras.

"To what do I owe the pleasure?" she finally managed.

Marie cleared her throat, then withdrew a sheet of paper from her briefcase and lay it with a flourish on Julia's desk.

It was a spreadsheet with a list of names with check marks, email addresses and phone numbers, dates—all within the last four days—and times beside them, and a final notation, yes or no.

Julia studied it. She recognized some of the names—people around town, a couple of courthouse clerks. Legislators. Cops. Claudette. A couple dozen names in all. But she couldn't figure out an overall theme, and the check marks, times, and dates made no sense at all.

"What is this?"

"Everyone I contacted about Leslie Harper and her committee. I tried to call or meet in person with everyone who had any contact with her on a regular basis."

Julia blinked. "But what does"—she chose a name at random—"Ginny Stevens have to do with it?"

"She and Harper were in the same book group. Along with Claudette Green, the prosecutor. Interesting, huh?"

"I wouldn't read too much into that. They've been friends for years."

Marie's laugh had an edge of hysteria. "Read—that's funny!"

Julia scanned the list again, paying particular attention to the times, and wondered if Marie had gotten any sleep at all over the weekend. Exhaustion smudged the skin beneath her eyes, battling the pride in her gaze.

"Impressive." Julia spoke carefully. The spreadsheet, for all its perfunctory categories, was devoid of detail. "How many of these people did you actually reach?"

"All of them. Even though not everyone—like Claudette Green, for one—would talk with me. It took me through the weekend."

"So I see." Julia ran her finger down the list. She tossed her another compliment. "Nice work. But what did you find out?"

Marie practically bounced in her chair. Julia wondered if she'd availed herself of coffee too, maybe something with a quad shot, before she bought Julia's latte.

"The committee? For all practical purposes, it's as dead as Leslie Harper. Sorry, that was rude."

"So?" Julia pretended indifference, despite a prickle along her spine. Committees came and went.

"She pushed for the committee last fall when the Democrats were still in the majority. But then we elected a Republican governor, who thinks law enforcement of all stripes walk on water. Anything that committee came up with would have been a wasted effort. But Harper wouldn't drop it. Now that she's gone, they'll probably just go through the motions and come up with some weak-ass bill they know will get vetoed. But even before she died, I heard on the downlow there was some pretty strenuous pushback."

Julia wondered whether Marie would ever abandon her love of jargon. "You didn't hear a name mentioned, did you? Because I heard"—she resisted saying *on the down-low*—"that Deputy Hayes was no fan of that committee."

Marie shot a glance toward the door, as though to check for hovering multitudes, and whispered, "I heard the same thing."

They looked at each other.

"It might not mean anything," Julia said finally. She sipped at a latte gone cold, hoping for a final jolt of caffeine that would trigger her synapses into a connection that made sense.

"Why would she object to a committee set up to see if the state needs a board to oversee the sheriff's departments?" Marie, gaming it out, just like she'd been taught in law school. Asking the obvious, which demanded the obvious answer.

"A board designed to crack down on corruption in the departments." Julia's hand went to her mouth. She thought of something Claudette had said. "I guess there were some allegations about our department."

Our as in the Peak County Sheriff's Office.

"What's the matter?"

Julia shook her head. "Coffee just went down wrong." She looked at the clock. "Shoot. I'm late for a meeting with . . . somebody." She hoped Marie hadn't noticed the hesitation when she failed to quickly embellish the lie with a name. "Thanks again for all your work. Truly."

"Where do we go next with this?" Marie called as she headed for the door.

"I'll let you know." She fled to the ladies' room, for the first time grateful for its single stall and a lock, which she turned behind her. She pressed her back to the wall and sank to the floor, repeating to herself in a hoarse whisper, "It's nothing, it's nothing, it's nothing."

Which might be true.

Just as it might be true that Mack Coates's appearance in the very tea shop where Hayes had been taking her lunch break meant nothing.

But if someone had wanted to shut down Harper's committee—wanted to shut it down badly enough to kill Leslie Harper and make it look like an accident—then Marie's little fishing expedition had just let everyone on her list know that Julia was looking into the matter.

A list that possibly included the person who'd stood in her back yard on a dark night and made a telephone call, who'd returned in daylight and peed a message into the snow.

31

J ULIA THOUGHT SHE'D battled insomnia before.

But those earlier bouts were a matter of waking too soon—maybe around four thirty AM—and being unable to fall back asleep before her alarm went off an hour later, leaving her fatigued and cranky for the rest of the day. Or maybe some difficulty falling asleep the night before an important court hearing as she obsessively went over everything in her mind.

But nothing had prepared her for hours of wide-eyed wakefulness, scanning the security camera images on her phone, and then—not trusting the grainy image of a raccoon loping away from the backyard trash can—rising to pace the house, checking the door locks and peeping behind the drapes and shades, holding her breath as she scanned the darkened yard for any hint of motion.

Jake stumbled behind her, not understanding this new game but willing to go along with it, leaping onto the bed as soon as she returned to it and falling asleep beside her in a matter of seconds as she sat, quivering and alert, phone at hand and ready to dial 911 at the slightest unfamiliar sound.

The next day, she incurred a crick in her neck from swiveling to check over her shoulder as she walked Calvin to school and herself to work, and then in the evening when they took the dog on his prebedtime ramble. Calvin complained that she held his hand so tightly it hurt. Jake objected to the newly abbreviated walk, pulling obstinately against the leash when she turned back toward the house after only a couple of blocks. And at work she endured comments on her haggard appearance from everyone from Deb to the barista at the coffee cart, who comped her latte and urged her not to come back until she'd gotten some sleep.

Which wasn't an option. Work continued apace, the daily overload of new cases and continuing cases as well as the glacial grind of Ray's case.

Julia suffered two teeth-grindingly frustrating meetings with Tim Saunders, during which they finally agreed to disagree about pushing for a plea and instead compiled lists of potential witnesses (few) and evidence (even less).

At least Saunders kept the meetings brief. A bout of spring crud was sweeping through the courthouse, laying low clerks and judges alike and causing delay upon delay in an already-snarled court schedule. Nobody wanted to spend any more time in close quarters than absolutely necessary.

All of which combined to erode Julia's initial terror to something resembling background noise, a low hum that grew easier to ignore by the day, so that by midweek she'd persuaded herself that she'd overreacted to Marie's findings. On Wednesday night she tucked Calvin and Jake into bed early, and only a little after eight PM she climbed into scalding, chin-deep water in the tub and fell promptly asleep, waking to find herself shivering in water gone cold as her phone rang and rang and rang.

*   *   *

Julia left the tub in a great splash, lunging for the phone, skidding across the tiles, crashing to her knees just as she grabbed it.

She lay there, kneecaps radiating pain, trying to control her breathing.

"Julia?"

She gave in then, a moan of both pain and relief.

"Julia? Are you all right?"

"Dom? Dom!"

"Julia, what's going on? Something's wrong. I can hear it in your voice."

Jake nosed open the door and galumphed to her side, shoving his nose against her face, breathing noisily into the phone.

"Um, Julia?" Dom's tone changed.

"Never mind. It's just the dog. I have a dog now. Oh, Dom. Wait a minute." She sat up, groaning again, and pulled a towel from the rack and wrapped it around her. "I was in the tub. I fell."

"Are you hurt?"

She gingerly stretched one leg before her, then the other. Each knee barked an objection but otherwise extended as commanded.

"Just my dignity." Not just that. He'd inflicted lingering pain upon her, a real kick in the gut, worse than whatever damage the tiled floor had just inflicted upon her knees.

"Dom, why are you calling? Didn't you say we shouldn't see each other?"

Jake stiffened at her tone. His ears flattened. His hackles rose. Whatever was wrong, he was ready to tackle it. Julia ran a reassuring hand along his back. "It's okay, sweetie."

"I'm so glad. Because I've missed you."

"I wasn't talking to you, Dom." Jake's hackles rose anew.

"Oh." The phone went silent.

Julia put it on speakerphone, toweled herself mostly dry, and donned her pajamas, a years-old flannel pair, soft and faded, that she generally saved for when she was sick or in special need of comfort, as she'd felt all during this interminable week. She picked up the phone, still silent, carried it into the bedroom, and climbed into bed. No way was she going to speak first.

Dom's voice finally sounded again, halting, hopeful.

"I don't suppose . . . would it be all right . . . I'd really like to see you. Elena's still at her mother's."

"So this is a booty call. Jesus, Dom." Jake, nearly asleep on the pillow beside her, gave a halfhearted growl, having sensed that whatever was causing her to speak in this new strange voice wasn't an immediate threat.

"No, no. Julia, how could you think that? I just want to see you. I'd meet someplace public if we could, but that wouldn't be a good idea. Julia, please. Can I come over? Just to talk? I'll leave the minute you say."

She rewarded him with another long silence even as she thought, *There are worse things than a man who begs.* She looked at the clock. It was only nine. Calvin was asleep. And damn it all to hell, she missed him too.

"Just for a little while," she said. "I'm exhausted."

"I'll be right there."

"Dom, wait." The last thing she needed was for him to show up, smiling and expectant, on Beverly's doorstep. "I've got a new place." She gave him the address.

Normally she'd have donned jeans and a sweater, maybe a little makeup. Poured drinks, put out snacks, touched a match to some candles.

Instead, she dragged a hoodie from a bottom drawer and pulled it on over her pajamas and left her hair, curling wildly from the steam in the tub, in its untamed state. But at least she was semipresentable five minutes later, when Dom knocked at her door.

* * *

In the movie version of her life, she'd have looked adorable in her pj's, childlike and sweetly vulnerable, her hair resembling a halo rather than a nest assembled by a large and careless bird. Dom would have swept her into his arms. They'd have kissed, shyly at first and then passionately, before heading up the stairs. Fade to black.

Instead, Jake launched himself at this nighttime intruder in a welter of uncertainty, circling Dom's feet, growling low even as his tail wagged, the epitome of how Julia herself felt.

Julia stood back. Jake looked to her for a cue.

"It's all right," she relented.

Dom produced a dog biscuit from his coat pocket, and Jake underwent an instantaneous transformation from wannabe guard dog to puddle of ecstasy.

"I keep them with me in case I run into aggressive dogs on the creek trail. It's happened a couple of times. Okay to come inside now?"

Julia stood wordlessly aside and watched his eyes widen as he took in the house.

"May I?" He headed for the kitchen.

"Go ahead. But be quiet. Calvin's sleeping—at least, he is if Jake didn't wake him up."

"This is Jake?"

The dog rewarded him with an adoring gaze, earning another biscuit.

"It is. A born con artist, as you've just found out. He's the reason we have this house."

They ended up at the kitchen table, Julia pouring a couple of glasses of wine, habit overcoming her cold-shoulder intentions. She briefly explained the rental setup, the deal that included Jake, who'd now plastered himself to Dom's legs.

"How old is he?"

"About six months. I guess this is about as big as he'll get. At least, that's what the owner told me."

Dom laughed and then tried to stifle it, casting a glance ceilingward. "Have you looked at the size of his paws? He's got a lot of growing to do."

Julia groaned. "He's already eaten his weight in shoes and anything else lying loose around the house."

Dom reached across the table and took her hand. "Do you want to keep talking about the dog. Or?"

She'd meant to pull her hand away. Instead, she gripped his like a lifeline, spilling out the frustrations and fears of the past days, opening the app on her phone that showed the security cameras' view of the yard, pointing to the heavy, room-darkening shades that made the large, bright kitchen feel oppressively closed in.

"Everything's so awful," she finished in a humiliating wash of self-pity. "I'm not getting anywhere with Ray's case. I've let myself get distracted by this business with Leslie Harper, even though it's not my case. I miss working with Claudette and—" She bit her lip to stop herself from saying, *I miss you.*

"I probably overreacted," she finished instead. "Nothing's happened since whoever it was peed all over the backyard." *My backyard,* she'd started to say, before reminding herself that the house wasn't hers and never would be.

"Jesus, Julia. You should have called me right away."

She gave him The Look she used on Calvin and, these days, Jake. He had the grace to apologize.

"I may have acted too hastily in saying we shouldn't see each other."

No shit, she wanted to say. Except the man faced the loss of his daughter.

"You did the right thing. The smart thing," she amended. "I've seen Susan in court. She pulls out all the stops. And when she loses a case, she doesn't forgive and forget. She knows she can hurt me by hurting you. For her, that counts as a win-win."

They fell silent, acknowledging the reality.

"You should go. You've got school tomorrow. I've got work."

"I don't want to. Especially not after what you've told me. No offense to Jake here, but I'm not sure how much use he'd be in a real emergency."

"How much use would *you* be?" She made her voice light, trying to turn it into a joke.

He didn't smile. "I'm serious. Another adult in the house would be good. At least when you were with Beverly, there was a gun in the house."

"You too? Wayne Peterson wanted me to get one. A deputy sheriff," she added, for his benefit. "I've got him on speed dial. Between that and the shades and drapes and the security cameras, I've made this place as safe as it can be."

"I hope you've kept me on speed dial." He rose.

"Always." Her voice caught.

"If anything like that happens again—anything at all, even something that seems innocuous—will you please call me? Even before you call the sheriff? Unless you're in some sort of immediate danger," he amended. "Then call the guy with the gun first."

He pulled her to him for a long hug, not the passionate embrace of her brief rom-com fantasy but nourishing just the same, better in its way.

"Can we do this again?"

She stiffened. "In this town? Speaking of which, where'd you park?"

He laughed. "Around the corner. Come on, Julia. I've lived here longer than you have. I know what this place is like."

She sighed. But even this visit, brief and constrained though it was, had lifted her spirits. "Maybe in a couple of weeks."

"I'll count the days." His kiss was so brief that later, she wondered if she'd imagined it.

Nonetheless, she fell asleep with a smile on her face and woke up the same way, the simple pleasure of contact vanishing only when she saw the slip of paper on the entryway floor beneath the mail slot with its hand-scrawled note.

Hope the sex was worth it, whore. Wonder what his wife will think?

"Ex-wife!" she screamed at the damning note, even as she dialed Wayne.

32

S HE EMAILED WAYNE a clip of the security camera footage, the
relevant piece thankfully occurring well after Dom's departure.
Wayne was waiting outside her office when she got to work.

Julia gave further thanks that it was one of Marie's law school
days so her intern didn't have to hear Wayne's lecture about destroying the note.

Which she hadn't, but she hadn't wanted to show it to him,
either. Courthouse gossip being what it was—and extending across
county lines to where Susan now worked—she didn't need it getting
around that she and Dom were still seeing each other.

"Just one word—*whore*," she told Wayne. Really, that was the
thing about the note that most frightened her. Well, the second-most
frightening thing, the first being the fact that someone had been
watching her. "I was so freaked out I flushed it."

She endured a second lecture on destroying evidence—"I honestly can't believe they let you practice law"—before they turned to
the grainy images she'd sent him.

At three in the morning, a hunched figure in a hoodie opened her
gate, scurried to the front door, illuminated by the flash of the security light, stuck something through the mail slot, and sloped away.

"The light didn't wake you up?"

"No." The downside of her overkill with the shades and drapes.
Plus the relief of Dom's visit had translated into the best sleep she'd
had all week.

He ran the abbreviated clip again.

"Damn. You can't see any facial features. Can't even tell if this is a man or a woman."

"You think it could be a woman?"

He raised an eyebrow. "Come on, Julia. You've seen the crazies in court."

She wanted to argue—those crazies were, after all, her clients—but he was right. When it came to crime, men might hold the edge in terms of numbers, but she'd seen her share of women accused of everything from embezzling the church kitty to driving blind drunk with unbelted kids tumbling in the back seat, and she'd even heard of a case where a woman blindfolded her husband on his birthday and then shot him between his bandanna-wrapped eyes. Surprise!

"And that damned hoodie. If I had my way, they'd be illegal. You ever seen surveillance video where the person wasn't wearing a hoodie?"

"There's something on it. Zoom in."

He spread his fingers on the screen, succeeding only in blurring the already-grainy image into unrecognizability. He restored the view and squinted. "Maybe part of a *D*? For *Duck Creek High*? Great. There's only about a thousand of those in this town."

She'd called Dom first, just as he'd asked, and emailed him the images too. He'd had the same thought about the sweatshirt.

"That's what—" she started to say to Wayne. But he knew Susan, knew she'd tagged Julia as her sworn enemy. She couldn't imagine he'd say anything that would get back to her, but you never knew. "That's what a friend of mine said."

Wayne almost dropped her phone. "You've talked about this with someone else?"

His disapproval vibrated between them, nearly palpable.

"I might have mentioned it to someone. Just in passing."

He took her arm. "Julia, you have to keep quiet about this. I can't emphasize this enough. If you've truly got a stalker—and it's looking more and more as though you do—you don't want to scare him off by gabbing around town about this. We want this person to make a move that allows us to nail him. Or her."

She looked him straight in the eye and lied. "Of course." Now that she and Dom had reestablished contact, she had every intention of keeping him clued in. But Wayne didn't need to know that.

He got out his own phone and snapped photos of the security cam images. "I'll add these to the file. Thing is, Julia." He hesitated.

"Spit it out, Wayne."

Wayne's hair was stiff with some sort of product, something he probably used in an attempt to tame the cowlicks that now stood up in defiance as he ran his hand across his head.

"There's nothing really illegal about this. It's not a threat."

"It's harassment! The phone call, the message in the snow, and now this. It's all part of a pattern."

He told her what she already knew. "*If* the same person did it. We have no way of knowing that."

She folded her arms. "We have no way of not knowing it. Are you going to fingerprint the mail slot?"

He held out his hand for her phone and enlarged the image again, this time just a little.

"Look at the hands."

In the video, the person yet again hunched toward her front door. Reached out. Shoved the note through. With—even the video's dreadful quality showed it—a gloved hand.

Julia slumped.

"Sorry. Wish I could be of more help. You don't have the slightest idea who this could be? You pissed off anybody lately? Some guy who didn't like his bail? What about a woman?"

She shook her head. "Don't think I don't lie awake at night going through all the possibilities."

"What about Susan?" Wayne, like most of the town, knew that Julia was involved with the former prosecutor's ex, and unless everybody in town had gone deaf, dumb, and blind, also knew that the principal and Julia hadn't been seen together recently. People would draw their own conclusions. She just hoped no one drew the right one.

"Not her style. She'll use the courts." A move she'd already threatened, but that was another thing Wayne didn't need to know.

"You're right. But if you think of anybody, no matter how wild a guess you take, let me know. Sorry you're going through this."

He put a hand on her shoulder.

She flinched.

He apologized yet again. "Didn't mean to scare you."

"It wasn't that. I'm just jumpy lately. Thanks for coming by."

She closed the door behind him and locked it, rubbing her shoulder. He hadn't scared her. But his touch on her shoulder had awakened a muscle memory.

Deputy Cheryl Hayes, her hands on both of Julia's shoulders. Shaking her. Shouting in her face.

Have you pissed off anyone recently? Wayne had asked. *What about a woman?*

Every encounter with Hayes had been tense, if not outright hostile.

She hadn't told Wayne about them. She wondered if it was time.

33

FRIDAY MORNING FOUND Julia detouring along the creek after she dropped Calvin off, for once not in search of anyone, counting on the rushing water as a distraction from her thoughts.

This time of year the creek rose daily, fed by mountain snowmelt, tumbling fast over rocks, surging up the banks, already so high that the county was offering sandbags to nearby businesses and home-owners. Some years the water even lapped across the walking path, but today it remained a safe few yards away, tearing at the creekside shrubbery, which bent and groaned in protest.

Julia wondered where Ray's friends stashed their belongings when the creek rose. Where they camped, where they slept. Transients had favorite spots all over Duck Creek. As the weather warmed, they lounged on the shady lawn of the courthouse, giving them easy access to the court appearances required by their citations for loitering.

In winter, the foolish found steam vents near downtown busi-nesses, earning both the wrath of the shopkeepers and persistent bronchial ailments from the combination of frigid air and hot, wet steam.

In the teasing warmth of spring and during the brief, achingly beautiful fall, they populated the parks like solid citizens, soaking up the too-few days of just-right sunshine, albeit wisely choosing the most out-of-the-way benches lest the good and generous people of Duck Creek reach for their phones to dial 911 and complain that dangerous characters were about.

But the creekside denizens were a special breed, long-termers as opposed to those just passing through, their fiercely guarded territory staked out by some unmistakable signal known only to those inhabiting Duck Creek's underbelly.

Julia cast her gaze along the bank, looking for places that might provide reliable shelter over the next few weeks until the raging waters finally calmed. She didn't see any. But farther up the path, a grimy red Chuck Taylor lay half-hidden in the bushes, probably left behind by one of Ray's friends as they decamped.

She hurried toward it, thinking to pick it up and sit out in plain view in case its owner came looking for it.

But when she reached into the shrubbery to retrieve it, the high-top sneaker stubbornly resisted, and she let go and fell backward, a scream rising in her throat as she realized it was still on a foot, attached to a leg, attached to the rest of Little Guy, floating half in, half out of the water and very much dead.

*   *   *

She didn't know the cop who responded to her 911 call, but she knew some of the others who followed, a regular gaggle of cops and sheriff's deputies and firefighters—a firetruck accompanied every ambulance call—and EMTs, even though their services were clearly of no use to Little Guy.

They stood at a distance while the police photographer did his work, bending low to get close-ups of Little Guy's face, a ghastly gray, hair in wet strings across it. The water had washed the blood away from the wound on one side of his head, his skull crushed from ear to crown. A magpie stalked nearby, angry at being kept from a ready meal.

A cop wearing blue rubber gloves sidled up to Julia. He thumbed through a billfold, worn and wet, extracting a couple of limp dollar bills and a Social Security card, its blue printing blurred and faded. He squinted and read aloud. "Craig Thompson."

Julia had forgotten his name. She nodded.

"You're the one who found him?"

Another nod.

"Your name?"

She opened her mouth and waited for the words to come. They didn't.

Wayne appeared next to the cop. "I'll handle this."

He took Julia's elbow and steered her away from the cop and his sputtering protest.

"Julia. Take a breath."

"I don't want to." Silly. Of course she was breathing, shallow sips of air, terrified that each one might bring a whiff of putrefaction that would seal the reality she was desperately resisting despite having found Craig facedown in the water, despite his caved-in skull: Little Guy was really and truly dead.

Wayne whacked her on the back, and she gasped. "What the hell?"

He shrugged. "They don't let us slap people anymore. Now. Deep breath. Good. Another. Okay. Tell me what happened."

She turned her back on the group around Craig's body, which was fast attracting onlookers, a dead body the one thing that could interrupt the relentless pursuit of fitness by the early-morning runners and cyclists increasingly populating the trail as the weather warmed.

"Not much to tell. I was taking the walking trail to work. Saw a sneaker. Recognized it as Craig's—at least, I'd seen him wearing sneakers like that. I thought maybe he'd dropped it, and I went to pick it up because I thought maybe he'd want it and—oh God."

She bent double, choking back nausea. Failed. Wayne, bless him, turned and walked a few steps away.

"Better now?" he asked after a few moments.

"I think so."

"Here." He offered her a stick of gum.

She bit down hard, the rush of spearmint reviving her.

"Look. You need to go to the cop shop and give a formal statement. And for sure you'll want to take the rest of the day off."

"No."

She couldn't imagine anything worse than going back to an empty house and sitting alone with the dog and her memories of Craig's face as they'd turned him over, his lips peeled back from his teeth in a frozen grimace.

She'd happily spend the rest of her life writing up plea agreements on bullshit cases if it meant she could chase that image from her mind forever.

*   *   *

Julia had finally gotten used to the presence of someone else in the office she'd briefly enjoyed having to herself.

On Monday, someone else greeted her, sparking a jolt worse than Marie's appearance had ever occasioned. Her boss, Li'l Pecker himself, occupied her chair, arms folded across his chest, eyes fixed on the doorway where she stood frozen.

Marie sat at her own desk pretending to stare into the computer screen open before her, the set of her shoulders telling Julia that Marie very much realized the seriousness of the occasion.

Even her worst encounters with Li'l Pecker, including the time he'd briefly laid her off during a round of budget cuts, had taken place in his office. Sometimes he dropped by, standing in the doorway making small talk and asking awkward personal questions—but carefully not too personal—in a way that Julia figured came out of some HR handbook: Let Your Staff Know You Care.

But seated at her desk? Never.

Her stomach twisted into the kind of intricate knots she should have learned in Girl Scouts but never had.

"Marie," she said without looking at her. "You should probably leave."

Marie snatched at her coat and purse, her face a study in pure gratitude.

"No, don't. This concerns you too."

Marie sank back into her seat with the expression of someone who'd just been informed the governor had denied a request for clemency.

"I understand you're a witness to Friday's, ah, unfortunate event."

"I found the man who'd been killed, yes." Li'l Pecker's delicate phrasing always brought out the worst in Julia. Why did the man have to dance around everything?

"Yes, indeed."

And that habit of agreeing with her on everything! When she knew that any moment he was going to dig a knife deep into her back and twist. Hard. What would it be?

"And that the man in question is—was—a potential witness in the case involving our Mr. Belmar."

Our Mr. Belmar, my ass. When had Li'l Pecker ever looked at Ray as anything but an impediment to his lovingly burnished reputation as the sort of public defender who guaranteed that only the most trustworthy defendants were released on bail?

"Yes, but Ray has nothing to do with this case. Clearly. Being that he's still in jail." Why were they even talking about Ray? She wished he'd just get to the point.

"Yes. Well." He rose from the chair. Her chair. "There may be some sort of tie-in. Even if he couldn't have done this, he may know who did. We can't risk actions by the Public Defender's Division jeopardizing safety in any way."

Of course not. Not when the head of the Public Defender's Division still hankered after a judgeship.

"I can't see what we have to do with it. The police will investigate. They'll turn their investigation over to the prosecutor, and—"

"I'm removing you from his defense."

"What?" Julia sagged against the door.

"The police will no doubt want to question Mr. Belmar about this case, just like they'll want to question you. It just doesn't look right to have you involved in a case with someone you're defending. Excuse me."

He'd taken a few steps toward her as he spoke and now looked past her toward the door she was blocking.

She took the hint.

Moved aside.

Watched him walk away, taking the biggest case of her career with him.

34

Tᵢₘ Sᴀᴜɴᴅᴇʀs ᴀʟᴡᴀʏs looked like the cat who ate the canary.

Now, only a few days after Craig Thompson was found dead, his usual self-regard was so over-the-top that Julia wouldn't have been surprised to see a feather peeping from the corner of his mouth.

He lounged in the doorway, leaning against the jamb, a *GQ* ad in a skinny-pants suit and a scarf knotted Italian-style around his neck, even though the weather had finally started to warm.

"Geary." He tossed a klieg-light smile her way. "And . . ."

Marie let several beats pass, not leaping in to help him the way he probably expected. "St. Clair."

If he was the slightest bit embarrassed not to have remembered her name, it didn't show.

"Right." He finally glanced at her nameplate. "Marie." Reinforcing her lowly status by using her first name.

Julia didn't dare look at Marie. She wondered if Marie had unobtrusively slid her hand to wherever she kept the gun Julia was sure she toted; wondered if Marie ever entertained fantasies of shooting the condescending asshole, not killing him but maybe sending a bullet whizzing past him, just close enough to pucker his backside.

"I've got good news for both of you."

He waited. Did he expect them to jump up, question him eagerly, eyes full of dewy anticipation?

Julia raised an eyebrow. Marie cleared her throat. Tapped her pencil on the desk, an auditory signal that they were busy people and for God's sake, out with it already. Julia felt one of those rare flashes of appreciation for her.

He straightened. Adjusted his scarf.

"I just came from the jail. I talked to Ray Belmar."

"What?" Julia's careful cultivation of cool dissolved. "Why were you talking to Ray?" She choked out his name, barely able to stop herself from saying *my client*. Because as far as she was concerned, he still was. She'd given herself a couple of days to settle down but had already begun outlining the argument she'd make to Li'l Pecker about staying on the case. Damned if she would let Tim Saunders take over.

But apparently that's just what he'd done, as his next words—delivered with a triumphant flourish, one with more than a hint of *Fuck you* in them—made clear.

"He's willing to plead guilty to William Williams' killing. In exchange, that leaves Mary Brannigan's death off the table, something that's even more urgent now that a third person has been killed."

Julia came up out of her chair. "Killed while Ray was in custody. So it's impossible for him to have done it, and it raises even more doubt that he killed the other two."

Tim waved his hand as though brushing away something small and unimportant. A dust mote. A buzzing fly. An unfortunate fact.

"I've talked with law enforcement. They're looking into the possibility that these killings are a gang thing, something like that case in Denver all those years ago."

"But those were kids! Preying on homeless people for fun. Why would Ray kill his friends?"

She'd have preferred outright contempt to the pitying look he bestowed upon her.

"These types have their own gangs. *Factions* might be a better word, fighting over territory or women or drugs or booze—or a combination of all those things. As you well know."

Which she did. Those cases took up far too much of her time.

"People," she said.

"What's that?"

"They're people. Not types."

He shifted smoothly from pitying to indulgent. "Of course. But the fact remains that Ray"—he paused and offered a sarcastic rephrasing in acknowledgment of her "people" comment—"*Mr. Belmar* and Mr. Williams had a very public dispute the night Mr. Williams was killed. Mr. Belmar is smart to cut his losses like this. I'm going to work up a plea agreement, something that'll give him serious time but not the life sentence he was facing before. I'll shoot it over to you when I'm done with it. As a courtesy."

And without so much as a good-bye, he was gone, leaving Julia and Marie staring at one another in mirrored narrow-eyed, clenched-fist poses.

* * *

Julia caught up with him in the hall, hating the optics of it—another woman pursuing Adonis—but under the circumstances not caring.

She swallowed the first words that came to her, phrases littered with curses and *How dare you*s, and forced herself to speak calmly, to pretend to merely be playing devil's advocate.

"Are you sure this is the way we want to go?"

Even though, according to Li'l Pecker, there was no more *we*. "After all, there's no real proof he killed anybody. It's still all circumstantial." She couldn't take her eyes off the scarf. So fucking pretentious. So soft and beautiful. Was it cashmere? She jammed her hands in her pockets to avoid the temptation to touch it. What sort of man wore a cashmere scarf in a place like Duck Creek?

"Julia." So she'd been downgraded to first-name status now too. He stared into her eyes in a way she supposed was meant to convey Deep Meaning. "There's no proof he didn't do it. If we put him on trial, that's all a jury's going to see. He could end up with forty years—which for someone like Ray, given the way he's abused his body all these years, could end up being the equivalent of life. Best-case scenario, he'd be up for parole in twenty years. It's not worth the risk. He's in full agreement."

Was he? Ray was many things, but he had an infallible bullshit detector. She could only think of one reason he'd agree to Saunders's proposal. He must be terrified. But of what? Of decades in prison? She did a quick calculation. Over the last few years, Ray had spent nearly as much time in jail as out, and while he was always glad to walk, he never seemed particularly bothered by his frequent sojourns.

It had to be something else.

"Julia?" Saunders brought her back to herself. He ostentatiously looked at his watch, another expensive accoutrement. "Is there anything else?"

"No."

There was plenty, not a goddamn bit of it anything that Tim Saunders needed to know about.

35

THE HOUSE JULIA had shared with Beverly had been full of her mother-in-law's possessions, including walls full of paintings and family photos.

But those in her new place were bare, and that night, after Julia had tucked Calvin into bed, she slipped into the spare bedroom she'd claimed for her work space and eyeballed the wonderfully blank acreage surrounding her. Two large whiteboards and a bulletin board, purchased earlier in the day at a downtown office-supply store, leaned against the walls.

Twenty minutes later, they filled most of a wall to the left of her desk, where she could see them whenever she turned her head or swiveled in her chair. She pinned a photo of Calvin to one corner of the bulletin board, then took up a blue dry-erase pen and stood before the whiteboards.

She drew a circle in the middle of one and wrote *Billy/Miss Mae/Craig* in the middle.

She drew another circle on the second board, with only a single name: *Leslie Harper.*

Then she went back to the first and drew lines radiating from the circle: *Ray. Angie. Ichabod*—she still had problems recalling his real name. All the people in the victims' inner orbit, including the necessary *Unknown Assailant.*

She drew longer lines for people with more distant ties. Cheryl Hayes. Wayne Peterson. That creepy Mack Coates, whispering to her in the courtroom. Even Claudette, for the simple reason that she, as well as the others, had mentioned Ray's name to her or had some involvement in investigating the case.

Her illustration resembled an ungainly spider, which in fact was the name for this particular exercise, one Michael had taught her when he worked for the local newspaper and was planning out longer-term projects. There was nothing new in it, only the questions and issues that tapped a daily drumbeat in her brain no matter what else she was doing. But sometimes a visual display would trigger an idea. Over the years, she'd used a similar system, writing bits of evidence on index cards and shuffling them until she came up with a coherent narrative. But that worked best for trial prep, an opportunity denied her in this case.

Hence the exercise Michael called Running the Spider: put your main subject in the middle and the people and things that relate to it all around.

"It looks more like a solar system," she'd observed the first time she'd watched him do it. Hers looked even more like one, especially when she drew a circle far to one side enclosing a remote planet labeled *Motive?*

Lacking even a guess, she took up her red pen to eliminate suspects.

She X'd out the obvious right away—Wayne and Claudette—and, after a moment, Cheryl Hayes. For all of Wayne's gripes about his colleague, he'd never once hinted that she was capable of murder.

She considered the two remaining creekside inhabitants—Angie and Ichabod—with an eye to whether either might be a killer. Fights were commonplace in the transient camps—alcohol- and drug-fueled turf wars, mostly—but she hadn't detected any tension among the group when she'd seen them all together before Miss Mae and Craig were killed. The idea that Angie could have killed someone Billy's size beggared belief. And she and Miss Mae had seemed good friends.

Johnny Harrow aka Ichabod had the sort of height that made him a potential suspect, but his arms were so spindly and stringy Julia couldn't imagine him swinging something like a tire iron with the force necessary to inflict the kind of wound she'd seen in his sidekick's skull.

Julia set the pen aside and hefted an imaginary bat. Could she put enough force into such a move to kill someone? Maybe—if she were scared or angry enough. If someone threatened Calvin. Her muscles tensed at the very thought. Jake, who had crept in from Calvin's room, sprang to his feet.

"It's all right, boy." She petted him, then drew a red X across Angie's name and a dashed X through Ichabod's, indicating doubt. While he hadn't said anything that implicated him, he hadn't offered an alibi either, probably because she hadn't asked him directly. She put an asterisk beside his name to remind herself to do that.

Mack Coates. She didn't know whether he'd known Billy or Miss Mae well, but she'd bet her new and too-reasonable rent that they were at least tangentially acquainted, given Mack's immersion in Duck Creek's demimonde.

But what would his motive be? Why kill a couple of transients who in no way threatened his tidy drug and trafficking operations? Word around the courthouse was that Mack ran his enterprises like the most ruthless Wall Street CEO. Get caught dipping into the product—or worse yet, the profits—and you'd be lucky to escape with a few missing teeth. He'd never faced a homicide charge, but Julia had represented defendants who were genuinely terrified of Mack; who'd asked if she could get them transferred into jails in other counties to escape his wrath or that of his minions.

Still, her breath caught as she stared at the board, with Ray's and Mack's names the only two—if she discounted Unknown Assailant—not crossed out. Was it possible? Had everyone in law enforcement focused on Ray because of his well-earned reputation as a fuckup and overlooked Mack despite his own notoriety as the most disciplined of thugs?

Except.

While Ray and Mack both had reputations as fighters, Ray had been seen arguing with Billy the weekend he was killed, and no one had mentioned a word about Mack so much as being in the neighborhood, let alone tangling with anyone there. She'd hated the circumstantial nature of the evidence against Ray, but the evidence against Mack was nonexistent.

Her red marker hovered over his name, but just before it touched the board, she flung it away. Then lunged to retrieve it before Jake could pounce upon it as some new and exceptionally flavorful chew toy.

*   *   *

Next, to Leslie Harper, despite the doubts that badgered her even as she started populating the second whiteboard with most of the same names. Claudette, Wayne, Cheryl Hayes, Mack Coates—the only people beyond Marie and Pinkham with whom she'd talked about Harper—and the shadowy Unknown Assailant, whom she favored more by the moment.

At least in this case, she could supply a possible motive for her far-flung planet. She settled on *Corruption*, even if she didn't know precisely what had piqued Harper's interest in the inner workings of Peak County's sheriff's department.

She stood back and looked at the two boards.

Nothing indicated the killings of the two transients and Harper were related.

But she couldn't ignore the timing, nor the fact that her questions about Harper, and her move into Harper's house, seemed to have triggered whoever was stalking her. People wanted her to back away from a vigorous defense of Ray. And someone wanted her not to look at Harper's death.

Every time she told herself to turn away from Harper, her gut urged her back.

"Always, always trust your gut," Claudette had commanded when they first started working together.

Once again, she X'd out Wayne and Claudette right away. Her pen hovered over Cheryl Hayes's name.

She should have been able to X out the deputy. Hayes had been visibly upset during Harper's funeral. But Julia couldn't avoid Wayne's comments about her and the fact that she'd objected to Harper's oversight proposal. Still, it was a long way from being upset about a proposed oversight board to murder—and of course there remained a significant school of thought that said Harper's death was accidental, despite Pinkham's caution. She drew a reluctant X through Hayes's name.

Which left her with a commonality between the two boards she couldn't ignore: in both cases, Mack Coates's name stood unmarred.

CHAPTER

36

JULIA'S PHONE, AUTOMATICALLY switched to vibrate at night, jumped in her pocket.

Her breath caught. Her stalker?

She withdrew it cautiously and held it away from her, afraid of what she might see. But the screen showed Dom's number. She punched it so hard the phone nearly flew from her hand.

"Julia? Are you there? Am I calling too late?"

He sounded anxious, afraid.

"I'm here. And it's not too late." She glanced at the clock. Ten PM. Not *too* late, but getting close, given her five-thirty alarm. She'd probably missed the window for a hot bath. "Is everything all right?"

"Fine. I mean, nothing new. I just. Well. I thought. Of you, I mean. I was thinking of you. This is probably crazy. I'm going out on a limb here."

She let him stammer on a moment longer. "Dom! Just spit it out."

"Remember the other night when you asked me if it was a booty call?"

She almost laughed, recalling her irritation when she thought it had been, and the slump of disappointment when she realized it wasn't.

"Yes?"

"Well." He cleared his throat, and laughter bubbled up within her again as she imagined him squaring his shoulders, stiffening his spine, preparing for whatever momentous pronouncement—one that apparently wasn't a disaster of some sort—had occasioned this late-night communication.

"Consider this a booty call."

Her laughter broke free, even as her mind ran through the obvious: Calvin asleep upstairs. The dog, prone to barking and leaping on the bed at inopportune moments. The neighbors, the neighbors, the neighbors. But it had been so goddamn long.

Misery leaked through the airwaves. "I'm sorry. That was inexcusable. I just . . ."

She grinned at the phone. "Shut up, Dom."

"I'm really sorry—"

"Dom. Seriously. Just shut up and get your ass over here."

*　*　*

They'd broken the main rule in the very slender book guiding their relationship: no sex with kids in the house.

Indeed, mere seconds after they'd finished—Julia's teeth clenched on a fat fold of quilt to muffle her cries of joy layered with a healthy dose of relief—she'd tiptoed from the bed and peeked into Calvin's room across the hall to ensure that he was indeed fast asleep, arms thrown above his head, eyelids twitching in some childhood dream that she hoped was a happy one. Beside him, Jake raised his head, then flopped back down at the sight of Julia, reassured that all was well.

Jake had gone briefly hysterical at the sight of this barely remembered intruder so late at night, then had succumbed to the offer of another dog biscuit, snatching it in his teeth and bearing his trophy to Calvin's room, where he'd remained—at least, Julia assumed he had—throughout their too-brief romp, thus earning absolution for the destruction of shoes and other household objects.

She slipped back into bed and Dom's embrace.

"All clear?"

"Yes. But you have to go soon. We shouldn't have." Even as she hugged him tighter, reluctant to abandon the luxury of touch, of shared pleasure, of—could she admit to love?

He stroked her hair. "You're right. But I'm glad we did. I promised myself I wouldn't do this. Now I'll promise that I won't do it again anytime soon. But Christ, Julia. The time we've had together has made it so hard to go back to going it alone."

"I know." She wanted to tell him about her frustrations with the case, her puzzlement over whatever relationship Leslie Harper's death might have to do with it, her suspicions about Mack Coates and lingering unease about Cheryl Hayes. But those were mere incidentals compared to the possible loss of custody of his daughter.

"Any word from Susan?"

"Not a peep. But Elena and I are talking again. Just barely—you know how those conversations go. 'How was school?' 'Fine.' 'What'd you do today?' 'Nothing.'"

She laughed low, remembering her own sullen responses to even the most innocuous questions from her parents during her teenage years.

"I don't want to do anything to jeopardize it." He started to get up.

"And yet here you are."

"And yet here I am." He fell back into bed, and though she should have shooed him out, she didn't.

*　*　*

Dom didn't leave until two in the morning, and then only because Julia briefly woke, triggered by a flash of light through the one-millimeter gap where she'd failed to completely lower the shade.

She held her breath, trying to hear over the pounding in her chest. Her stalker?

But the motion-activated light dimmed immediately and stayed dark. Probably an animal, she told herself, and finally looked at the clock.

"Holy shit. We fell asleep. Dom, you've got to go!"

He scrambled from the bed and into his clothes, his uncoordinated haste an echo of the panic in her voice.

"I'll let myself out."

"No. I have to throw the deadbolt behind you." She wrapped herself in a blanket, peeked into Calvin's room again—still asleep, thank God—and followed him down the stairs, the dog tumbling sleepily behind.

"Back door," she hissed.

He opened the door. The motion sensor light flashed, illuminating him as he sprinted across the backyard toward the alley's dark shelter. She watched until he faded from view, then twisted the lock until she heard the deadbolt's reassuring clunk.

She sighed again, touching a fingertip to her lips, still warm from the final, fierce kiss he'd bestowed, before she closed the door behind him.

"Good-bye, love," he'd said.

That word again, first in her mind, then spoken aloud by Dom. Was it?

She cast a final look at the clock before collapsing into bed. The morning—the whole coming day—would be a brutal slog through a morass of exhaustion. But at this moment, she didn't care.

37

H ER PHONE BUZZED again just as she was dropping off.
Dom, probably, letting her know he'd arrived home safely.

"Hey," she murmured into it without looking at the screen.

"Julia. Tell me you're all right." The voice jolted her upright. Sleep fled.

"Wayne?"

"Are you okay? Is anyone there with you?"

Not anymore, she thought. "Just Calvin and the dog."

"I'm just outside. Let me in."

"What the—?"

She took a moment to find her pajamas, tossed across the room in her haste with Dom, and shrugged into a robe.

As soon as the deadbolt slid free, Wayne pushed through the door. He slammed it behind him and locked it, then peered into her face. "You're really all right? There's nobody here ordering you to tell me that?"

"God, no! Wayne, I'm fine."

He withdrew his gun.

"Wayne! What are you doing?"

"Making sure. Stay with me."

He moved through the hallway, flinging open the doors to the hall closet and half bath, circling the dining room and opening the doors in the built-in hutch before turning to the kitchen, where the lower cabinet doors got the same treatment.

"Basement?"

She pointed.

He clicked on the light and headed down the stairs with Jake, too startled to bark, scampering at his heels. She followed him halfway down, and she watched as he circled the room, stepping over Calvin's toys, peering into the recessed nook that held the washer and dryer.

He left the basement and headed for the second floor. He stopped at the top of the stairs and looked a question toward her. "My room," she whispered, pointing left. She jerked her thumb right. "Calvin's. My office."

She stood in the hall and watched as he flung her door open and burst into the room, checking beneath the bed and opening the doors to the half-empty closets, pushing aside the clothes hanging there.

She stepped out of his way as he moved to the bathroom, where he shoved the shower curtain to one side, and then silently opened Calvin's door, letting the hallway light illuminate the room as he again checked the closets and beneath the bed.

He moved on to her office, where he took a long glance around, holstered his gun, and announced, "All clear."

"I could have told you that. Wayne, what's going on?"

He paced the room. "I'm on nights this week. Was driving back at the end of my shift. Swung by your street just . . . well, just a feeling."

"Because? Wayne, has something happened?" Her hand went to her throat. Was somebody else dead?

"Those things that have been happening to you, the calls and notes. I know it sounds like I've been blowing you off, but I didn't want you to worry."

So she hadn't been crazy. Scant comfort, under the circumstances.

"I've made it a habit to do a few drive-bys. So far, it's been quiet. Until tonight when I saw someone running away from the direction of your house. I drove around the block in the car. Then I got out and walked around but didn't see anybody. Thought I'd better check on you, just for safety's sake. Okay to take a look at the security camera footage?"

She bit her lip. The footage would indeed show a man sprinting across her backyard, maybe recognizable as Dom, maybe not. Thank God the snow had melted, so at least there was no damning trail of man-size footprints coming and going.

"No need," she said. "The motion lights went on and woke me up a few minutes before you called. I checked the footage and it was just a raccoon. Thank God. Given that it's trash day, I was worried it might have been a bear."

They were ubiquitous in Duck Creek, skulking down out of the foothills to the weekly feast that was trash day—pizza boxes with scraps of crust, waxed paper around half-eaten sandwiches, beer cans with dregs sloshing within—all irresistible, especially this time of year, when the bears awoke famished from their winter's hibernation.

He hesitated.

"Whoever you saw running never came to my door. I'm sure of it." She held her breath and crossed her fingers behind her back. "Can I get you anything before you go? Want a cup of coffee?"

Just the act of making it would probably rouse her to the point where she'd never get back to sleep, but it would be worth it if it made him forget about looking at those images.

"No, thanks. What's this?"

He stood in front of the whiteboards.

"What's my name doing there?"

Hell and damnation. "It's a system I have. Sort of a written version of throwing everything against a wall and seeing what sticks. I jotted down everyone I've talked to who's even tangentially involved in these cases. As you can see, your name is crossed out."

"But why is Harper's name up here? You don't have anything to do with her case. There isn't even a case for the public defenders, given that they haven't arrested anyone. And I thought I heard you were off Ray's."

Damn the courthouse hotline. "I am. This is something I started before I was pulled." Another lie, adding to the one about the raccoon. Julia was a confirmed skeptic, but vestiges of her Catholic girlhood lingered, manifesting themselves in the heavenly disapproval she felt directed her way. "As for Harper, I'm curious. Just like everyone else."

"Huh." He studied it a moment longer. "Interesting."

"Any thoughts?"

"With a plea agreement already in the works? I know you law-yers have to jump through all your legal hoops, but it seems pretty cut-and-dried to me, at least as far as Ray is concerned. Sorry." He gestured for her to go ahead of him back down the stairs but lingered in the room. She waited for him at the bottom of the steps.

He stood at the top, looking down at her and shaking his head. "If this is what floats your boat, go for it. It's actually not a bad sys-tem. I might try it myself."

He came down and walked with her to the front door. "Guess I overreacted tonight. I saw that guy and jumped to conclusions. Hope somebody else's house didn't get burgled while I was here. Didn't mean to cause you any trouble."

"Are you kidding? The fact that you went out of your way to check on me—that means the world, Wayne. I know you guys get a bad rap sometimes. People should see this side of things."

He threw her a grateful smile, and she watched as he opened the gate at the end of the walk and latched it carefully behind him in the bright glare of the motion sensor light.

She closed and locked the door, trying not to think about how soon her alarm was going to go off, and how endless the coming day would feel as she dragged herself through the hours wanting nothing more than a full night's sleep.

A line glowed beneath her office door. She'd forgotten to turn off the light. She almost ignored it but reminded herself that the electric bill was not included in the rent.

She trudged upstairs and reached for the switch, glancing at the whiteboard as she did so. Her hand fell. She walked over to the board. She'd X'd out Cheryl Hayes's name, reasoning that whatever Hayes's involvement might be in either case, it surely fell short of murder.

But now the X was largely gone, just a few faint traces remain-ing, all that was left after Wayne Peterson—it had to be him—had smeared it away just a few minutes earlier.

38

S HE MADE IT through the day—barely—and swung through a McDonald's drive-through after picking up Calvin, muttering the "Just this once" mantra that every overworked parent knows.

But Calvin, with the unerring instinct of every child of overworked parents, was having one of his bouncing-off-the-walls days, and her suggestion to play in the basement with his Legos or to run around the backyard with the dog met with a near-meltdown.

"Playground!" he insisted.

"But it's dark," she countered weakly. It wasn't, not completely, the sun sinking a little later each day behind the ski mountain outside town, something Calvin pointed out to her with unassailable logic.

"Playground." He stomped his feet. Jake sat beside him and turned a pleading gaze upon Julia, who wasted a few moments wondering if it was possible to drown in self-pity.

"Fine." If nothing else, maybe it would wear out both Calvin and Jake and give her an excuse to put them to bed early.

Calvin raced around the living room, the dog on his heels, and grabbed his coat and flung open the front door.

"Wait!" Julia caught up with them halfway down the walk, lecturing Calvin the rest of the way to the playground about the perils of running off like that, only to be rewarded with him mockingly chanting "Stranger danger! Stranger danger!" at the top of his lungs, Jake barking a joyful chorus.

* * *

At least she could relax at the playground, pushing herself languidly to and fro in one of the swings while Calvin attacked the swing next to her, then the slides, monkey bars, and that awful relic from Julia's own childhood, the spinner.

She'd refused to join him on the seesaw—another piece of equipment she deeply distrusted for the irresistible temptation it posed to legions of kids to leap off as their end rose to its height, leaving their partner to crash ignominiously to ground.

She felt the same way about the spinner. Some called it a merry-go-round, although her own private name for it was death trap; too many memories of mean kids pushing it faster and faster until she flew off, landing dizzy and nauseated. But Jake—who'd planted himself in its center, ears flapping as Calvin twirled the diabolical thing—appeared to have no such reservations.

She pumped her legs and swung higher, thinking of her white-board exercise the night before, of Mack Coates's unmarred name, of the X erased from Cheryl Hayes's. Despite her Occam's razor lecture to Marie, her mind skittered among wild possibilities. Was Hayes in some way part of Coates's trafficking operation? Did she steer women toward him after detaining them on minor charges?

It seemed farfetched, but it wouldn't be the first time a cop had joined lucrative forces with the very people he arrested. Nearly every department dealt with such issues at one time or another, and for sure, such an allegation would merit Leslie Harper's push for an oversight agency—and Hayes's apparent objections to it.

Her phone dinged, interrupting her musings just as she was beginning to take them seriously. She twisted in the swing to check on Calvin—the spinner was behind the swing set—and then clicked on the incoming text.

Busy night! Two men, one right after the other. Do you charge by the hour or by the fuck?

Her hand shook so badly that it took her a few tries to bring up the security footage, swiping through the grainy images to see if she could detect anyone or anything beyond Dom's surreptitious arrival and departure—shoulders hunched, coat collar turned up around his face, hat pulled down low—and Wayne's far more confident stride to the front door, his fist striking it three times.

She looked again and again, repeatedly rewinding the images, but saw nothing other than the two of them. She started to forward the text to Wayne but thought better of it, still not wanting him to know about Dom's visit. She glanced around, wondering if someone was watching her from behind a tree, hiding in the small building housing the restrooms, or masquerading as another parent.

But the playground was deserted.

It was deserted.

The fact sank in as she rose from the swing in one of those slow-motion maneuvers that seemed to take forever even as she called, louder and louder, trying to drown out the sound of her jackhammering heart:

"Calvin? Calvin! *Calvin!*"

Julia ran to the spinner and stared at it, as though looking hard would cause her son to materialize.

"Calvin! Calvin!" And, taking a chance, "Jake!"

Maybe the dog would come running, sink his teeth into her jeans and tug her toward her son and one of those cinematic reunions where mother, son, and dog collapse in a happy heap.

Jake was not that dog.

This was not that movie.

*   *   *

Julia sprinted to each of the park's four corners, scanning the damnably empty streets leading away from it. Where the hell was everybody? Had the rest of the world, like Calvin and Jake, been swept up in some cruel, cockeyed form of a rapture?

Stay put. She'd taught him that from the moment he could understand his first few words. If you ever get lost, stay put. Don't wander around trying to find your way back.

Useful, even lifesaving information in a place like Duck Creek, surrounded by wilderness and full of people who liked to spend their summers hiking and camping, their falls hunting, and their winters backcountry skiing. Every year, people reliably stepped off trails to investigate something that had caught their eye, or took shortcuts, and then kept moving until hypothermia or some even more unpleasant fate caught up with them, leaving searchers no clue as to which direction they'd taken. *Stay put.*

She jogged back to the spinner, still half calling, half sobbing Calvin's name, fumbling for her phone, taking one last desperate glance around before calling 911, only to see a trio approaching.

Calvin.

Jake.

And Cheryl Hayes.

* * *

For a moment, she was in the movie she'd imagined, clutching Calvin even as he laughingly tried to squirm away from her kisses, the dog performing ecstatic arabesques around them as she showered her son with the mixture of relief and fury familiar to all mothers.

"Where did you go? I was so scared! Calvin, I told you never to wander off."

"Why weren't you watching him?"

Hayes's words dripped like acid, dissolving their happy reunion.

Julia loosened her grip on Calvin, although not entirely, keeping one hand clamped around his wrist, wrapping the other in Jake's leash. She maneuvered to her feet and met Hayes's eyes.

The woman's gaze flashed anger. She was in her running clothes, fists jammed deep in her sweatshirt's kangaroo pocket. She withdrew one hand and pointed an accusatory finger toward the creek.

"I found him on the creek trail. Alone—well, except for the dog. He was chasing him. It's almost dark now. A few more steps and he could have ended up in the water. Or one of the people who hangs around down there could have gotten him. Not all of them are as harmless as your friends. A lot of sex offenders camp out there because no one in town will rent to them. What kind of mother are you?"

Hayes's voice rose throughout her lecture until she was nearly shouting, her face mere inches from Julia's.

"Get out of here. Keep hold of him the whole way home, and once you get there, stay there. Jesus Christ. If you can't protect your own son, how can you hope to protect yourself?"

She whirled and stalked away, shaking out her arms, jogging a few steps before breaking into a steady run.

Julia stood frozen, almost as shocked by Hayes's last words as she was by the Duck Creek High logo emblazoned across the back of Hayes's sweatshirt.

S HE WAITED UNTIL Calvin was splashing in the tub, steering his
ducky through floes of bubbles, flicking an occasional bit of foam
toward Jake, who shook his head in bafflement at the way it disappeared whenever he closed his jaws around it.

She'd put extra bubble bath in the water and brought out a toy
she'd been saving for a special occasion, a plastic tugboat that sucked
up water when squeezed, then squirted it out when squeezed again.
She wanted him relaxed and distracted as she chatted away about
mundane things—school, his friends, Jake.

"Where'd you go today, anyway?" she asked, finally getting
around to what truly interested her.

"To school." *Squirt!* The ducky took a direct hit in the eye. Calvin crowed in triumph.

"No, after school. In the park this evening."

Calvin cast her a doubtful look. Sometimes he was a little too
smart for his own good. She grabbed the duck and clobbered the
tugboat with it. "Take that, you mean boat!"

The resulting naval war left Julia nearly as soaked as her son.
She tried again. "Where did you say you went? Hey, look, the duck
is getting away."

He grabbed for it, and she put up a brief fight before letting him
wrest it from her.

"Jake runned away."

"Ran away. So you chased him?"

Another sideways glance.

"Because you were worried about him," she reassured him. "Just like I was about you."

"Uh-huh."

"How did you catch him?"

Bubbles slid from his shoulders as he hunched away from the question.

She tried again. "Where did you catch him?"

He brightened. He knew this one. "By the creek! Man helped."

He caught himself and looked away again, chin trembling.

"Calvin, what is it? Did something happen? Did the man do something?" Her mind pinwheeled through the awful possibilities, heightened by Hayes's warning about sex offenders camping along the creek.

He was sobbing, tears mingling with the bathwater, his toys forgotten.

"Oh, Calvin. It's all right." Even though it wasn't. "You can tell me."

"You told me . . . you told me . . ." Calvin blubbered. "No strangers."

Oh God. "Did the man touch you? Hurt you? What did he look like?"

She would find him, this faceless, nameless man. If it took the rest of her life. She would find him and confront him and with her bare hands she would . . .

"He looked like . . ." Calvin twisted his lips, one side drooping. "Funny mouth."

The tugboat fell from Julia's hand.

She drew an imaginary scar across one corner of her lips. "A line here? Like this?"

Calvin nodded, his smile returning. He'd gotten something right.

Julia turned away so he wouldn't see her face, the horror written there at the thought of Mack Coates in any proximity to her son.

"He was nice!" Calvin crowed behind her. "He givved Jake back."

"Gave." Julia rearranged her face and turned back. The bathroom's steamy heat bordered on discomfort, but she suppressed a shiver. She sat back on her heels, trying to see it. Jake on the spin-ner, maybe seeing a bird or a squirrel—or maybe being lured by a grinning man with a treat—leaping after it, Calvin in pursuit as she stared oblivious into her phone. The man, once safely out of Julia's sight, grabbing the leash, offering it to Calvin, waiting with that same crooked smile as the boy came close.

"Did the man say anything to you?"

Calvin shook his head firmly, happy to cooperate now that he could tell he wasn't in trouble. "Police lady came."

But Hayes had been in her running gear—and that damn sweatshirt.

"Calvin." It took an extreme effort to keep her voice low and calm. For good measure, she took up the toys again, filling the tugboat with water and squirting it toward Jake, who sneezed and shot her a look of betrayal. Calvin rewarded her with a cascade of giggles.

"How did you know she was a police lady?"

"She told me."

Julia's breath caught. Hayes could have been anyone.

"And I 'membered her. From before. When we saw the people with the fire."

"The people under the bridge! Yes! You remember them and her!" In her relief, she was babbling. "That's good, Calvin. That's really good. But the next time someone tells you they're a police officer, make sure they have the police uniform. And the badge—the shiny star." She struck her chest. "And if Jake ever runs away again, don't you chase him. You call me and I'll chase him for you. My legs are longer and I can run faster."

She lifted him from the tub and wrapped him in a towel, her sweet boy, safe in her arms, slippery and wet as a seal.

"Mom! Stop kissing!"

She released him, and he ran naked to his room, Jake at his heels, the two of them making the kind of joyful racket that never would have been tolerated in Beverly's house.

It took her four readings of "Strega Nona," his current favorite, before his eyelids grew heavy and he finally slept. Thanks to Strega

Nona, she had to sing over the stove whenever she cooked pasta, with Calvin blowing the necessary kisses before she drained it.

She sat with him a long while after he fell asleep, stroking his hair with one hand, the other wrapped around his arm, unwilling to let him go, as though he might disappear again when she turned away to go to her own room.

"Stay," she finally commanded Jake. "And bark like hell if anything happens."

What did she think might happen? That someone might lean a ladder against the house and whisk Calvin away before the motion sensor lights had fully awakened her?

She walked through the house, checking the locks, pulling the drapes tighter, the shades lower. She checked her phone app for the security cameras. Peered through the peepholes in the front and back doors, just in case.

But when she finally fell into bed and closed her eyes, the paired images of Cheryl Hayes and Mack Coates rose before her. She'd entertained the possibility of coincidence the day Hayes had shown up at Coates's initial hearing. Again when she'd seen him emerging from the tea shop where she'd found Hayes.

How'd the saying go from that old James Bond movie? "Once is happenstance, twice is coincidence, the third time it's enemy action."

She'd brushed aside as fanciful her notion of Hayes and Coates being involved in some sort of criminal operation, just as she'd given no more than a cursory follow-up to Wayne's broad hints about the woman.

No more.

Time to take action against the enemy.

CHAPTER

40

Before she figured out her next move, she had to ensure her son's safety.

Julia debated long and hard about how to approach Calvin's teacher before coming up with a story she deemed both vague and suitable enough.

"I've been getting some threats," she said when she dropped him off the next morning. "It happens occasionally in my line of work, and it's probably nothing. But could you please make sure the playground monitors keep an extra eye on Calvin when he's outside? And of course, the school is not to release him to anyone but me or his grandmother."

She thought she'd soft-pedaled it enough, hit the sweet spot between too scary and too casual. Apparently not.

The teacher's pursed lips conveyed both concern and disapproval. "If one of our students is in danger, that means the other children could be. Or our teachers. We can't have that."

"Oh, no." Julia hastened to undercut her own words. "If it was that serious, there'd be a restraining order. I'm probably being overly cautious. You know how it is."

The woman had two decades on Julia and was exactly the kind of person she'd have imagined as a kindergarten teacher, plump and grandmotherly, a warm smile her default expression. Now the smile was nowhere to be seen and Julia glimpsed another side of her, the one that daily rode herd over a dozen five-year-olds with little or no impulse control and somehow managed to keep the days from devolving into chaos.

"I suggest you try and see it from my point of view." Her tone made it clear it was a command, not a suggestion.

Try seeing it from mine. "Of course. I understand completely. Gosh. Look at the time. I'm going to be late for work."

Julia, ready to confront a rogue sheriff's deputy with metaphorical guns blazing, turned coward when faced with a teacher's disapproval. Scattering demurrals, she fled.

* * *

She *was* late. But she couldn't walk into the office in this agitated state. So she took the long way, heading for the creek trail, hoping despite recent experience that its distractions would this time soothe her into the readjustment necessary for radiating an attitude of being firmly In Charge.

For a few moments, it worked. A great blue heron caught her attention, standing statuelike on a single leg on a log jutting into the creek, its yellow eye fixed on the water rushing past. A couple of mallards paddled in a placid backwater, gabbling to one another, seemingly oblivious to the chaos just a few feet away.

The creek snatched at things as it passed, tearing shallow-rooted trees free and sending them downstream like so many ungainly vessels. Sometimes a trailing root would snag on a rock, pulling the log low in the water, where it would bob nearly undetectable until it grabbed an overeager boater who'd launched too early in the year, the centrifugal force of the rushing waters dragging the craft under with a savage and lethal swiftness.

Julia looked past the logs and focused on the egrets, the ducks, an osprey hovering high overhead, vying with the heron for the trout newly freed from their winter somnolence.

Spring, a teasing flirt in their part of the world, today bestowed upon Duck Creek an abundance of sunshine, the temperature climbing by the moment, the kind of morning that invoked thoughts of daffodils and budding fruit trees, of hats and mittens tossed aside, of the reappearance of sidewalk buskers and patio tables—all the things to make one think that life this close to the Canadian border made sense after all.

Julia unfastened her coat. Slowed her pace. Turned her face to the sun. And nearly walked into Angie.

"Watch where you're going, lawyer lady."

Julia stumbled and refocused, blinking her eyes, trying to chase away sun-blindness.

"Sorry. Guess I was daydreaming."

"Sun-drunk," Angie said knowingly. "Happens to everyone at this time of year. Better than the real thing, if you ask me."

Indeed, she was clear-eyed, unburdened by the pained expression, the pretzeled posture, the shaking hands of so many of Julia's clients when they showed up for court appearances scheduled the morning after the night before.

Julia studied her. She wasn't like the others who huddled in downtown doorways, hands hopefully extended for spare change; others who wandered the streets, muttering and gesticulating, lost in their own private world of misfired synapses. Clean up Angie Barrett, supply her with some teeth, put her in one of the ramshackle apartment buildings on Duck Creek's outskirts, out on a postage-stamp balcony watering plants in an old coffee can, and she'd have fit right in.

"Angie, do you mind if I ask you a question?"

"Shoot." She shielded her eyes against the sun's glare.

Julia struggled for tactful phrasing and ended up going with direct. "How'd you end up out here?"

She favored Julia with a sly smile. "Heading downtown just like you are."

"I don't mean today. What I mean is—"

"Oh, I know what you mean. You want to know why I don't live the way you do. Or all these people." She swung her arm wide, the gesture incorporating the whole town.

"I guess."

"Guess, nothing. That's exactly what you mean." Angie's grin was gone, replaced with the implacable expression of someone calling bullshit.

Busted. "So why do you?"

They stepped aside to allow a runner to pass, along with a bicyclist pedaling so fast they felt the breeze. Julia wondered at these people who had time for such workaday jaunts. Neither runner nor cyclist looked anywhere near retirement age.

Angie pointed to their retreating forms. "Same reason they're out here. Only difference is, I don't go to a house at night. Or"—she shuddered—"an office. I tried. I really did. Worked a few jobs, nothing special, fast food or stocking shelves in a supermarket, stuff like that. I still take a little job now and then, but it doesn't last long. I always either get fired or quit. Don't like people telling me what to do." The sly smile reappeared.

"But isn't it dangerous out here?" Julia kept the obvious—*given that you're a woman alone*—to herself.

Angie bent and slid a hand into her beat-up boot. Something flashed silvery in the sun, then disappeared back into the boot.

"Was that a switchblade? Aren't they illegal?"

Angie ran her tongue over her gums. "Yeah. So's what some people want to do to me. And if they do it, they end up with somebody like you defending them in court, telling them I asked for it. Let's just say my friend"—she nodded toward the boot—"is way more reliable than any judge and jury. Miss Mae told me years ago to always have one on me, and it's the best advice I ever got.

"Besides." Her expression softened. "Ray was usually out here with me. Anybody hassled me, they'd have to deal with Ray, and if he wasn't around, one of the rest of us. Now half of us are dead or in jail. It's just me and Johnny out here on our own. Everyone leaves us alone now after what happened to Billy and Miss Mae and Craig, either out of respect or more likely they think we're bad luck. Wonder how long that'll last, what with Ray in jail now."

Ray. Julia had been so caught up in her own worries that she'd nearly forgotten about him.

"I'm trying my best with Ray. Or at least, I was. Do you have any idea why he decided to plead guilty? He won't talk to me at all."

The wind went out of Angie, so defiant just a moment before.

"Because he doesn't have a choice."

"He does! He could have let me defend him. I'd have worked my ass off for him. I'm worried about him, Angie. Last time I saw him, he'd been beaten up."

Angie moved close and lowered her voice. "Beaten is bad. But killed is worse."

Julia tried to sound casual. "What do you mean?"

She looked around. "Nothing. I don't mean nothing."

Julia grabbed her wrist. "What are you saying? Angie, if you know something, you have to tell me. You have no idea how important this is."

Angie didn't pull away. Just looked at Julia's hand and laughed, a grim, rusty sound.

"I have no idea? Billy, Miss Mae, and Craig are all dead and Ray's in jail. Don't talk to me about important. I have a better idea than you ever will."

Julia went out on a limb. "I know Cheryl Hayes is mixed up in this, but I don't know how. If you tell me, I can do something about it. And I promise I'll keep you out of it. Keep you safe."

Angie shook her wrist free. Contempt chased the despair from her face.

"You couldn't even keep your own kid safe, letting him run loose down here in the dark. What are you going to do for me?"

Julia gaped. "How do you know about that?"

Angie ignored her. "Only person you ought to be worried about keeping safe is yourself."

She reached into the shrubbery, retrieved a day pack and slung it over her shoulder. "And leave Deputy Hayes out of this. She's about the only friend we've got out here."

* * *

"Like hell I'll leave Deputy Hayes out of this," Julia muttered. Hayes's shtick might have worked on Angie's alcohol-soaked brain, but Julia had finally come to her senses.

Hayes's lunch break was at twelve thirty. Julia was at the tea shop by noon.

This time she ordered Earl Grey, which came in a pint-size tea-pot decorated with—what else—tea roses. Julia, no fan of cuteness, turned it sideways so as to avoid the showiest of the painted flowers.

"I never took you for the tea-and-crumpets type," Coates had said. He was right. But the shop offered crumpets, and out of curi-osity, she ordered one. It turned out to be something like a spongy English muffin, browned on one side, pale on the other. Butter vastly improved it, marmalade further still.

She nibbled at it, licking a bit of sticky marmalade from her fin-gers, and sipped her tea and tried not to think how much she missed the instant caffeine kick of coffee. She'd stop at Colombia on the way back to the office.

The bell on the door tinkled, and she hastily turned her chair away. She'd left her wool cap on, tucking her too-recognizable cop-pery curls beneath it, a subterfuge that apparently worked because the voice responding to a cheerful "Your usual?" was that of Cheryl Hayes.

Julia became very, very interested in the remnants of her crum-pet, bending over her tiny plate—with its own rim of painted roses—until she heard a chair scrape at a nearby table and the rustle of Hayes removing her coat.

She waited for the first faint slurp and made her move.

Two long strides brought her to Hayes's table. She grabbed one of the adorable wrought-iron chairs, spun it around, and sat facing Hayes, who froze with her teacup halfway to her lips.

"What's the deal with you and Mack Coates?"

Give the woman credit. When Julia had first confronted her in the tea shop, she'd been shaken. Now Hayes lifted her cup, drank, and set back in its saucer (this one rimmed with violets) with a rock-steady hand.

She glanced at her book—still working her way through *Crime and Punishment*, Julia noted—gave the corner of her open page the tiniest crimp, and closed it with possibly more force than necessary. Julia braced herself to be clocked upside the head with nearly five hundred pages of Dostoyevsky.

But Hayes merely folded her hands before her and waited. An old trick, one Julia had used herself.

Hayes was better at it.

"You were with him the other night down by the river, weren't you?" Julia said finally. "After he took my little boy."

"You mean the night I found your little boy wandering alone."

"After Mack had lured our dog away."

Hayes lifted a brown-clad shoulder and held her gaze. "So you let both your child and your dog wander off. At night. Near the river. I could have ticketed you."

Two could play this game. Julia rested her arms across the back of the chair. "But you didn't. Why?"

Hayes's eyes crinkled at the corners, signaling a smile that never made it to her lips.

"I'll let you figure that out."

She rose, slipped into her coat, tucked Dostoyevsky under one arm, and headed for the door in a *Fuck you* saunter, maneuvering around tables and shelves laden with fragile, pretty things as nimbly—despite her heavy coat and clumsy work boots—as she'd dodged Julia's questions about Mack Coates.

41

BRIEF AS HER fruitless conversation had been, Julia nonetheless had missed her window to duck into Colombia for a necessary dose of what she thought of as real caffeine.

She picked up her pace, rounded the corner to the courthouse, and stopped.

A knot of people stood before it. Two SUVs sporting local television station logos waited at the curb. The imposing double doors with their polished brass handles opened, and Claudette Greene descended the wide marble steps toward a phalanx of microphones. Julia sprinted, elbowing her way through the onlookers until she stood among the reporters at the front of the pack, arriving just as Claudette began to speak.

"These are difficult days for our community. Three of our citizens have been violently taken from us in recent weeks. Allow me to speak frankly."

A reporter turned her head at Julia's snort. When had Claudette ever soft-pedaled a single thing? Frank was her default position, with the adverb *brutally* usually appended. Julia braced herself for ballistic.

"These deaths, these vicious *homicides*—and the arrest we've made in connection—have occasioned little interest from the local press other than short stories reporting they'd occurred. Yet by contrast, the death—at first thought accidental—of a local legislator merited a half page of type."

All around Julia, shoulders hunched. Nobody liked a public scolding. Julia wondered how much of Claudette's speech would make it onto the evening news, or the front page. She stole a glance at Chance Larsen. He'd written all the stories in question, including the one in which a host of prominent citizens had sung Leslie Harper's praises. *An appreciation*, the newspaper had called it, their term for something that went far beyond a generic obit.

Chance bent his head over his notebook, his hand a blur as he took notes. Julia knew he'd have placed a recorder on the portable podium that had been toted outdoors for the event, but he'd once told her he had never fully trusted them. "Best to go old-school as a backup," he'd said, waggling his pen.

"That story about Representative Harper—I myself was quoted in it—told us so much about her. Her years of service to the community and our state. The many awards she'd received over the course of her career. Her close relationship with her sister and her niece and nephew, even though two thousand miles separated them. Her wizardry in the kitchen. It even mentioned her new puppy."

Claudette took a breath and drew herself to her full six-foot height, enhanced today by the four-inch scarlet heels she kept in her desk drawer for just such occasions, when she wanted to push intimidation to DEFCON 2, a level just short of thermonuclear.

"Even if I hadn't already known Leslie Harper, I would have felt as though I did by the time I'd finished reading that story. I didn't get that feeling from the newspaper or television stories about William Williams. Or the ones about Mary Brannigan. Or the even shorter ones about Craig Thompson. Maybe they weren't state legislators. Maybe they didn't have shelves full of awards. From what I gather, they didn't even have shelves.

"That doesn't mean they didn't have dreams. Aspirations. People they loved and people who loved them in return. But I don't know any of those things about them because"—her normally booming voice lowered to a hiss—"because apparently nobody bothered to ask."

She paused. Julia counted the beats.

One.

Two.

Three.

"Because apparently nobody cared."

One more very long beat.

"But the Peak County Attorney's Office cares. It cares very much. We don't give our prosecutions short shrift just because they happen to involve the least among us. We've already filed charges in two of these cases and are working hard to develop information that will lead to an arrest in the third."

Julia scanned the group of reporters until she found a face she didn't recognize. Someone new, with the fresh-out-of-journalism-school mixture of cockiness and eagerness—not unlike that of her intern—that would serve her purposes. She sidled up to him. "Think she wants a story about the guy they arrested?"

His eyebrows shot up. He too glanced around, taking in his colleagues' cowed expressions. His shoulders straightened. His hand went into the air. Julia moved away, fast. She didn't want him to be able to find her when Claudette was done with him.

"What about the person who was charged? Wasn't he a transient also?"

No, Julia whispered from her new location in the back of the crowd. *Not a transient. Not someone just passing through. He lived here too. Just not in a house.*

The reporter pressed on. "Would you like to see more stories about him too?"

The other reporters took a few steps away from him, leaving him alone in the white-hot spotlight of Claudette's glare. Criticizing coverage generally guaranteed an even sharper focus from the press, but if Julia correctly read the shamefaced expressions around her, Claudette had a point.

She raked Julia's hapless victim up and down with her gaze.

"No questions," she said. "I know you all are busy people. You have stories to write. *Legitimate* stories."

Julie hurried around the corner and entered the courthouse by a side door before he could find her and give her the tongue-lashing she deserved, but in avoiding him, ran straight into Claudette.

"What the hell, Julia?"

Because she'd shared an office with Claudette for so many years, Julia was one of the very few people in the courthouse unafraid—mostly—of her former colleague.

"What the hell yourself? What was that all about? A news conference? What was the news? And why here instead of at your own office?"

Even though she knew the reason. Claudette's office a few blocks away was befittingly imposing, but it didn't have the made-for-TV backdrop of the courthouse.

"For exactly the reasons I said. Pisses me off that Billy Williams and Miss Mae and Craig Thompson got short shrift when they were killed. I know you feel the same way." She stabbed at the elevator button, flashing a new manicure that matched the color of her pumps.

"I do. I just don't understand . . ." Julia stopped. She did understand. In just a few short months, Claudette would face the election that could see her ensconced as the county's official, rather than acting, prosecutor. But her job left her precious little time for campaigning. While it was illegal to campaign on work time, she was following a time-honored tradition of public announcements about her office's—extra stress on *office*—priorities and accomplishments, which basically achieved the same thing.

Julia tap-danced away from what she'd been about to say. "I just don't understand what brings you to the courthouse today. Now that you're done with your no-news news conference."

The elevator door opened. Claudette stepped inside. "Just visiting with Tim Saunders to iron out the details of Ray's plea agreement. Sorry they took you off the case."

But the grim smile she flashed as the doors closed told Julia she wasn't sorry at all.

42

JULIA SLUMPED AT her desk without even taking off her coat.

She didn't want to talk with Marie. She didn't want to talk with anyone. Ray was in jail and was going to plead guilty, which would see him sent—apparently willingly—a hundred miles away to the state prison, and there didn't seem to be a goddamn thing she could do about it.

She was dimly aware of motion behind her, a rustle as Marie rose, the door opening and closing. She was alone. Thank God.

She shed her coat, booted up her computer, and pulled one of the files from the stack on her desk. A drunk driver, only his second offense, nowhere near the felony level yet. But the guy had blown a .16, well over the .08 considered impaired, the kind of proof that sealed his guilt. At least he was a solid citizen, a sales clerk in an appliance store, thankfully not a job that required driving or being any sort of role model. She'd try to get the prosecution to go along with an Alford plea, where her client would maintain his innocence but agree that he'd likely be found guilty in a trial. It'd be chancy, given his prior conviction, but she'd seen clients with as many as seven DUIs. This one would lose his license for six months, and maybe he'd even be that one in a hundred who mended his ways.

She selected another file. A typical Saturday night special, drunk and disorderly upon his return to town after a kegger in the woods, something she'd see a lot more of as the weather warmed. She checked the name against her files. First offense, at least in their state. That would help. Also, he was only twenty, and while he'd done a lot of shouting and flailing in the course of his revelries, he'd apparently injured nothing but his own pride, so this would be an easy OR release, and he'd have to pay the ticket for underage drinking. Judges, most of them male, tended to go easy on college boys, viewing their antics as harmless and predictable shenanigans, the sort of thing they'd outgrow. Never having been college girls, it didn't occur to them that some men only got worse.

She made some notes and selected a third file, trying to lose herself in routine, the things she knew how to do rather than the ones that stubbornly resisted solutions.

The office door opened again, revealing Marie, in each hand a go-cup of coffee emblazoned with Colombia's logo. She bumped the door closed with her hip and put one of the drinks on Julia's desk.

Julia grabbed the coffee with unseemly haste, taking several swallows before she set it aside and eyeballed her unlikely benefactor.

"Twice in two weeks? What's the deal?"

"What do you mean?" Marie had removed the lid from her own cup and was busy demolishing a floe of whipped cream atop her drink. Hot chocolate again, Julia guessed by the scent drifting her way.

"I mean, what's the occasion?" Why would a penniless and obviously unappreciated intern suddenly start sucking up to her harpy of a boss?

"You looked like you needed it. Like you *really* needed it."

She *really* did. But damned if she wanted Marie to know her mounting but still vague fear.

Marie slurped her whipped cream–topped hot chocolate, never taking her eyes off Julia. "You know, I'm not as stupid as you think I am." Said with equanimity, not even a tinge of resentment or hurt.

Julia raised an eyebrow and mentally awarded Marie points for a plain statement of fact. She tossed one of her own back.

"I don't think you're stupid. I just don't think you're as smart as you think you are. It's a baby lawyer thing. You'll get over it. God knows, I've had to."

A little more information than she'd intended to divulge.

"Like now, you mean? With this case?"

Julia gestured to the stack on her desk. "Which one?" Marie was probably talking about Ray, but that didn't mean Julia had to make it easier for her.

Marie acted as though they'd already agreed they were discussing Ray. "Tim Saunders seems to think it's settled."

Julia waited.

"He acts like it's a big deal, getting Ra . . . Mr. Belmar to plead guilty. Is it?"

Julia finished off her coffee. The caffeine hit had raised her spirits just enough to entertain this conversation with Marie.

"Normally, yes. It's always preferred over a trial. Saves the county time and money, not to mention you never want to roll the dice on a jury. But you know that."

Marie nodded gravely, her solemnity at odds with the child's drink in her hand. "I do. But I had a thought."

Julia braced herself for a pronouncement sure to highlight her own shortcomings and Marie's legal brilliance. She searched her mind for a task that would take Marie out of the office for the rest of the day.

"Let him," Marie said.

"Excuse me?"

"Let him plead guilty. I mean, you don't really have a choice in the matter, given that you're off the case. But don't try to go around Saunders' back and talk him out of it."

Julia crushed the empty paper coffee cup in her hand and hurled it toward the trash can. It bounced off the wall with such force that she had to duck its ricocheting return.

"Look. I haven't said anything about this until now in the hope that I'd see a change. But it's become increasingly clear that you should be interning with the prosecutor's office."

"Hear me out," Marie continued, implacable. "He pleads, they schedule a sentencing hearing. Buys us some time."

Us? Marie persisted in thinking they were a team. Julia folded her arms across her chest and waited.

"Takes the heat off, lets everybody think we've moved on. But just to make sure, find some innocuous case and make a big deal about it. Say something in the press. Bury any public thought of Mr. Belmar deeper than whale shit."

"And?"

Marie crumpled her own cup and made a perfect bank shot.

"Then, while everyone else goes about their business, we keep investigating on the down-low. If we come up with something, Mr. Belmar can withdraw his plea."

We.

Julia didn't realize she'd spoken aloud.

"It'll go faster and better with two of us. You can review every-thing I do."

This time, Julia's equally brief query was deliberate.

"Why?"

Marie turned away and spoke to her desk.

"You don't like me. You don't trust me. You think I hang around too much with cops. Well, I've known cops my whole life. They're the ones who pulled my dad off my mom again and again and again, until the night they got there too late. I don't hold it against them—they couldn't be with us twenty-four seven—but for a long time they saved me and my mom, and they checked in on me when I went into foster care, made sure I was all right there."

"I'm sorry about your mother." But Julia couldn't help herself. "All of that seems to be a reason you'd make a better prosecutor, though. Go after guys like your dad and put them behind bars where they can't hurt anyone."

Marie blinked rapidly. "You'd think. We lived in a trailer park. Pretty sure half the people there were in the criminal justice system somehow—DUIs, petty theft, the usual. But they couldn't get out. Their fees would mount up, or they'd skip a court date because they finally got work that same day and they needed the money. Or they'd violate some impossible parole condition, like somebody picked up for passing a bad check and then prohibited from drinking or going into bars for six months. Once they got into the system, it seemed like they were stuck there forever."

Her voice grew smaller and smaller as she spoke, until Julia could barely hear her.

"It just didn't seem fair." She turned her head away. "Anyway, they were a lot like Mr. Belmar. Screw-ups but not killers. I don't know why he's so insistent on pleading, but it doesn't smell right. Does it?"

Julia was so taken aback by Marie's revelation she couldn't focus on Ray.

"How'd you make your way to law school? And what's it like being there?"

She'd taken Marie for the sort of people who'd surrounded her through her own law school years—people whose parents paid not just their tuition but covered their rent and sometimes car payments too—or even those like Julia, paying down an Everest of debt. But at least she'd had parents who raised her in a calm, crime-free household in a comfortable middle-class neighborhood, where college was a given and advanced degrees encouraged, even if they couldn't offer much in the way of financial support.

The strength returned to Marie's voice. "I never wanted to live that way again. And I didn't want other people to either. You tell that to a guidance counselor and they get all smiley and say, 'You should go to law school and make a difference!' So far, I'm not seeing how this makes much of a difference for anyone."

No shit, Julia almost said.

But Marie wasn't done. "What's law school like for me? Like a foreign country."

Of course it was. No wonder she liked to hang out with cops. If nothing else, they represented familiar territory. And the whole fascination with guns—they probably gave her a sense of security, even though Julia was getting the feeling that Marie knew at least as well as she did that security was an illusion.

"So why tell me all of this now?" And was she telling the truth? Julia had faced enough master manipulators in the jail's interview rooms to be tempted to tattoo a maxim on her arm: *If your mother says she loves you, check it out.*

She'd check out Marie's story. If the young woman's father had truly killed her mother, it'd be in the courthouse files, along with the domestic violence incidents—if indeed charges had ever been filed against him. Although attitudes and policies had undergone a sea change over the years, Julia still knew cops and prosecutors who were inclined to back away from pursuing cases when the understandably terrified woman didn't want to press charges—even though the prosecutors were supposed to file them anyway, so as to take the pressure off the woman in question.

"I wanted you to judge me on the quality of my work, not because you feel sorry for me. But I got sick of waiting for you to realize that I can actually do you some good." Marie held her face impassive, but the hurt leaked through in her voice. "You're like everyone in law school. You took one look at me and made a snap judgment. Sure hope that's not how you handle your cases."

Julia held up her hand. "Enough. You've made your point."

Marie turned away, but not quickly enough to hide her triumphant smile. "Thank you."

"Now let's talk about your idea. And let's come up with a plan—and a way to keep it from being completely obvious to the whole world what we're doing."

43

B UT BEFORE JULIA could put her part of the plan into action, she
had to deal with Mack Coates, with whom she hoped to fare
better than she had with Hayes.

Her mission with Coates was simpler. Maybe she'd get information from him. Maybe not. But for sure, she'd issue a warning.

Finding him would be easy, although the timing was tricky. A
quick scan of his file, whose thickness rivaled that of Ray's, informed
her that Mack's two business interests, women and drugs, converged
at the Mother Lode, a dingy strip club in an industrial area on the
edge of town. Julia had her own share of clients who'd run afoul of
the law there, although she sometimes wondered if the club's reliable
appearance in affidavits owed more to the fact that the cops preferred
arresting people there over a less entertaining locale.

Her best chance at finding Mack there was late at night, when
things would be in full swing. But even when Beverly was still babysitting on a regular basis, dropping Calvin off at nine at night would
have raised her meticulously plucked and penciled eyebrows. Julia
would have to slip in during the scant hour between leaving work
and picking up Calvin at after-school care.

She crossed her fingers, hoping for a Friday evening after-work
crowd, and headed for the Mother Lode.

The club owed its name and existence to Duck Creek's silver mining history. It stayed true to its roots, resisting any urge to
remake itself as a "gentleman's club" even as Duck Creek papered

over its gritty, blue-collar history in its headlong transition into a
ski resort whose service industry jobs paid a fraction of the miners'
union wages. Most of the Mother Lode's green paint had flaked off
the cinder-block facade, and something was wrong with the neon in
the two blinking babes in bikinis who bumped and ground against
its sign. They buzzed and fizzed, their bright-red outlines intermittently going dark.

Julia wrenched her attention away from the sad sign and forced
it to the task at hand, pushing through the door and into a world of
eardrum-busting darkness. Sir Mix-A-Lot? Really?

A half-dozen men sat widely spaced along a bar, eyes trained on
a small stage where a weak spotlight highlighted a woman shaking
a butt that likely wouldn't have occasioned a second glance from
Mix-A-Lot. Then the woman grasped the pole and somehow flipped
upside down and spun in an undulating maneuver that left Julia feeling both impressed and slightly seasick.

"Hey. No looking for free."

Julia hadn't noticed the woman behind the bar. Now she wondered
how she'd missed her. Like the woman onstage, she wore a G-string so
minuscule that Julia winced at the thought of all that waxing.

Julia shouted above the music. "I'm looking for Mack."

The men at the bar glanced back toward her, ascertaining that
she was dressed and that she wasn't anyone's wife, and ignored her.
The dancer flubbed a move and tumbled to the stage.

The men guffawed. She scrambled to her feet, found her balance
on her clear plastic platform heels, and shot Julia a look that sent
Julia fumbling in her purse for a five-dollar bill.

She handed it to the bartender. "For her," she nodded toward the
stage.

The bartender took it and waited. Julia found another five,
thought twice, and switched it out for a twenty. "And for you."

The woman jutted her chin toward a room in the back. Julia
thought again of the deserted playground. Of Calvin in the tub,
twisting his face to mime Mack's scarred lips. That was all it took.

She strode across the sticky floor and banged into the room.
Mack sat at a metal desk, giving her a rare height advantage. Better

yet, his chair was wheeled, which made it easy for her to slam it against the wall when she grabbed him by the collar.

Shock flashed across his features before they assumed their characteristic sneer. "You're about to be very sorry," he began, half rising from the chair.

Julia shoved him back down.

"Not half as sorry as you'll be if you go near my child again."

He gave her that grin, flicking his scar with his tongue. "He *ran* to me."

Julia had always looked askance at so-called crimes of passion. Really, how hard could it be to drop the gun, loosen the fingers around the throat, lower the arm holding the knife?

Impossible, she now knew as she grasped the chair's arms and smashed it again into the wall, harder this time.

"Knock that nasty shit off. Show me that tongue again and I'll rip it from your throat."

Where had that come from? Julia was one step away from the misdemeanor assault line, if she hadn't already crossed it.

Phrases floated through her mind. *Malicious intimidation. Harassment. Terroristic threats.* Sanity belatedly reappeared.

Julia spun on her heel and got the hell out of the Mother Lode.

* * *

If Mack was her stalker, surely he'd strike again after her shenanigans at the Mother Lode.

She spent a restless weekend with an unnervingly silent phone in hand, clicking the app for her security cameras, which showed only a ragged-eared tomcat wisely backing off from a brief confrontation with a skunk.

Monday morning meant putting in motion her part of Marie's plan. It involved a return trip to the medical examiner.

Maybe she was imagining things, but Pinkham had always seemed uneasy about the investigations into Duck Creek's recent deaths.

Julia found Pinkham at her desk instead of wrist deep in a cadaver, which was where she'd rather be, she informed Julia.

"Paperwork," she said, glaring at her computer screen before swiveling to face Julia. "It's the bane of my existence. You understand I deal in science, right? Facts. And yet the minute I finish a report, you guys—not one of you a scientist—start trying to pick it apart."

"With precious little success," Julia reminded her. "Which is why I'm here today."

Thus mollified, Pinkham relaxed, her inky brows unknotting, lips curving into a slight, sanguine smile. "And why is that? Coffee? I just made fresh."

"Sure."

Pinkham poured from a coffeemaker within easy reach and handed the mug to Julia. *If it's breathing, we're leaving,* it read.

Julia took a careful sip, half expecting the tang of blood. Pinkham liked her coffee strong. She took a bigger sip.

"I'm just checking on the most recent death. Craig Thompson."

Pinkham quirked an eyebrow.

"Thought you were off the case."

Julia choked on her coffee. "News travels fast," she said when she'd recovered.

"So . . ."

"Call me curious."

"Right." Having established her skepticism, Pinkham delivered the basics. "Head injury, but that's not what killed him."

Julia sat up. Finally, something different.

"Are you going to tell me?"

"Given the alcohol in his system, it's possible he'd have died of exposure before he recovered consciousness from the blow to his head. But there was water in his lungs. He was alive when he fell into the creek. Or when someone put him in it."

Julia very much hoped Craig Thompson had stayed unconscious, that his last few moments hadn't involved an awareness of a battle he couldn't win. She turned to rote questions to steady herself.

"Any drugs in his system?"

"The usual suspects. Weed, meth."

She thought yet again of the bruise on Ray's arm.

"Nothing IV?" she persisted. "Can you inject meth?"

"You can. But somebody who does that is usually pretty far gone. Craig Thompson may have used once in a while, but I doubt he was a hard-core addict to anything beyond his alcoholism. Despite what the billboards tell you"—their state's anti-meth campaign featured a series of billboards, each more lurid than the last—"it's possible to use without become immediately addicted. Assuming there's an arrest, it'll come up at trial, or at the sentencing hearing—that is, if the charges aren't dismissed. Just like in the case involving Mary Brannigan."

Julia nearly choked again. It would have been unprofessional for Pinkham to come right out and say she had doubts about Ray's guilt. But the fact that the medical examiner was entertaining her questions at all told her what she needed to know.

She finished her coffee, slid the mug back across the desk, and rose.

They smiled bleak understanding at one another. Julia left without saying good-bye.

* * *

She'd left it up to Marie to find a case she could take to the press.

She figured it would take a few days, given that most of her cases were of the low-level variety, discouraging in their banality.

But Marie waved a file as soon as she walked in the door.

"Walker Bennett," she announced.

Julia shook her head. "Doesn't ring a bell."

"There's no reason it would. He was Dave Pearson's case." She named a public defender who'd recently found a job in private practice. He'd had to move two states away, but the raise involved would allow him to buy his first home at the age of forty, he'd told his colleagues with the stunned look of one who'd just won the lottery.

"Bennett's got a hearing in a couple of weeks for nonpayment of fines. Listen to this. Dude's got nothing but municipal citations for things like loitering, along with a couple of drunk and disorderlies, the usual. But he's homeless, sort of—I think he's couch surfed all over town—and doesn't have an address and can't afford a phone. He uses the public computers at the libraries, but still, he misses the notices for his court appearances, and every time he doesn't show up, his fines double. He does odd jobs for under-the-table cash, but he's on the hook for a couple grand by now, and facing a jail sentence because of it, which means he won't be able to work to get the money to pay off the fines, let alone eat or save up on a deposit for a place to live—you get the picture."

Julia got it. She could have papered her office walls with similar pictures.

She held out her hand for the file and let out a sigh of relief when she saw Bennett's mug. He was youngish, early thirties, past the age when people tended to refer to men as thugs but not so old that he'd started losing teeth, accumulating scars, or acquiring the cauliflower ears and veined noses of drunken brawlers, the occupational hazards that signaled life on the margins.

He didn't sport the facial and neck tattoos that people found so off-putting, and he didn't have any violent crimes in his file. Best of all, he didn't have any DUIs. While their state had what in Julia's mind was a ridiculous tolerance for drinking and driving, people frowned on repeat offenders.

"Where is he now?"

"Where do you think? In jail, awaiting his hearing."

Julia clicked on her phone's calendar and started to log in a date to interview. She stopped and looked at Marie.

"Tell you what. Why don't you talk with him? Make sure he's the guy we want for this."

Spring was finally making itself felt in Duck Creek, the creek rising higher every day, trees budding, the sun intermittently shoving its way through the lingering dark clouds, and the temperature creeping upward to almost warm.

But Julia could have sworn that it took a ten-degree jump due solely to the wattage of Marie's smile.

44

CHANCE LARSEN'S STORY on Walker Bennett, splashed across the front page of Thursday's *Bulletin*, exceeded expectations.

Bennett, by his own admission, was no angel. "I lived to party," he told Chance. "And look where it got me."

Julia had laid the groundwork for Chance's story carefully. First, she'd gone to the legislature's website and looked at the criminal justice reform bills that Leslie Harper had sponsored, catching her breath anew at the one that would have ended onerous fees for people convicted of minor crimes.

In addition to the fines for the crimes, people found themselves saddled with fees for their public defenders—assigned to them because they'd already been deemed indigent by the court—as well as the vaguely worded "court costs" and further fees for jail admin-istration and probation supervision, all of them mounting with each failure to pay in full or even the monthly payment set up by the court. Sometimes that failure to pay landed people in jail, further adding to their overall bill.

She'd looked at Harper's cosponsors for the bill—it had, of course, failed—and contacted one, asking if he'd be willing to spon-sor a similar bill in the next legislative session.

With his assurance in hand, she'd called Chance and told him she had a story, one about carrying on Harper's work, with Walker Bennett as exhibit A for the need for such work.

"Christ," he'd said when she called. "Do you think I have a death wish? Claudette already tore me a new one over my first story on Harper."

She let the silence go to the edge of uncomfortable before responding. "And you did a big-ass story on Claudette's rant the other day and then followed up with stories about the dearly departed murder victims. I'd say you're even. Besides, you can't tell me this isn't an issue. Isn't criminal justice your beat?"

His laugh plumbed depths of bitterness.

"Criminal justice, city and county government, development, and every so often I've got to shoot over to the next county and write about the goings-on at the university. Oh, not to mention the occasional weekend editing shift. In case you haven't noticed, we're a little short-staffed here. Michael was smart to leave when he did." A pause as he belatedly remembered that Michael had left the newspaper to join the military, which led to him stepping on the IED in Iraq that killed him. "God. I'm sorry."

Now Julia had guilt on her side. She slathered her words with magnanimity. "It's okay. I know you didn't mean to cause me further pain. And Michael would have hated to see what's happened to the newspaper. I think it's half the size it was when he was there."

"Even less."

Julia tried to steer the conversation back on track, away from the seemingly never-ending series of layoffs plaguing the *Bulletin*. "This guy I told you about, Walker Bennett. He's about to go back to jail, not for any crime but just for failing to pay his fines. But how's he going to pay them off if he can't work because he's sitting in jail? Swear to God, Chance, I was nearly in tears just talking with him."

Which was crap. Julia couldn't remember the last time she'd cried. Lose a husband young—probably at any age—and you cry yourself out of years' worth of tears.

"Fine. Shoot me an email with the particulars. If I can get a spare moment, I'll take a look. But don't hold your breath. Yesterday my editor suggested I shove a broomstick up my ass so I could sweep the floor as I run back and forth, and I'm not entirely sure she was joking."

She knew then that she had him. And Chance had gone the extra mile, not just talking with her and the legislator and Walker but researching reform movements well under way in other states and combing jail records to see how many nonviolent offenders were being held in Peak County for similar reasons. The story included a chart showing the surprising total of money flowing into county coffers from such fees, nearly always assessed from the people least able to pay.

Oh, and he'd called Claudette to obtain the county prosecutor's take on the matter.

"Let's not forget," Claudette had said stiffly, "that these people are in the system due to their own actions. There's an easy way to stay out of these situations, and that's by obeying the law."

Chance had called Julia afterward. "If I were you, I'd go into a witness protection program when that story runs. I think she wants your head on a plate. Right after she gets done removing my manhood with a rusty penknife."

Julia held the newspaper up in triumph when Marie walked in. "Looks like we've bought ourselves some time."

Marie gave a little skip.

"Great! What do I do first?"

Someone tapped at the door.

Julia grinned. "You answer that and get rid of whoever it is as soon as possible while I pretend to be on the phone so they can't bother me." She grabbed the receiver, held it to her ear, and started nodding and *uh-huh*-ing as though in actual conversation.

Marie crossed to the door, tossing an answering grin over her shoulder. "Time me. My money's on less than a minute."

But when she opened the door, Angie Barrett stumbled in, grabbing at Marie for support and sobbing a plea to Julia.

"You've got to help him. Enter that plea and get him sentenced right away. Do it now. Tomorrow. Just do whatever it takes to get him out of that jail and into prison."

45

Aᴺɢɪᴇ ʟᴇᴛ ɢᴏ of Marie and fell across Julia's desk, scattering papers, pens, and a half-full mug of coffee.

Julia leapt back, but Angie scrambled after her, succeeding only in falling from the desk into the narrow space between it and the bookcase behind it. She curled into a fetal position and mumbled between gasps, "You gotta. You gotta," as coffee slid in slow drips from the desk onto her body.

Marie unfroze first, throwing Kleenex onto the puddle. Julia stooped beside Angie and lay a cautious hand on her heaving shoulder.

"We gotta what, Angie? What's going on?"

Angie's eyes rolled back in her head.

"Christ. I think she's having some sort of a seizure. Can you call 911? Or better yet, just run downstairs and grab someone from the sheriff's office. Wayne's an EMT."

"Nooooo. Not that bastard. Not anyone." The words escaped in a low groan, barely coherent. Angie struggled to sit up but fell back.

Julia slid an arm under her shoulders and gently raised her up again.

"Angie, you're not fine."

"I think she's really, really drunk," Marie whispered. But Angie heard.

"Not drunk. Not a drop since . . ." She waved a hand. She could have meant yesterday or five minutes ago. Her head lolled.

Julia bent closer still and inhaled the mingled scent of extreme poverty—dirt, sweat, clothing worn too many days in a row. But not booze.

"I don't smell it on her."

"High, then?"

"Could be."

Angie nestled her head against Julia's shoulder, curling into her like a small child. Julia stroked her hair. "Pinkham told me she found traces of meth in the other three but nothing indicating they were hard-core users."

"I still think we should call someone."

"No shit."

Angie stiffened in her arms.

"No!"

Marie's hand jerked away from the phone. "What should we do? She needs help. And she's scared to death of something."

"Or someone."

Angie nodded, her eyes closed again.

"Who, Angie?"

Angie wrapped Julia in a grip so hard she struggled for breath. "Uh-uh. They'll kill you too."

Marie and Julia stared at one another.

"Does she even know what she's talking about?" Marie whispered.

"Damned if I know. But we've got to get her out of here. Angie, I want to take you to the emergency room."

Angie moaned a long and emphatic no.

Julia tugged at her. "Can you stand? Let me help you."

Marie came around to Angie's other side, and together they pulled her to her unsteady feet.

"Now what?"

Julia blew a breath. "I think I'll take her to my house. Make her some coffee, maybe even get some food into her. Help her sober up to the point where she can tell me what's going on."

She took a tentative step forward. Angie's feet dragged on the floor.

"How are you going to get her all the way to your car?"

Julia's shoulder was already beginning to ache from Angie's weight.

"Let's get her into my chair, at least."

Angie flopped into it like a rag doll.

"You stay with her. I'll get my car and bring it around." Calvin had been in a mood that morning, and she'd been so late leaving the house that she'd driven the few blocks to work.

Marie posed the question Julia had been avoiding.

"How do we get her past Deb?"

Julia felt nearly as deflated as Angie. Deb had probably already broadcast to the world that a drunk homeless woman had stumbled down the hall to her office. For all she knew, Deb had alerted the sheriff's department to be on standby in case there was trouble. She went to the door and peered down the hall. "She's not at her desk now."

Marie's voice squeaked with excitement. "That's right! I just remembered! She's got some sort of training today, something to do with a new computer program. She'll be out of the office all day."

Julia very nearly crossed herself, a reflexive throwback to faith long abandoned. "Maybe there's a merciful God after all. The freight elevator is in the hall just outside Deb's desk. It ends up at a side door by the trash cans. Nobody goes back there, not even to smoke. I'll text you when I get to the car, and then you take her downstairs. I should be pulling up by the time you get down."

Marie nodded, eyes bright. Somewhere along the line, Julia realized, they'd crossed the line into true partnership, even if they didn't have much to show for it yet.

She stopped in the doorway.

"And Marie? Thanks."

46

ANGIE SEEMED A little more awake when they got to Julia's house, able to sit at the kitchen table, albeit occasionally swaying so severely Julia feared she'd end up on the floor.

Julia hurried to make coffee, despite the truism that pouring coffee into a drunk only resulted in a wide-awake drunk. She popped a couple of pieces of bread into the toaster.

"Smells good," Angie mumbled.

Julia, wary of spills, only half filled Angie's coffee mug. She thought a moment and added a glug of whiskey, resisting the temptation to do the same for her own. She slathered the toast with butter and added cinnamon and sugar. What Angie really needed was protein—a proper eggs-and-bacon meal with fresh-squeezed orange juice, or maybe even steak and eggs—but she feared it might all come back up on her kitchen table. Save that for later, she thought.

She watched carefully for signs of sick as Angie nibbled at her toast. So far, so good. Jake had dogged her steps as soon as they'd come in the door but now sat quivering at Angie's feet, training his most winsome look upon her.

"Cute dog." Angie held out a bit of toast, and he took it politely before backing away a few steps and wolfing it down.

"He's your friend for life now."

Angie nodded, her eyelids at half-staff. She needed sleep. A bath. Clean clothes. All of which Julia was happy to supply, but first she had to know what was going on.

"Angie, why are you so eager to see Ray sent off to prison?"

Angie's eyes snapped open, fear flaring anew.

"You've got to get him out of that county jail. You've got to." She reached across the table, clutching at Julia's hand, for the second time in a single hour upending a cup of coffee despite Julia's precautions. Julia grabbed a kitchen towel and mopped the table and herself.

"Why?"

"Because he was in cahoots with that woman. The one who died."

"Miss Mae?" Julia wondered if she should have held off on the whiskey. Miss Mae had a good fifteen years on Ray. Maybe more. "I thought Ray was with you."

"No." Angie slumped again in her chair. She was fading again. Julia resisted the urge to shake her. "Not Miss Mae. The big one. The lawyer lady."

"Lawyer lady?"

"Not lawyer. Something else. Something important."

"The legislator? Leslie Harper? And Ray?"

Now Julia wondered just how drunk or high Angie really was. Nothing the woman was saying made sense. She'd be better off waiting for her to sober up.

"Angie, how would you like a nice hot shower? And some clean clothes? Then a long nap."

Even as she spoke, she wondered what she could possibly offer Angie. Her own clothes were barely above child size.

Angie nodded dazed acquiescence to a shower. Julia hadn't dared offer a bath, fearful Angie would drown in the capacious tub. It would make more sense to let Angie sleep first and then shower, but in the confined space of the house, Angie's lack of recent acquaintance with soap and water was becoming more noticeable by the moment.

When Angie saw the tub, though, her eyes widened in near alertness. "Oh my. Would you look at that?"

She gazed at it with such longing that Julia, who'd cringed at the reality of having to help Angie undress, realized that a shower wouldn't do and furthermore that she was going to have to stay with Angie for the whole process. She twisted the faucets on the tub and set about helping Angie remove layer after layer of clothing, more than necessary now that temperatures had finally begun to lift. She turned her back while Angie used the toilet, then retrieved her recently purchased jar of bath salts and added them to the water.

She helped Angie into the tub, averting her eyes from Angie's ribby frame. Angie sank in up to her chin, murmuring, "Oh, oh, oh. Only time I ever get to take a bath is in the creek, and no matter how hot it gets in the summer, that water is never warm."

Julia tried to imagine it, how Angie would have had to wait until full dark, when the townspeople finally abandoned the creek, then strip naked and vulnerable, knowing all too well the unsavory types who haunted the creek at night. Would Angie keep her knife in hand even as she bathed? Would she creep step by step into the frigid rushing creek or plunge in at once to get the worst of it over with? And would such a necessarily quick and furtive process ever really leave you feeling fully clean?

"Sit up a little, if you can," Julia said. She squirted liquid soap onto a washcloth and began to scrub the back of Angie's neck and around her ears, just as she did for Calvin. But even the surprising amount of dirt accumulated by a small boy in the course of a single day washed away easily compared to the weeks—months?—of ground-in grime layering Angie's skin.

"Lift your arms." Angie, somnolent, responded in slow motion, water sheeting from them.

Julia soaped the tangle of hair there, thinking how shaving, something she considered a necessary annoyance, would be an impossibility for someone like Angie, probably along with brushing, flossing—two things Angie no longer had to worry about—shampooing, moisturizing, deodorizing, the daily grooming routine she took for granted. She had some disposable razors somewhere. She'd offer them to Angie later.

"Can you lift a foot?"

It was a horror, the skin tough and cracked, the nails blackened and misshapen. Julia ran the cloth between each toe, thinking that Angie's feet were roughly the size of her mother-in-law's. She wondered if Beverly, whose footwear tended toward ladylike pumps and serviceable winter boots, had a single pair of sturdy shoes that might be practical for the kind of life Angie lived. She intended to find out.

"Here." She finished with Angie's feet, discarded the begrimed washcloth, found a fresh one, and prodded Angie awake. She wet the cloth, soaped it, and handed it to her. "So you can clean down there." She turned away until the splashing stopped.

"Thanks." Angie's voice was thick with mingled sleep and embarrassment.

"One more thing." She squirted shampoo into her palms and then rubbed it through Angie's hair, working hard at her scalp, trying not to think of things like lice. Surely it was too cold?

She fetched the cup from the sink and turned on the water again, pouring cupfuls over Angie's head until the water ran free of suds. She pulled the plug on the tub, grasped Angie under each arm, and helped her from it, wrapping her in a towel and seating her on the toilet.

"Almost done. You can sleep in just a few more minutes. But if we don't get this hair untangled now, you'll wake up with a rat's nest that we'll have to cut out." She kept her voice soft and low and constant, an effort to soothe herself as much as Angie. Because what was she going to do with this woman in her house? Angie couldn't stay. She worked a wide-toothed comb through the snarls, apologizing when she tugged especially hard.

Maybe she could call a shelter. Definitely not the police; Angie had been vehement on that point, and especially about Wayne. *Not that bastard.* Julia made a mental note to ask Angie about that when she was awake.

"Can you sit here for one more minute?"

She feared Angie would topple from the toilet. But Angie, eyes closed, slurred, "I'm warm. I'm clean. I'm dry. I can sit here all night if I have to."

Julia ran to her bedroom and ducked into the closet, rooting around in the back for the boxes of Michael's clothes she'd been unable to bear to give away, feeling past the layers of folded sweaters and flannel shirts for—"There!" She retrieved an old sweatsuit, soft with use and age.

Angie would swim in it, but it would be better than anything of Julia's, which would barely cover her and be too tight besides.

She led Angie to her bed and drew the blankets close around her chin, resisting the impulse to kiss her cheek as she did Calvin's at night. Jake appeared and leapt onto the bed, curling himself against Angie's shoulder, somehow sensing vulnerability and appointing himself as protector.

Just as Julia started to tiptoe away, Angie's eyes flew open and she sat up, looking wildly about the room. Jake crouched stiff beside her, hackles raised.

"Where am I? What happened?"

Julie hurried back and knelt beside the bed. "It's me. Julia. You're in my house. You're safe here."

Angie sank back onto the pillow, whimpering. Julia decided to press her advantage.

"Angie, what are you so afraid of? Why is it so important that I get Ray out of the jail and into prison?"

Angie rolled over and clutched the pillow, curling herself around it like a child with a teddy bear and muffling her voice. Julia strained to hear.

"Because they think he's going to tell."

47

Julia shook her hard, practically screamed in her face—"Tell what, Angie? Tell what?"—but she couldn't get any more out of Angie, who fell into a sleep so profound that Julia pulled a chair beside the bed lest sleep change into something more ominous.

But Angie's chest rose and fell with long, deep breaths, although her eyes twitched wildly beneath her lids and the occasional moan escaped her open lips.

Julia punched a number on her phone and spoke in a near-whisper.

"Beverly? I'm sorry to bother you with so little notice, but could you possibly pick Calvin up at school and take him tonight? I've got a . . . a . . . situation. Sort of an emergency. No, I'm fine. It's just . . . something came up that I have to deal with. Really? Are you sure? Thank you so much. It should just be for the one night. I'll let you know when things settle down. Yes, Beverly. Yes, I'm safe."

She hurried on before Beverly could detect the doubt in those last words. "One more thing. Do you have a pair of old shoes that you don't wear much anymore? Something sturdy? You do? Could you please drop them off here? Just leave them next to the front door. Yes, I know they're too big for me. What's going on? I'll explain later."

Though no matter how long she waited, she couldn't imagine an explanation that would make any more sense to Beverly than it did to herself.

Then she called the office, thankful that she had no court appearances today and even more thankful when she got Deb's voice mail, where she left her lie that Calvin was sick and so she'd be working from home for the rest of the day. It would be another black mark against her, compounding her error of having a child at all. Julia kept waiting for attitudes toward working mothers to change, but so far, the new millennium had brought only profound disappointment in that regard.

To transform her lies into a half-truth, she called Marie and asked her to drop off some files so she could at least work on cases at home.

"Don't ring the bell or anything—the more sleep she gets, the better. I've got a set of spare house keys in my top left drawer. Just open the door and leave them inside. If we're lucky, the dog won't hear you. Please be sure and lock the door when you leave. You're sure it's all right? Thanks. I really appreciate it."

But the files sat untouched at her elbow as she doodled on a legal pad, wondering about the secret that Ray was guarding with his life.

*   *   *

Angie slumbered on and on, so long that Julia finally felt safe in leaving her side.

She stuffed Angie's clothing into the washer, added extra detergent, and set the washer on an extra-long cycle with extra-hot water. True to her word, Beverly had found a pair of brogues that must have dated to her time on the dairy farm, which she'd fled in favor of Duck Creek the moment she was widowed. She'd also tucked in two pairs of wool socks, thick and new, in silent acknowledgment of the unspoken need behind Julia's request.

Julia busied herself in the kitchen, readying a meal in anticipation of Angie's eventual waking. Bread, to soak up whatever alcohol was still sloshing around in Angie's system. Pasta for the same reason. She found a container of Dom's Sunday sauce in the back of the freezer and nuked it in the microwave. Thick and meaty, it would provide the necessary kick of protein to reactivate Angie's senses. At least, she hoped it would.

Just in case, she kept the whiskey handy. If Angie had the shakes, it would help. Finally, she brewed another large pot of coffee, as much for herself as for Angie.

Who, when she looked up, was standing in the doorway, the hems of Michael's too-long sweats bagging around her bare feet.

Angie blinked, dug her knuckles into her eyes, and blinked again.

"Where the fuck am I? And what the fuck are you doing here?"

* * *

The whiskey was a good idea.

Angie's hands stilled after a couple of shots.

"Thanks," she whispered, wrapping them around a fresh mug of coffee. Julia hoped it wouldn't meet the others' fate.

"Don't know that I've ever had a hangover this bad, and that's saying something. Weird, 'cause I only had a couple of beers yesterday. Smoked a little weed, though. Maybe shit was bad."

"Mm." Julia issued a noncommittal response that she hoped Angie would interpret as agreement. Over her years in the Public Defender's Division, she'd learned that a "couple of beers"—an amount readily volunteered by any number of drunk drivers—usually amounted to several more.

She pushed a plate of spaghetti and sauce across the table, meatballs and ribs piled prominently atop it. Angie took a wary forkful. Her eyes widened.

"You cook this?"

"Mm." No need to credit the sauce to Dom. It would only confuse things.

"Damn! Next time you come down to the creek, why don't you bring us food instead of whiskey? Because this right here"—she shoveled in another mouthful and spoke around it—"this is the real deal."

Her Adam's apple jerked as she swallowed. The look she cast Julia was tinged with embarrassment. "You got a knife? Because the meat . . . my teeth . . . I can't."

"Of course."

Julia waited as Angie clumsily separated the beef from the ribs. Her foot jiggled with impatience. She needed Angie to talk about something other than the damn food. But she also needed her to be relaxed.

She poured a glass of wine, fetched a plate, dished up some pasta and sauce for herself, and sat down across from Angie. Just two friends having dinner together, talking about the weather and whatever else might come up—quickly, she hoped.

But for safety's sake, she started with the weather. "Looks like it's finally going to be spring. The Weather Service said we could hit fifties, even sixties by the end of the week. Sunshine too. My daffodils are already starting to come up." *Her* daffodils. That was a stretch. She supposed Leslie Harper had planted them, along with all the other mysterious things beginning to make their appearance in the yard.

"The trees are even leafing out." She nodded toward the window with its view of the fast-darkening yard, wondering how long she could keep up this inane chatter.

"Spring." Angie offered a final bit of meatball to an ardently grateful Jake, then polished her plate with a piece of bread and held it up for seconds. "Guess I got through another winter. Not like Billy or Miss Mae or Craig."

Julia's hand jerked as she ladled sauce onto Angie's plate, christening the counter with a splash of red. She handed Angie the plate and sponged up the mess, biting her lip to enforce a silence she hoped Angie would fill.

But Angie turned her attention back to her plate, so determinedly that Julia couldn't help herself.

"Billy and Miss Mae and Craig gone and Ray in jail," she nudged.

Angie dropped her fork. Now Julia had her full attention.

"But you're going to get him out, right? Send him off to prison where he'll be safe."

"That's an odd way to look at prison," Julia began.

But the terror that had sent Angie staggering into Julia's office that morning was back. "You don't know. You don't know," she gasped. She twisted her shaking hands together, holding them up prayerfully. "Please. How fast can you do it?"

Julia gently pulled Angie's hands apart. "You said they thought Ray was going to tell. Who thought it? And what was he going to tell?"

Angie's entire body quaked. She shook her head so vehemently that her newly washed hair lashed her face. "I can't. I can't. I can't."

"If you want me to be able to help him, I have to know. This goes no further, Angie. Promise." She dropped Angie's hands, pinched thumb and forefinger together and zipped them across her closed lips, a child's symbol of secrecy, feeling silly as she did so. Would Angie take it as an insult?

Angie drew a deep breath, then another.

"You swear?"

"I swear."

Another breath, her shoulders heaving with the effort of finally divulging her secret.

"Well," she began.

The doorbell rang.

48

Every curse she'd ever heard in her life rattled around in Julia's head. She considered not answering it, even as it rang again and again.

Angie wrapped her arms around herself and rocked in her seat.

"Don't worry. I'll get rid of whoever it is."

Julia ran for the door, followed by Jake, reminding herself not to let the curses escape. She peered through the peephole, blinked in surprise, and twisted the deadbolt open.

"Wayne? What's up?"

He stepped through the door without waiting for an invitation. "Hey, buddy." He stooped to pet Jake, who went into paroxysms of glee, finally falling onto his back and presenting his belly for a final rub.

"You weren't at work today. Just wanted to make sure everything was okay, especially with all the crazy stuff you've been dealing with."

"I'm fine. Calvin wasn't feeling well." She spoke in a low voice, casting a worried glance toward the stairwell, hoping to convey a sick child in a room above them.

"I'm sorry. Is he going to be okay?"

"He'll be fine. Just one of those twenty-four-hour bugs, probably. Thanks for checking on me, Wayne. I appreciate it."

Julia waited for him to take the hint. He didn't.

"Sure smells good in here? What's cooking?" He headed for the kitchen.

"Wayne, wait!"

But it was too late.

"Hey, Angie. Fancy meeting you here."

*   *   *

Angie jumped up so fast the chair fell to the floor. Jake yapped in surprise.

Wayne cocked his head. "You're looking good, Angie. What's different about you?"

Julia looked from one to the other, Wayne standing relaxed, hands in his pockets, feet apart, rocking a little on his heels; Angie backed against the kitchen counter, eyes wide, teeth audibly chattering.

"It's all right, Angie. Wayne just came by to check on me because I called in sick. Someone's been harassing me and he's been keeping an eye on my place."

Angie's mouth worked. Her voice emerged hoarse. "Yeah. I'll bet he has."

Wayne walked to the stove. Angie cringed as he brushed past her.

He lifted the lid from the pot and inhaled. "So this is what smells so good. I'm starving. You don't mind, do you?"

Without waiting for an answer, he started opening cupboard doors until he found a plate, then repeated the process with the drawers until he had a fork and tablespoon in hand.

Angie retreated to a corner of the room. She pressed her back to the wall, slid to the floor, and wrapped her hands around her knees.

A colander in the sink still held some spaghetti. Wayne dumped it onto his plate, then spooned sauce atop it. He dropped the spoon on the counter, leaving it in a puddle of sauce, and brought his plate to the table.

"Oh, hey. And you've already opened some wine. That'll come in handy." His glance fell on the whiskey bottle on the counter. "That too. Even better."

He sat at the table and proceeded to fork up the pasta, ignoring the wine he'd praised seconds earlier.

Julia reverted to the automatic pilot of good manners. "Let me get you a glass for the wine."

He waved a hand. "No need."

She stopped trying to make sense of the performance playing out before her. She swallowed hard. "Then what do you mean, the wine will come in handy?"

Wayne tore a hunk of bread from the baguette, dipped it into the sauce, and stuffed it into his mouth, chewing exaggeratedly. He swallowed, leaned back, patted his belly, and belched. Then he snapped his fingers.

Julia jumped.

"That's it. Angie, I've been trying to figure out what's so different about you, and it just came to me."

"No, no, no," Angie murmured. Her head fell to her knees.

"Yes, yes, yes. It's that you're clean. You don't reek. That's why I was able to enjoy this good food. Otherwise, you'd be stinking up this whole damn room."

Which was when Julia knew Wayne was not there to help her.

*   *   *

She felt the pressure of her phone, safely in her pocket, against her hip. But even if she could somehow use it without Wayne seeing, who would she call? 911?

Whatever was going on, if a cop were to arrive at her door, what would she say? *Your buddy Wayne was rude to my guest?*

Her mind was already running through the sort of standard questions she usually posed to someone on a witness stand.

"Did he physically hurt you?"

"No."

"Touch you?"

"No."

"Threaten you in any way?"

"No."

"Then what is your complaint, exactly?"

"I'm afraid."

"Of what?"

"I don't know. But it's bad."

She'd always thought that business of the hair standing up on the back of your neck was no more than a handy trope. Now she fought an urge to rub her hand across it, to smooth the hair back into a semblance of order in hopes that these last few cockeyed moments would also revert to normalcy.

Wayne pushed his plate away with such force that it scooted across the table and sailed off the edge, bouncing once against the tile floor before breaking neatly into three pie-shaped pieces.

"Well, would you look at that?" Wayne guffawed.

Jake, ever alert to falling food, ran to it. Julia finally unfroze, reaching the dog a second before his tongue could swipe the razor-sharp edges.

She straightened, clutching the dog to her chest. He squirmed briefly then quieted, sensing the tension in the room and rolling his eyes toward hers, his brow creased in worry and confusion. She hugged him tighter and tried to keep her voice low and calm so as not to frighten him further.

"Wayne, what the fuck is going on?"

He belched again and looked toward Angie.

"Wanna tell her? Or should I?"

Like an answer to a prayer, the doorbell rang again.

49

JULIA HAD NEVER been so glad to see her mother-in-law in her life. Nor—once she glimpsed Calvin standing behind Beverly and Gregory—so terrified.

"Julia, we're so sorry to bother you. Calvin has everything he needs at my—" She stopped. The smile she turned on Gregory dripped rainbows and songbirds. "At *our* house except for Bear-Bear. We were out running errands, so we stopped by to get him."

"Jake!" Calvin crowed. The dog leapt from Julia's arms to the floor, where he fell into an immediate wrestling match with Calvin.

"Listen, Beverly." Julia pulled her close. The hair on her neck stood at attention again.

"Who do we have here?" Wayne stepped past her and extended his hand, first to Gregory and then to Beverly. "Deputy Sheriff Wayne Peterson. I just stopped by to check on Julia. She might not have told you, but she's been having problems with some harassment lately."

"How very kind of you. I'm Julia's mother-in-law, Beverly Sullivan, and this is Gregory Abbott, my, my . . ."

"Her betrothed," Gregory finished with his characteristic twinkle.

"Congratulations!" Wayne pumped Gregory's hand again. "You're a lucky man."

Beverly flushed and tried to recover her equilibrium. "You might know him. He owns the bookstore downtown."

"Of course." Gregory nodded recognition. "Standing order for the weekend *Wall Street Journal*, right?"

Julia turned to Wayne in surprise. "I'd have taken you for the *Guns & Ammo* type." Then wanted to kick herself. The last thing she needed, under whatever circumstances these were, was to antagonize Wayne.

But he took it in stride. "Helps me talk with the movers and shakers," he said easily.

Julia reminded herself that Wayne had his eye on the top job in the sheriff's office. The election was still some months away, but she was already tired of these campaign machinations. When would people go back to being themselves?

Although—this time the prickling sensation ran all the way down her spine—she'd thought of Wayne as one of the good guys. Now she just wanted him out of her house.

"Wayne was just leaving," she said. She motioned Beverly and Gregory inside. Anything to get them out of the doorway, impeding Wayne's departure.

But he stepped back, farther into the house. "Come on into the kitchen. You won't believe what Julia has made."

"Yes, come in."

As much as Julia wanted Wayne out of the house, if he was going to stay—which appeared to be his intent—she wanted as many people with her as possible. Whatever Wayne was up to, Beverly's and Gregory's genteel presence would certainly put a stop to it.

But Beverly shook her head. "No, we still have several stops to make. Nice to meet you, Deputy Peterson."

"Gamma, can I stay and play with Jake? You can pick up me and Bear-Bear on your way home."

"No!" Julia's refusal emerged in a near-shriek.

Beverly glanced at her, but Gregory was already staring indulgently down at boy and dog. "That sounds like a fine idea. Julia, it won't be any trouble, will it? We won't be long, an hour or two at most."

"No trouble at all." Wayne stepped into the fray. "In fact, I can stay here with Julia until you get back."

That earned another curious glance from Beverly, sharper than the first. She knew about Julia's months-long relationship with Dom. Now here was another man, acting perfectly at home in Julia's new house.

Julia threw her a pleading look, but Wayne was already shepherding Beverly and Gregory toward the door, showering them with inanities on the way. "You two crazy kids have a good time. Don't do anything I wouldn't do."

The door closed. Wayne turned to Julia, an unseemly gleam in his eye.

"Now," he said. "Where were we?"

* * *

Jake ran back toward the kitchen, Calvin in pursuit. He stopped in the doorway, staring a question at the open back door.

Wayne shoved past him. "Goddammit."

Halfway across the yard, Angie stumbled in her too-long sweatpants and fell.

"Wayne, no!" Julia ran after him, grabbing at his heavy-duty belt, trying to pull him away. "Angie, run!"

Wayne reached back, gripped her arm, and flung her aside. He kicked Angie's feet from beneath her as she tried to scramble away on all fours. He wound a hand in her shiny clean hair and hauled her to her feet. "Bitch. What were you thinking?"

Julia recovered her balance and looked back toward the house, where Calvin stood in the doorway, his mouth an O of surprise, face scrunched with fast-growing fear.

"Hey, Calvin," she called. "It's okay. The lady fell and Deputy Peterson was just helping her up. Isn't that right, Angie?"

She locked eyes with Angie, willing her to understand that from this moment forward, everything was secondary to Calvin's safety.

Angie ran a hand across her face as though trying to wipe away her own terrified expression, an effort betrayed by her shaking hand, her trembling lips. But her voice, when it emerged, quavered only a little and her words added further cover.

"I scared myself when I fell down."

"Is that what happened to your teeth?" Calvin asked with the frankness of the young. "Did you fall down?"

Angie stretched her lips in a vague resemblance to a smile. "Something like that."

Wayne twisted her arm behind her back, where Calvin couldn't see, and marched her toward the house. "Probably because she ran her big fucking mouth," he muttered.

Julia's blood iced her veins.

Whatever was happening was worse than she'd thought, and now her son was in the middle of it.

She waited until they were all back in the kitchen and said to Calvin, "Why don't you and Jake go wrestle in your playroom in the basement while the grown-ups talk?"

She held her breath. Wayne nodded assent. "Good idea."

Julia's shoulders sagged. Whatever was going to happen next, at least her son wouldn't see it.

* * *

Wayne forced Angie into a kitchen chair and sat next to her, clamping her arm so tightly she cried out in pain.

"Shut up," he said. "Unless you want that kid to come back up here and see what's happening?"

"What *is* happening, Wayne?"

Ignorance was anything but bliss. Julia figured she might as well find out what was going on.

"I didn't tell her nothing, Wayne," Angie said. "She doesn't know."

"But you know. And that asshole boyfriend of yours knows. And he was going to tell her, wasn't he?"

"He wasn't. He wasn't." Tears streaked Angie's cheeks.

Wayne put his face close to hers. "He was. I heard him trying to meet up with her."

Angie gasped for air. "He was upset about Billy. About what you all did to him."

Julia knew that the less she understood, the safer she was. But she couldn't help herself. "Meet up with who? What did you do to Billy?"

"Doesn't matter. He was just a big dumb drunk. He was going to buy it one way or the other."

Angie's head snapped up. Her eyes blazed. "He was our friend. What you did to him, it was wrong."

Julia's head whipped back and forth as she tried to follow the conversation.

"Are you saying that . . ." No. It was impossible. But she couldn't think of any other explanation. "That Wayne killed Billy?"

Wayne laughed, jarring. "Big dumb fuck practically drank himself to death. Just like you're going to."

*   *   *

"Wayne, what the hell are you talking about?"

The conversation had veered from improbable to surreal, something Julia found oddly steadying.

"Yeah." Angie chimed in. "I tried to drink myself to death all those years ago and it didn't work. Besides, what's my drinking got to do with Billy's fighting?"

"Billy's fighting? You mean with Ray the night he was killed?"

Now it was Angie's turn to laugh, though hers held no more mirth than Wayne's.

"Tell her, Wayne. You're so worried about me telling her." She straightened and spoke in mincing, formal tones. "Why don't you be the one who, ah, enlightens our hostess?"

Wayne cast her a warning look. "Shut the fuck up, Angie."

"Why? You just said we're goners anyway."

He had?

Julia's mind shied away from the prospect. Her son was playing in the basement. Beverly would be back soon. Surely Angie was overreacting.

But Wayne nodded agreement.

"Another homeless person gets clobbered while blind drunk. Claudette Greene can jump up and down and hold all the press conferences she wants, but nobody in this town gives a shit when one of you dies. One less cockroach is how most people see it."

"Wayne!" Julia's head reeled. Had he always been this person?

Angie's words came out in a rush. "They make them fight. In jail. They bet on it. A fight club sort of thing. Big money. Real money. Billy was so big, he usually won. But he got sick of being everybody's punching bag. He was going to tell. Well, Ray was. He was afraid Billy was going to end up dead one of these days. So one of you guys"—she turned a poisonous look upon Wayne—"saw to it that Billy ended up dead anyway and put it on Ray. You figured that would shut him up and it did. But you didn't count on Miss Mae. That woman wasn't afraid of anything."

Julia waited for Wayne to deny it. He merely shrugged.

"Guess she should've been, huh?"

"Wayne, what are you two talking about?" Angie couldn't possibly be saying what Julia thought she was saying. And Wayne wasn't denying it. Which meant that he was . . .

And he was in her house . . .

And her little boy was downstairs . . .

She didn't want to know.

She couldn't afford not to.

"Wayne. Are you saying you know who killed them?" Too vague, too vague. She gulped oxygen and tried again. "That you did?"

He turned to her with an easy smile. "Aw, hell, Julia. You know me better than that."

A wild hope soared within Julia. Crazy talk, all of it. Drunken ravings from Angie. As to Wayne's treatment of Angie, she knew that the daily grind of policing, seeing humanity at its most inhumane, ground even the good ones down. She'd never think of Wayne the same way again, would certainly never trust him, would slot him into the "just another asshole cop" category. She'd always thought Duck Creek's two law enforcement agencies remarkably free of assholes. One more thing she'd been wrong about. Her cartwheeling thoughts tripped over something Angie had said.

"A fight club?"

He rolled his eyes.

"Angie here really needs to lay off the sauce. People fight in jail all the time. It's one of the biggest problems our guys deal with. It's why I'm campaigning on extra pay for them."

Angie snorted. "So they can bet even more money that'll just end up in your pockets—owwwww."

Wayne gave her arm a vicious twist.

Angie's face contorted. "It's true! That guy Mack Coates helps him. Scouts big guys like Billy for him to arrest. And now he's got Ray fighting. Ray knows if he doesn't, he'll end up like Billy and Miss Mae and Craig."

"That little prick'll end up like them anyway. So will you."

He smiled amiably at Julia.

"And you too."

50

Julia stood in her kitchen in the evening gloaming, everything beyond the window black, the light within warm and soft and welcoming.

The plates sat on the table, waiting to be taken to the sink and rinsed and placed in the dishwasher. Julia moved automatically to the broken plate on the floor, picking up the three pieces, placing them in the trash, dampening a paper towel and running it across the floor to pick up any lurking shards that might endanger Jake's soft paws or her son's bare pudgy feet.

The bottle of wine sat beside the whiskey on the counter. Calvin's artwork, stick figures in bright primary colors, graced the refrigerator. The pot of sauce still bubbled cheerily on the stove. She'd heated far more than two, or even three, people could eat. She switched off the flame beneath it, the click echoing in the room's absolute silence.

She twisted the faucet, let the water run hot, and picked up the wineglass to rinse it, intent upon performing mundane, everyday tasks until she awoke from this nightmare.

"Don't touch that." Wayne's bark locked her into the nightmare and gleefully away tossed the key.

"I want everything here just the way it is now, wine and whiskey already out on the counter, glass half-full. Shame you drink so much."

Just a little earlier, Julia had been able to control her voice, had marveled at the calm she projected. Now she was surprised she could speak at all.

"What do you mean?" Her words climbed an octave.

"Must be something about this house," he continued in a musing voice. "Women who live here plumb drink themselves to death."

"No," she said. "No."

What was he going to do, hold a gun to her head and force her to drink? She might get really, really drunk, epic-barfing-and-a-hangover-of-monumental-proportions drunk, but she was pretty sure there wasn't enough booze in the house for her to drink herself to death.

Besides, it would take forever, and Beverly and Gregory would be back soon.

"That's crazy." Her voice still sounded like a cross between a toddler's uncertain pitch and an elderly woman's quaver, but at least she'd regained some focus, enough to hit him with logic.

"How are you going to explain two more people dead in this house? And anyway, Beverly and Gregory—"

He cut her off. "As if those two old farts could help you. And besides."

She wanted to see his preternaturally calm smile as that of a psychopath. But he wasn't, she thought. He was just someone trying to protect what he saw as rightfully his, with the casual assurance of someone who believed he deserved it, no matter what it took.

"Besides?" she prompted.

"There won't be two bodies here. Angie will end up along the creek, like Billy and Miss Mae and that other guy. It's starting to look more and more like a serial killer, maybe somebody just like them, riding the rails. Watch the local paper for editorials about how Duck Creek needs to do more to protect"—he wiggled air quotes—"its most unfortunate citizens. Oh, wait. I forgot. You won't be around to watch."

Julia's mouth went dry.

"You can't. My son. My *son*."

"Shoulda thought of that before you started poking around. Just say your prayers that he stays in the basement. That way, the worst that'll happen is he finds his mom dead on the floor and grows up thinking she was a drunk, which is a whole lot better than what'll happen if he were to come upstairs in the next few minutes."

"Are you insane? Who's going to believe that? In the same house where Leslie Harper was found dead? You told me a long time ago that coincidences are like unicorns. Even with law enforcement on your side, the public won't believe it. You'll never get away with it."

He leaned back still farther, the chair tilting precariously on two legs, and began ticking off reasons on his fingers. Julia realized he was enjoying this. Her internal temperature dropped further still.

"Well, let's see. Your career is in the shitter because you just had a big case taken away from you. And your love life is even worse. Your boyfriend dumped you because his daughter caught the two of you having sex in the same bed where he used to sleep with her mother—yeah, I know about that. Susan Parrish couldn't keep that tasty morsel to herself. You'll be named in the custody case. You're sitting around, drinking wine or whiskey or maybe both, feeling sorry for yourself. You overdid it. It happens."

She fell back on practicalities. "Am I going to hit my head too? Isn't that a coincidence too far?" She nodded toward the service weapon on his belt. "And you can't shoot me. That'll make a big mess. You and I both know that nobody, *nobody*, ever succeeds in cleaning up every little drop of blood and brain matter." Something Amanda Pinkham had told her early on that she'd never forgotten. "Besides, no matter how much you make me drink, I'll still be alive when Beverly and Gregory come back."

"About that. What's your mother-in-law's phone number?"

Julia folded her arms across her chest and shook her head.

His demeanor, so easygoing seconds before, changed in a flash. His eyes narrowed. He spat words through thinned lips. "What's the number? Make me ask again and I'll get your little boy up from the basement and make him watch what happens next."

Julia bent double, gagging, gasping out the number between dry heaves.

"That's better." Wayne left-handed his phone. "Miz Sullivan? Deputy Peterson here. We just met over at your daughter-in-law's house. She's had a rough day. I told her to go on to bed and that I'll bring her little boy back to your house. That way she can rest without people traipsing in and out. You all right with that? You sure? We won't be long."

He rang off, all pleasantness again. "It's good to be a trusted member of law enforcement. But I told her I'd be quick. Let's get this show on the road."

"Wait." Julia tried a Hail Mary. "The security cameras. They'll show you coming and going."

"Oh. That. Let me show you something." He tapped at his phone, then held it up so she could see the screen. It showed her own front door, the image revolving among views of the side of the house, the rear, the backyard, then returning to the front walk.

"Speaking of shared custody, you and I share custody of this account."

"What? How?" But she remembered the oh-so-helpful locksmith standing beside her, making her run through the system's functions on her app, watching as she punched in her passcode. The same locksmith who was the FOW—friend of Wayne.

"The guy who set it up," she said through lips gone stiff.

"He owes me a favor or three. If it wasn't for me, his ass would be in jail."

He'd been able to log in with her password and watch all of her comings and goings, along with Dom's.

"Does that mean you're my stalker? Let me guess. You've got a Duck Creek High sweatshirt or three in your closet."

"Guilty as charged." He grinned. "By the time they find you, that footage will be deleted back to before Angie's arrival. It'll be like neither of us was ever here."

Julia reached for the back of a chair for support. "What happens now?"

"This."

He laid his phone on the table and shoved up Angie's sleeve. "This didn't work last night. You fought me like an alley cat. Probably got only about half the dose. You gonna fight me now?"

Angie had gone nearly catatonic, eyes blank, lips partly open. She lifted her arm like an obedient child.

"Why bother?" she murmured. "Why be the last one left alive?"

Wayne fumbled at a pouch on his belt. "First smart thing you ever said in your life."

He withdrew a length of rubber tubing, tying off Angie's arm with the speed and dexterity of long practice. A large hypodermic flashed in his hand, jabbing deep into the soft flesh of her inner arm even as, despite her words, she screamed and tried unsuccessfully to twist from Wayne's implacable grip.

"Mom?" Calvin's voice floated up the stairs.

"Oh, no," Julia moaned.

"Keep him down there," Wayne hissed.

Julia ran to the top of the stairs, glanced over her shoulder, and ventured a few steps down, out of sight. "Honey," she called, loud enough for Wayne to hear, "I just dropped something. It scared me. But it's all right. Are you and Jake doing okay? You're not getting into any trouble down there?" She forced a laugh.

Even as she spoke, she slid her phone from her pocket, punching feverishly. Calvin stood at the bottom of the stairs, looking uncertainly upward, the dog standing stiffly beside him, absent his usual bouncing enthusiasm.

A heavy step sounded. She thumbed the phone's ringer off and jammed the phone back into her pocket.

She turned. Wayne loomed in the doorway. "Good job. Come on back up."

"But Mom?"

"It's okay, buddy," Wayne said. He put a finger to his lips, miming an exaggerated *Shhhhh*, and spoke in a stage whisper. "Your mom is working on a surprise for you up here. But if you come up too soon, you'll spoil it. So stay down there until I call you, all right?"

Calvin nodded, brightening.

"You promise? Cross your heart?"

Calvin drew his finger across his chest and then down.

Wayne stepped aside and waited for Julia to pass, then closed the door behind him and wedged a chair under the knob. Calvin wouldn't be able to get out unless someone let him out.

Julia choked back a sob. She hadn't even been able to tell her son she loved him.

* * *

Back in the kitchen, Angie slumped in a chair, eyes glassy.

Anger, blessedly reviving, flared within Julia.

"What did you do to her? Whatever you shot her up with, it's going to show up in the autopsy. Amanda Pinkham is going to own your ass."

With the brief threat posed by Calvin resolved, Wayne was relaxed and expansive.

"I could have shot her up with strychnine and it wouldn't matter. These people down by the river, they use every substance known to man. But this is better yet. Pure alcohol. By the time they find her body, it'll be out of her system. They'll think she drowned in the river, just like that last guy. Happens this time of year, what with the creek rising the way it does."

He frowned. "It doesn't help that you cleaned her up. I'm gonna have to drag her through some dirt, get her looking the way she used to look. And I'll probably undress her again, the way I did Miss Mae, so people will think some pervert's on the loose. At least this time I won't freeze my ass off while I'm doing it."

He withdrew another hypodermic from his pouch and waggled it toward her. "All that paramedic training came in handy. Get on over here. Make it easy on yourself."

In the few murder cases she'd followed, Julia had wondered when the victim finally gave up and accepted his or her fate, stopped struggling against the hands around the throat, let the deflecting arms fall away from the descending knife, turned away so as not to see the gun go off.

She wasn't there yet.

At least if she struggled, she thought, there'd be bruises. She'd rake her hands down Wayne's face, get a good scrape of his skin beneath her fingernails, give Pinkham something to work with. She closed her eyes and steeled herself.

She opened them and looked into the barrel of a gun.

"Don't even think about it. You can be the unfortunate victim of a break-in with the added tragedy of your son finding you with your head blasted to bits. Because the last thing I'm going to do before I leave this house is put that chair back where it belongs."

She grasped at a final, forlorn straw. "But my mother-in-law and Gregory. They saw you here."

"They saw me checking on you after a disturbing series of events. You can't imagine how sorry I'll be that I wasn't able to prevent a terrible tragedy. Now get over here."

Julia stayed rooted. "Ray never killed anyone, did he?"

Again he beckoned.

"Does it matter?"

"It does to me," she whispered. So much mattered.

It mattered, so very much, that she'd wasted her last seconds with Calvin on a Hail Mary that wouldn't work rather than telling him she loved him more than anything in the world.

That he'd spend the rest of his life without a father or a mother.

That Beverly, just as she was beginning a new life, would have to incorporate full-time care of a new grandson—and a dog—into her routine.

That she'd never told Dom she loved him, refusing to take that last step into a new life of her own after Michael's death.

Even, for Christ's sake, that on the long, long lists of things she wished she'd done, she'd never apologized for her behavior to Marie.

Who now strolled into the kitchen as though she were just stopping by for coffee.

"Hey, Julia. Hey, Wayne. Hey, Angie—although you don't look like you're in any condition to say hey back. What's going on here?"

* * *

Julia, who thought she'd been beyond emotions other than sheer terrorized panic and sorrowful regret, experience a twinge of spiteful glee at the look on Wayne's face as he slid his gun hand behind his back and dropped the hypodermic on the table, covering it with his other hand.

"What the hell are you doing here? How'd you get in?"

She held her hand high, Julia's spare key dangling from her fingers.

She was, Julia thought, the most beautiful sight she'd ever seen. Julia's last-ditch ploy—texting 911 to Marie's number as she stood briefly out of Wayne's sight on the basement steps—had worked. Except for one thing: Marie was alone.

But then, who would she have called? The police? The sheriff's office?

According to Angie, now drooling and listing dangerously in her chair, they were in on Wayne's scheme, maybe not the killings but the fight club for sure, and they'd probably believe any explanation he offered, no matter how unlikely, over anything she might say.

Marie walked past the table to the counter, set her purse on it, and turned to face Wayne with her hands shoved deep in the wide pockets of her oversize blazer.

"So? Anybody care to enlighten me?"

Julia took a chance. Marie and Wayne went way back. Marie liked him, at least as much as and maybe more than she had herself until, oh, about an hour ago. Who would Marie believe? Yet she had to try. After all, she had nothing to lose.

"Angie said Wayne and Mack Coates have been running some sort of fight club at the jail, something the cops and deputies would bet on. Billy was their stooge. Ray was going to tell. That's why they killed Billy, and the others, and pinned it on Ray—to shut him up."

Wayne's laugh, so free and easy before, sounded forced this time.

"What's going on is that I stopped by to check on Julia because I was worried about her, and found Angie here, drunk and spewing all sorts of crap, which for reasons that escape me, your boss seems inclined to believe."

Julia tried to read Marie's expression, but the woman had a poker face that would serve her well when it came time to try a case in court.

"Huh. What's with the gun? For sure that's not your service weapon. Would I be wrong if I guessed the serial number's gone?"

Julia jumped. She hadn't even noticed that Wayne's service weapon remained securely holstered.

Another brittle laugh.

"Angie got a little rammy. Took it out to calm her down. That usually does the trick."

Marie slid a quick glance toward Angie without moving her head. "I'd say you calmed her down, all right. She looks damn near unconscious."

Julia jumped in again.

"That's because he just shot her full of alcohol, enough to kill her. It's what he did to Billy and Miss Mae and"—the realization came to her—"probably Ray, too, the night Billy died. For all I know, Ray was supposed to die too, but it didn't kill him, so they pinned that homicide charge on him. Am I right, Wayne?"

"Whatever." He waved the gun toward the wine and whiskey on the counter. "Looks like Julia and Angie made quite a bit of headway on those before I got here. Maybe that's why she's spinning all those wild tales."

"Wild tales, huh? Wayne, what's under your hand?"

They locked eyes. Julia held her breath. The hand holding the gun twitched.

"Put the gun down now, Wayne. Mine's right on you"—she moved a hand within her pocket, and the outline of the gun within became clear—"and if you move your hand one more millimeter, you're done."

Wayne froze.

Julia breathed a prayer.

But Wayne recovered his equilibrium far more quickly than she would have imagined possible.

"And you'll be a cop killer. Trust me, nothing Julia says about what happened here will matter stacked up against that. No one will believe either of you. They'll think the two of you cooked up some cockamamy story."

The poker face vanished, replaced by a smile that Julia found more terrifying than anything Wayne had said or done.

Marie lifted her free hand from the blazer and felt behind her for her purse. Her hand emerged with her phone.

"Except I've got one of those apps that uploads video—well, audio in this case—in real time to the ACLU. They developed it for all those cases where cops kill Black guys. Black women too—well, anyone—but we all know it's usually Black guys. Works for this too. You can kill all three of us here, but it's too late. This is you on this recording, with your own voice and your own words, admitting to what you've been up to."

"You fucking . . ." Wayne snarled, coming halfway out of his chair.

"Mom? Mom!" Calvin's voice sounded, closer than Julia would have thought possible. He had to be nearly to the top of the stairs. "Is my surprise ready yet?"

Wayne and Julia both lunged for the basement door.

Wayne got there first, kicking the chair away.

Marie shot. The gun spun from Wayne's hand.

"Julia, get it!"

Julia dove. Got to it just as Wayne got to Calvin and Beverly's voice sounded from the open front door.

"Julia?"

"Beverly, what are you doing here? Oh God, and Gregory too?"

A few moments earlier, Julia had thought she'd never felt such terror in her life. Now fate had just presented Wayne with two more victims.

"This man's message. That nonsense about you needing sleep and him bringing Calvin home. It didn't ring true."

Beverly's nose crinkled as though the odor of bullshit hung nearly visible in the air.

Julia had always prized her mother-in-law's ability to cut through crap. *Oh, Beverly*, she thought now. *Why couldn't you have been more gullible?*

Beverly looked at Wayne and Calvin and read the situation immediately.

"Let go of that child this minute."

She'd once been a teacher, skills she'd refreshed in her time with Calvin, and the command she issued had such authority that Wayne flinched before locking his elbow tighter around Calvin's neck. His other arm hung limp by his side, blood darkening his sleeve and dripping onto the floor. He moved it experimentally, and his face contorted. "Sonofabitch!"

Marie lifted her gun again.

"Whoa, whoa, whoa." Gregory looked from Marie to Julia, who also held a gun, though it dangled from her hand as though she were terrified of it, which she was. His own hands flew up, though neither weapon was pointed his way.

"You heard her. Let him go."

"Or what, Ree?" Wayne's previous cockiness had vanished. "You'll shoot me? And hit the boy too?"

"Mommy?"

Calvin's voice, small and trembling, broke Julia's heart.

She tried to channel Beverly's authoritative tone. "Don't worry. No one's going to hurt you. We won't let that happen."

Wayne's forearm flexed. Calvin cried out.

"How are you going to keep that from happening?" Wayne cocked his head toward Marie. "She can't shoot. She doesn't dare."

He looked at Julia. "And you won't. You probably don't even know how."

He turned his gaze on Beverly and Gregory. "And these two old people? What are they going to do? Beat me up? I'll break this boy's neck if any of you so much as takes a step toward me."

Calvin's eyes overflowed, his sobs all the more frightening because of their silence.

Julia took a breath.

Ray's was the first homicide case she'd handled and possibly the last. She might never defend a homicide suspect at trial, might never have a closing argument with life and death at stake.

But if she did, she'd approach it unafraid. Because no argument she'd ever put to a jury would carry the significance of the one she launched now.

She locked eyes with Wayne and lay the gun on the table with an audible *thunk*.

"Marie might as well put her gun down now too. In fact, go ahead, Marie." She didn't dare look at Marie, holding her breath until she heard an echoing thud.

"It doesn't matter whether either of us can shoot you or not. Because Marie's phone is still uploading every minute of this. Right, Marie?"

"Afraid so." Marie sounded entirely too chipper.

"And even if it weren't, what are you doing to do? Kill all of us? A kid, a mom, an intern, and two old, frail people?"

"Hardly frail." Beverly's interjection was astringent as a sucked lemon.

"Add to the body count you've already racked up? Billy and Miss Mae and Craig? And . . ." She paused as it came to her. "Maybe Leslie Harper too?"

She spoke slowly, sussing it out.

"She formed a committee to come up with a bill to root out corruption in law enforcement. And you said there was a complaint about your department. You told me Cheryl Hayes was involved. But the complaint wasn't about her, was it?"

All of her interactions with Hayes came back to her, this time in a new light. Angie's defense of the woman: *She's about the only friend we've got out here.*

Hayes had tried to tell her what was going on: *Ray was fighting. He was FIGHTING.*

The way Hayes, her eyes rimmed red, had sat apart from the other deputies at Harper's funeral. She'd probably thought then that her best hope of stopping Wayne's scheme was gone and, worse yet, that her efforts had put her own life in danger.

She could have quit, left Duck Creek entirely, found a department several states removed. And yet she'd stayed, still trying in her own way to let someone—in this case, Julia—know what was going on. And, until this very moment, Julia had failed her.

"Jesus, Wayne. Did you shoot Harper up too? Bash her head against the kitchen counter? Where was this all going to end?"

Wayne clung to his plan like a drowning man hanging on to a two-by-four in the face of a tsunami.

"With Ray pleading guilty and her"—he jerked his head toward Angie—"taken care of."

"Taken care of," Julia echoed. "Ray's not going to plead guilty now. The only one who's looking at any sort of a plea is you."

"No." He shook his head.

"Yes." Beverly again.

She strode to him, ignoring Julia's gasp—"Beverly, wait!"—and held out her arms to Calvin.

"Gamma!" The next minute, he was in her embrace.

"Calvin!" Julia rushed forward, but Marie stopped her. "I need you to hold this."

She put her gun in Julia's hand. "Keep it on his gut. You won't be able to miss it. Be careful. It doesn't have a safety. But if he makes a break for it, shoot."

The gun jumped and bobbled in Julia's hand.

"For God's sake, hold it in both hands and keep it steady. I don't want to end up full of holes."

"She won't shoot." A last-ditch burst of bravado from Wayne.

Julia thought of her son in Wayne's grip. Of Ray, bruised and bloodied, in his jail cell. Of Craig bobbing in the creek, Miss Mae stripped naked as a final insult, Billy bludgeoned on the bank. And Leslie Harper, a ghostly presence in this very kitchen.

"Oh yes I would. With pleasure." The gun stilled in her hand. Her eyes fastened on Wayne's midriff. Right there. Between the third and fourth buttons on his shirt. She angled it a lower. Her finger caressed the trigger.

"Easy there," Marie said.

She removed the handcuffs from Wayne's duty belt. "You know the drill." When he didn't move, she wrenched an arm behind his back, fastened one cuff on his wrist, then repeated the move with his second arm, the metallic click loud in the silence.

CHAPTER

52

I N THE END, they double-teamed it.

Marie called 911 and asked for an ambulance for Angie, and for good measure called Cheryl Hayes, while Julia dialed the Highway Patrol, whose officers functioned as state police in their state, stressing her position as a state-employed public defender and using her most authoritative voice in an explanation she hoped didn't make her sound like a crazy person. Then, for good measure, she called Claudette.

They all arrived at once, and the house, which had seemed so spacious when she moved in, suddenly felt too small.

Beverly, as usual, took charge, brewing coffee, prying Calvin from Julia's arms, and calling the dog, who'd plastered himself to Julia's legs.

"The police will need to talk with you," she reminded Julia, who started to follow her from the room, her hand wrapped around Calvin's wrist. "And they'll need to talk with him, too, but not tonight." She stared down an officer who'd approached them. "I'm going to draw Calvin a hot bath and then read him as many stories as he wants before bedtime. And don't worry. Even after he falls asleep, I won't leave him."

Their eyes met, each of them reading the same thought. Calvin likely would have nightmares, maybe not immediately, but soon and for a long time. Or maybe not.

"Children are resilient," Beverly said, repeating the prayerful mantra of every parent dealing with a child's trauma.

Julia forced herself to release her son.

"Gregory," Beverly called. "See that everyone has coffee. Come on, Calvin. Let's get your bath started. If you squirt me in the eye with that tugboat, you're going to be in big trouble."

Calvin responded with a wan smile, far removed from his usual exuberant burst of laughter. But it was a start.

Julia turned to find the highway patrolman at her side.

"We called the sheriff's department," he said.

"But they're all involved in this!" Julia gasped. "They'll let him go!"

"No. They won't. I've listened to part of your friend's recording. Besides, I called the police department too. They'll handle the initial procedure, due to the conflict of interest with the sheriff's department. Oh, and given that the sheriff's department runs the jail, I've notified the jail in the next county and arranged transport. He'll be held there."

He'd done the right thing. Still, Julia had to tamp down a bit of disappointment that Wayne wouldn't be jailed with the inmates he'd tormented and used for his own purposes for so long.

Claudette joined them. "May I speak to you outside for a moment?"

The farther Julia got from the bedlam in her kitchen, the better. "Of course."

Once outside, Claudette eyeballed the security cameras. "Come on." She took Julia's arm, then dragged her down the walk to the sidewalk and a few steps farther, until she was sure they were out of range.

She pulled a flask from her pocket and handed it to Julia. "Figured you could use this."

The shakes ran from Julia's head all the way down to her feet, arms and legs jerking so violently that Claudette reached out a hand to steady her.

"Booze was going to be what killed me," she managed. "It's how he did it. He injected people with alcohol. Billy. Craig. Mae. Ray, but I guess it didn't take. And maybe—probably—even Leslie Harper."

Claudette drew a sharp breath. "Oh, I'm going to love prosecuting this sonofabitch."

She tilted the flask to her own lips and handed it to Julia. "Here. You're in shock. Get hold of yourself. The next few hours are going to be rough. Thank God Marie recorded everything. She's a sharp one."

The streetlight illuminated a gleam in her eye. Julia knew that look.

She took the flask, gulped, and handed it back to Claudette. "No," she said, after she caught her breath. "You can't have her. At least, not until she's done her internship with me. But after that . . . all yours. You'll be lucky to get her. She's got prosecutor written all over her. Or at least, that's what I thought when she started."

"Fair enough. I'm going to head on out of here and let the police do their work. Maybe get a little sleep so I'm fresh when this lands on my desk in the morning. I'll write up a statement for the press. Might be a good idea for you to do that too. I've learned that if you throw them a bone, they generally back off."

Julia thought of Chance Larsen, and of her husband, of his years at the *Bulletin* before he'd joined the military. Pit bulls, both of them, when it came to a story, "backing off" a wholly foreign concept.

"Not all of them. But it's a good idea. Claudette, wait. There's something else."

Claudette turned. "You don't even need to say it. I'm starting the process first thing. By the time you drag your ass in, Ray Belmar should be a free man."

53

Cheryl Hayes stood just outside Julia's front door, smoking.

"You smoke? What does that do to your running?"

Hayes held the cigarette away from her and regarded its glowing tip.

"I quit smoking years ago. That's when I started running—something to take my mind off how badly I wanted a cigarette. But guess what? No matter how fast or far I go, I've never outrun that craving. Figured if ever there was a time to relapse, tonight is it."

She took a deep drag, then tilted her head back and blew a series of smoke rings that wavered and dissolved in the air above their heads. "Ah. I was afraid I'd forgotten how."

"You knew," Julia said. "All along, you knew."

Hayes took another drag, so deep that a cough racked her body.

"I suspected," she said, when she'd recovered. "I was trying to get hard evidence. But people kept ending up dead."

"You saved my son, didn't you? That night Mack Coates got him away from me on the playground?"

"Maybe I just happened to be running by." Said in a way that let Julia know there was no happenstance about it.

"Thanks." Such an inadequate word. "Why didn't you say anything about Wayne?"

Are you really that fucking stupid? Words left unspoken, but Hayes's look made them clear.

She blew a few more smoke rings. "You know what it's like being the only woman in a department that runs on testosterone? All the *Just kidding, don't be so sensitive* remarks I heard all day, every day?"

The end of the cigarette burned perilously close to her fingertips. She studied it, then dropped it onto the walk and toed it into near-oblivion. "Don't suppose you've got any of those on you? I bummed one from a highway patrolman."

"I never smoked. But if I did, I'd give you the whole pack."

Hayes stared at the bits of paper and flakes of tobacco on the walk as though wishing she could reassemble them.

"I didn't have any problem with turning all of their asses in. But God, Julia. They were killing people! I thought Billy was a one-off. I knew Ray didn't kill him but figured I could take my time, get rock-solid evidence, and then bring it to Claudette. But then there was Miss Mae. And I started wondering about Leslie Harper. I'd been talking with her, you know."

Julia started. "I didn't know."

"She wanted to meet with people in law enforcement about reforms. I was happy to volunteer. God know there's more than enough that needs fixing. I hinted to her, without telling her out-right, that there needed to be some mechanism to handle corrup-tion within departments. You know how it works now—each agency handles its own oversight. And they wonder why nobody ever finds anything wrong."

She snorted and paced a few steps. "I finally came right out and told her that maybe our own department could use a look-see. You knew Harper, right?"

"A little. I always liked her."

"Then you know how sharp she was. She was all over it in a flash. And then she was gone." Her lips twisted. "If she'd had the same security camera setup that you installed, my guess is the recording would show our own Deputy Peterson showing up on her doorstep the night she died."

Wayne. Her friend, in the casual sense of workplace friend-ships. Wayne, who joked with her in the courthouse hallways, bought her the occasional coffee, and sometimes even shared juicy tidbits about his work, as long as it didn't involve someone she was defending.

Hayes looked at her as though she were reading her thoughts. "He wasn't a good guy, Julia. Or maybe he was, but in that humans-are-complicated way." Offering her an out.

Julia, still trying to reconcile the joshing, helpful Wayne of old with the man who'd threatened to snap her son's neck, took an easy mental step across a line.

"No. You're right. He wasn't a good guy. What happens to you now? You've got to go back into a department where everybody knows the part you've played in upending their lucrative little game. It could be worse now than it was before."

Hayes spread her hands wide. "Could be. But I doubt it. They'll all be scrambling for cover. That giant sucking sound you'll hear tomorrow? It'll be half the department trying to make out like I'm their best friend and always have been. Hell, I wouldn't be surprised to find flowers and chocolates and maybe even a sheet cake waiting for me when I come in."

Julia offered the obligatory smile. But . . . "Half the department?"

"Probably not that many. A handful. For sure the sheriff didn't know. I almost went to him. He's the one who brought me on, who mentored me. Told me he knew they'd hassle me but to just ignore it. In retrospect, it wasn't the best advice, but to be fair, I don't think even he could imagine how far they'd go. Anyway, I couldn't stand the thought of him turning up dead too."

Julia's mind rebelled. "They'd never have gone that far."

Hayes arched an eyebrow.

"They took out a legislator." She paused, and then she and Julia blurted simultaneously, "Allegedly."

"They may never be able to pin Harper on him unless he confesses, and I don't see that in his makeup. But the recording from that intern of yours will give them more than enough to put him away for the others."

"It doesn't seem fair, though. A jury might go easier on him for killing homeless people. A legislator, not so much."

Hayes sighed and jammed her hands in her pockets. "I've got to go. I've barely slept in weeks, worrying over all of this. This might be my night to finally get"—she lifted her wrist and looked at one of those oversize watches that all the runners seemed to wear—"oh, a good two or three hours before my alarm goes off."

She started to walk away but turned back.

"Fair? Our justice system? What planet have you been living on?"

54

B EVERLY AND GREGORY opened the door as she headed back into
the house.

Beverly held Calvin and Bear-Bear in her arms, while Gregory
cradled Jake.

"Your house is a crime scene now," Beverly said. "Calvin and
Jake are going to stay with us for a few days until things calm down.
I think it's better for everyone. Right, Calvin?"

Calvin nodded sleepy assent.

Julia looked to the dog, wriggling in Gregory's arms. "Are you
going to be all right with the dog there? What's your cat going to
do?"

"Adjust," Beverly said tartly. "Just like the rest of us." Her voice
softened. "Your little dog has already seen one crime committed in
this house. Now another. I can't imagine leaving him here. Don't
worry, we'll take good care of him. We'll probably be asleep when
you get done here."

"Or we might not even see you until tomorrow." Gregory, twinkling again.

Julia gawked at him. Whatever was he talking about? She knew
the police would let her wait until morning to give a full statement.
Crime victims' memories were notoriously scattered and unreliable
immediately after a traumatic event. The police would like her to be
well rested as much as she'd like it herself.

Gregory looked down the walk. She followed his gaze.

Dom stood by the gate.

* * *

"Claudette called me. Beverly too."

His voice sounded muffled, far away.

Julia had collapsed into his arms, burrowing her face into the slick fabric of his spring-weight down jacket. She knew she'd be embarrassed later about her movie-cliché near-swoon, but everything caught up with her when she saw him—the attack on Angie, the danger to her and Calvin, the revelations of Wayne's desperate perfidy.

He held her close, murmuring nonsense words until she stopped shuddering.

"They told me a little bit about what happened. You can tell me the rest later. But for now, let's go home."

She pulled back. "Home? Whose home?"

"Mine. Beverly knows you'll probably stay there tonight. In fact, she suggested it."

"Absolutely not." Strength returned, stiffening her spine, tensing her jaw. "I need to be with Calvin. Dom, he threatened him. I was afraid he was going to kill my son before my very eyes."

She freed herself from his embrace and headed down the street after Beverly and Gregory and Calvin, almost running. Dom caught up with her after a few paces, reaching for her hand and swinging her to face him.

"Beverly's right. She's afraid—let's see, how did she put it? That you'll cling to Calvin every waking moment and scare him even further. Her aim is to get him back into a routine as quickly as possible."

"No." Julia shook her head, but her steps slowed.

"Trust me on this one, Julia. I taught school for years, and I've been a principal for even longer. I've seen kids in every situation imaginable, kids who've lost parents, siblings, friends. Kids who've been abused—physically, sexually, emotionally. The last thing they need after something like this is for their whole world to change. Calvin needs to see tonight as an aberration; to know that life goes on as normal. Beverly left voice mails for both his teacher and his principal, explaining the bare basics of the situation so they'll be prepared. Calvin will be taken care of. It's you everyone's worried about."

"I'll be fine." Her knee-jerk response, so patently untrue, would be laughable under any other circumstances. "Besides, what about Susan and the custody case?"

"The hell with Susan. Something I should have said right away. If Elena really wants to live with her mother because of this, I'll survive. But I don't think she will. I'm just sorry I didn't stand up to Susan earlier." He took both her hands and looked into her eyes. "I'm sorry, Julia."

Words that, at this moment, meant even more than *I love you*.

Or maybe it was the same thing.

55

JULIA MET RAY and Angie at Colombia, damn the anonymity of
Starbucks, not caring who saw them.

She'd offered to buy them dinner at the best restaurant in town,
but Ray waved her off. "Don't want to be around alcohol."

Angie, too, was on the wagon. "That shit almost killed me," she
said. "Bit of a wake-up call."

Julia smiled up at the barista, who delivered a whole triple-berry
pie with three plates and three forks to their table.

"Dig in," she told Angie and Ray. "If you wouldn't let me buy
dinner, at least let's go big on dessert. Angie, I think it's great that
you've quit. But you'd have to drink a whole bottle of whiskey, maybe
more, before you hit the equivalent of the dose Wayne pumped into
your veins."

Angie shivered. "Don't remind me." She turned her head and
discreetly removed her new dentures, wrapping them in a napkin. "I
don't want to stain them," she explained. An anonymous benefactor
had funded Angie's trips to a prosthodontist, along with the dentures, after reading Chance's stories in the newspaper.

Chance had gone far, far beyond reporting the arrests. He'd
delved into the fight club allegations, his story buttressed considerably by quotes and financial records from Wayne's ex-wives, who
were only too happy to dish dirt.

"Word to the wise," he'd said when Julia called to compliment
him on his work. "If you're going to get involved in any sort of

criminal enterprise, never, ever piss off the significant other. Make sure it's roses and chocolates and plenty of great sex into infinity."

Julia apologized now for ordering a pie that posed such a danger to Angie's bright new smile. "I'm sorry. I should have ordered banana cream. Something like that."

"No apology necessary. This is my favorite. Worth the inconvenience."

Angie looked good, her hair clean and glossy, its color newly discernible as a dark auburn compared to Julia's frank ginger. She'd gained a couple of pounds, and even that little bit, along with the dentures, had erased the hollow-cheeked look. No longer did her very appearance telegraph homelessness, and indeed, she no longer was.

"How's the new place working out?"

Angie and Ray looked at each other. "Tiny," they said at the same time, then burst out laughing.

They'd been approved for Duck Creek's experiment with tiny homes. A settlement of about a dozen of the portable houses, set in a circle with a small park with picnic tables and barbecue grills in the center and anchored by a washhouse with showers, toilets, and laundry facilities, was the town's first step in getting transients permanently off the streets.

Predictably, a small but exceedingly vocal group in town had lost its shit over the project, railing against handouts and issuing dire warnings that it would only attract more vagrants to Duck Creek. Others had volunteered donations of cash, food, and clothing. And the majority of people in Duck Creek went about their lives, possibly vaguely aware that there were fewer people seeking handouts outside the downtown businesses than before.

Just outside the tiny house complex, a portable office building housed city social services workers who assisted the residents with finding health care and jobs, even acquiring suitable clothing, and— because many, like Ray, had ongoing legal issues—managing their court dates and fines and fees.

The people living in the settlement were required to police the grounds, keeping the area and the washhouse clean. Alcohol was

discouraged but not forbidden, but public drunkenness or fighting—
any brush with the law, in fact—was grounds for immediate eviction.

"Seriously, it's great," Ray said. "It beats a tent, or just a tarp, any
day."

"Heat and hot water on command," Angie marveled.

"Our first day there," Ray said, "she turned up the thermostat to
about eighty and lounged around in her underwear all day, pretending she was at the beach."

"Other than those summer heat waves we get every once in a
while, it was the warmest I'd been in years," Angie said.

"We've had to learn a few things," Ray said. "Like, never to cook
onions. Every single thing in the place—our clothes, the sheets, I
swear even the walls—smelled like onion for days."

Julia felt almost guilty, thinking of her spacious kitchen with
its efficient vents and fans that sucked away odors within moments;
guiltier still that Ray and Angie owed their recent good fortune to
near-death experiences at the hands of someone who was supposed
to protect people.

She served up another round of pie. "I do believe we're actually
going to finish this thing."

Angie poked at her slice with her fork. "When do you think the
medical examiner will be done with her report?"

Amanda Pinkham was reviewing her findings in Leslie Harper's
death. She'd noted the damning bruise on Harper's arm that could
have been an injection site, as Ray's had turned out to be, but so far,
nothing tied Wayne to Harper's death.

"Everything's still circumstantial," Julia said, and she could tell
that, just like her, Angie suddenly found the surpassingly flaky pie
crust tasting of nothing at all.

"I wasn't going to bring this up here, because I wanted this to be
a happy occasion," Julia said finally. "But I might as well. Ray, what
were you going to tell me back before all of this happened? Was it
about the fight club?"

Ray stared into his pie as though trying to retrieve the answer
from among the glistening berries. "Sort of. Mostly, I wanted to tell
you about Billy. He was Wayne's secret weapon, a guy so big that

everyone would bet on him. Then Mack Coates"—he wrinkled his nose as though he'd just bitten into a berry gone bad—"would scout around until he found some little guy, someone like me, but who knew how to use not just his fists but his feet and knees and elbows and even teeth if need be. He'd let Wayne know, and Wayne or one of his goons would pick him up on some sort of trumped-up charge. Then, when it came time for a fight, Wayne would place his own bet on that guy and cash in. Plus he took a cut of everybody's bets for running the whole shebang."

"I don't get it. So many people must have been in on it. How'd he get away with it for so long?"

Ray gave her a pitying look. "How do you spend all day defending criminals and not pick up on some of their tricks?"

She noticed he didn't include himself in that phrasing.

"They didn't do the fights very often, and only a few people were in on it each time. Besides, he picked guys like him, guys with a lot of debt, guys who boosted some of the take from drug busts, those kinds of guys. If any of them told, they'd be busted right along with him. As for the guys doing the fighting, bad things happened to people who got squirrely. Remember that guy a year or so ago who gouged out his own eye?"

Julia flinched. "God. That was awful. What was he on, bath salts? Something like that."

"Bath salts, my ass. They put one of Mack Coates' finds on him. A sneaky little shit, just like Mack. Where other guys punched, this guy used his thumbs, went straight for the eyeballs. Billy nearly lost one of his. That's when I started calling you."

Someday Julia would get over the way she'd put Ray off. This wasn't that day. Would Billy still be alive if she'd returned Ray's calls? Leslie Harper had already been dead by then, but what about the rest of them?

She tamped the guilt deep inside, to be dealt with later. "Speaking of Billy. What happened that night? Did you guys really get into a fight?"

Ray pushed his plate away. "Oh yeah, we fought. Not physically, though. Argued. He was giving me crap about fooling around in the parade the day before. I told him to quit worrying about me and start worrying about himself. Said I was going to tell. He said they'd kill him, but I told him it looked like they were going to kill him anyway. It was only a matter of time before Wayne picked him up on some sort of bogus charge and set him up for another fight. So then he said he'd just leave town. 'I'm going right now,' he said, and off he went. Like he could get anywhere in the middle of the night."

Julia had hoped for something more. "So you didn't see what happened to him after that."

But Ray surprised her.

"Oh, I saw it all right. I walked around a few minutes, trying to give him time to cool off. Then I went after him, thinking maybe to talk some sense into him."

All this time, Julia had thought the case against Ray circumstantial, given that by all accounts—albeit discounted by authorities—he and Billy had gone their separate ways after their argument. She stiffened, hoping she hadn't been wrong. Ray's next words doused that flash of fear, although she would have preferred her belated suspicion to the scenario he sketched next.

"I caught up with him right about the same time Wayne did. Here we go again, I thought. That fucker's down here to scoop him up for another fight. Except he must've heard us arguing, heard what we were saying. Knew what was afoot. But he didn't let on, just told us he was taking us in for vagrancy and cuffed us."

Julia's fork fell from her hand. "And you just went along with it? That's not even a misdemeanor. It's just a municipal citation. All they can do is write you a ticket."

Ray and Angie turned deeply pitying looks on her.

Angie pushed a strand of hair behind her ear. "They can do whatever they want to the likes of us."

Of course they could. It was why Leslie Harper had been pushing so hard for reform.

Julia was still trying to puzzle it all out. "So he cuffed you, but then he let both of you go?"

"Yeah. Eventually. He just stood there and stared at us for a while. Understand, it was nighttime. We were down by the creek, off the trail, no lights there. He had us sitting on the ground in the snow. It was fucking freezing. I'd dragged Billy away from the fire to talk to him, so we didn't even have that to keep us warm."

Julia remembered how cold it had been just a few short weeks earlier, the sky hard and blue during the day, the sun a cheat, illuminating without warming. Then, at night, the temperature plunging further still, the air crackling with cold.

She tried to imagine the two men, their butts slowly freezing in the snow, hands—probably bare—cuffed behind them, the metal cuffs colder by the moment. Wayne looming over them, seeming even bigger than normal in his bulky winter coat, his warm boots, his thick gloves.

The pie sat forgotten before her. Her coffee grew cold.

"He pulled something out of one of those pockets on his belt. A needle. He uncuffed one of Billy's hands and told him to sit still or else, and like the big dumb fuck he was, Billy just sat there and took it." Ray took a breath. "Then he came for me."

Angie put a hand on his arm. "You don't have to talk about it if you don't want to."

Julia held her face very still, because yes, he did. As far as she was concerned, he very much had to talk about it. Anyway, it didn't matter. Ray was too deeply immersed now, reliving that night, his words coming in staccato bursts.

"I didn't know what was in that damn thing. Figured it was something that would kill us right off. I screamed and hollered and kicked for all I was worth. Tried to scoot away on my ass. Almost went into the creek—if I'd gone through that ice, it would've killed me for sure. But he finally got me."

Ray's breath made a tearing sound.

"After that, I just lay there, waiting to die. But he unlocked me and went over to Billy and uncuffed his other hand. Soon as those things were off me, I ran. I heard Billy running too, the other way, Wayne chasing after him even though he'd just uncuffed him. I got lucky. Ran into Angie, and she'd found another unlocked car we could sleep in that night. Woke up with a hangover like I'd never had before, even in the worst of my drinking days. But at least I was alive. Best as I can figure, he didn't get the whole dose in because of the way I was carrying on."

Angie broke in. "Like me, the first time he tried."

"Yeah." A ghost of Ray's old, cocky grin crossed his face. "You and me, babe. They couldn't take us down."

"Meant for each other." Tears wobbled in Angie's eyes.

Julia went to the counter to order another round of coffee, hoping neither had seen the moisture in her own eyes.

Ray took up his narrative when she returned, his coffee sitting untouched.

"I tried calling you and calling you. Somehow made it to my court hearing. Tried to figure out what had happened, but none of it made sense to me until they arrested me and tried to hang Billy's death on me. Then it made all kinds of sense. I was supposed to be dead, but since I wasn't, Wayne must have figured on pinning Billy's death on me. But what was I going to do? Who could I tell? Not the police."

Me, Julia thought. *You tried to tell me. And I let you down.*

"I'm so sorry," she said.

With his story purged from his system, Ray's face regained a little color. He straightened in his chair and shrugged. "You got him in the end. That's what counts. And can't say as I blame you for avoiding me. I know I can be a pain in the ass."

Angie, too, cheered up. "I try to tell him it's his best quality." She renewed her attack on the pie, finishing the piece before her, then running her finger through the berry juice on her plate and popping it into her mouth. "What happens now?"

Julia suspected that, given their intimate knowledge of the court system, they already knew the answer.

"We wait. Multiple victims—alleged victims—means multiple investigations. Could take weeks. Months. I don't see them letting him out of jail, though."

Resignation tinged Ray's words.

"Are you kidding? He's lawyered up with Tibbits. He'll be out of jail tomorrow."

Dan Tibbits, Duck Creek's most prominent and most expensive defense attorney, produced such reliable results that the slogan whispered behind his back was *If you did it, better call Tibbits.*

"You're forgetting something," Julia said. "Tibbits will be up against Claudette. You think the fights Wayne engineered in the jail were bad? This will be a legal bloodbath. For the record, my money's on Claudette."

56

I N THE END, they were both right.

Tibbits successfully argued at trial—with Wayne nodding solemn agreement from his chair at the defense table—that while Marie's recording was very problematic indeed, whatever blunt instrument had bashed in the victims' skulls had never been found, and furthermore, there was no actual proof he'd shot them full of alcohol at all.

"Known alcoholics and drug users," he thundered. "Their word against that of an officer of the law."

Julia, fresh off her own turn on the witness stand, half rose from her seat in the gallery, restrained only by Dom's firm hand on her arm. What about her own word? Didn't that count for anything?

Marie's recording hadn't been as helpful as they'd hoped. Although Wayne hadn't denied killing anyone, he'd never actually admitted it either. And the hypodermics and tubing he'd had with him that night had mysteriously disappeared somewhere between Julia's house and the booking room.

"Palmed 'em to one of his buddies, no doubt," Ray groused, and Julia was inclined to agree with him.

Tibbits had rolled the dice on taking the case to trial instead of negotiating a plea deal, betting that a jury—the most unpredictable body on earth—wouldn't be able to stomach the thought of a man of the law locked up with lawbreakers.

Those twelve good men and women deliberated for three days, during which time Julia nearly wore a groove in the kitchen's floor tiles as she paced—with Jake, puzzled but faithful at her heels—and swore and drank so much coffee that Dom threatened to cut her off.

Beverly and Gregory kept Calvin. "He doesn't need to see you in this state," Beverly said.

"Great," Julia said. "Someone else who knows what's best for me."

"I always have," Beverly responded, ever imperturbable.

Julia supposed she should be grateful when the jury came back with a negligent homicide verdict, rather than convicting Wayne on the mitigated deliberate homicide charge Ray had once faced.

She could tell Claudette was pleased by the twitch of her lips, the quick flick of her gaze that took in Tibbits's dangerously reddening face.

And yes, the sight of Wayne being led from the courtroom in handcuffs satisfied.

But she knew the drill—a maximum sentence of only twenty years, sure to be argued down by Tibbits at the sentencing hearing, with usually only half that served before moving to probationary status.

"Relax," Claudette said that evening.

They were in Julia's kitchen, Dom at the stove, stirring a pot of Sunday sauce that he'd cooked during the interminable wait for a verdict and was reheating. Jake hovered at his heels, his patience rewarded as bits of sausage mysteriously slid from the spoon to floor.

Dom offered Julia a taste and, when she pronounced it satisfactory, dished up bowls of rigatoni and topped them with sauce.

Claudette poured more wine. "There's still the trial on the fight club charges. They'll nail him on those for sure—unless he does the smart thing and takes a plea agreement. Even Tibbits knows that's in his best interest. Turns out plenty of deputies knew about it and were disgusted by it, and now that our boy has been publicly disgraced, they're willing to testify against him. That blue line isn't as impermeable as they'd have you think."

"What about Leslie Harper? Will they ever be able to pin that on him?"

They fell silent, thinking of the woman who'd died just a few feet from where they sat.

"Maybe," Claudette said finally. "Amanda Pinkham's doing her best." She took a bite, then another. "Dom Parrish, so help me God if I weren't already married and you weren't wasting time with Julia, I'd sweep you off your feet."

Dom raised a glass. "That may be the best compliment I've ever gotten. Happy to have your whole family over as soon as Julia and I get settled in our new place."

Claudette gasped. "I didn't think anything could top this meal, but that news does it. You two are moving in together? It's about damn time. If I'd have known, I'd have brought champagne!"

Julia tried to play it cool. "Didn't have much choice. Leslie Harper's sister sold the house a lot faster than she anticipated."

"Couldn't let her and Calvin and this little guy here"—another bit of sausage hit the floor—"end up out on the street," Dom said. "Besides, it gave me the push I needed to sell my house. That place is full of bad karma. It's where I lived with Susan and where I nearly lost custody of Elena."

"Please." Julia groaned and covered her face with her hands. "Can we never talk about that again? I'm just glad Elena's forgiven us."

"So she'll be living with you too? You're going to need a lot of room. Have you found a new place?"

Julia looked to Dom. "Have you? He's the designated house finder. I'm still trying to get caught up at work from all the time I had to take off during the trial."

"I've got a couple of leads. I think you'll like the ones I'm looking at."

"Change upon change upon change," Claudette said. "I was kidding about the champagne, but I'm not now. I just ordered some. We all deserve it."

"Yes we do. You especially."

The conversation veered into banality—the weather, plans for the coming summer. Safe topics, salving the pain of the past weeks. But Claudette deserved more. Julia knew her own disappointment in the verdict against Wayne had been both evident and unfair. "You put that asshole behind bars. I'll be glad when you rack up some new convictions against him."

"About that," Claudette began.

The doorbell rang.

"That'll be the champagne. I'll get it." Claudette went to the door, and Julia found the slender glasses, a never-used wedding gift from her too-brief marriage to Michael.

"High time we christened these," she said when Claudette returned.

Dom tried to ease the cork from the bottle, but it flew from his hand and ricocheted off the ceiling, much to Jake's delight.

"To new beginnings," he said.

Julia lifted her glass and turned to Claudette, still trying to make up for her earlier recalcitrance. "To our new county prosecutor."

Julia would never have described Claudette as lighthearted. Yet her smile, as she lifted her glass, was positively mischievous.

"To our new county prosecutor—whoever she, or he, may be."

Julia quaffed her champagne and topped off everyone's glasses.

"Oh, it'll be you. Nobody else stands a chance."

Claudette stared into her glass, the unnerving smile still on her face.

"I don't know who it will be. But one thing's for sure: it won't be me."

Dom caught on before Julia. His eyebrows climbed toward hair badly in need of a trim. Julia, though, remained in loyal best-friend mode.

"It has to be you. No matter who they primary you with, you'll outwork them. Outsmart them."

Claudette held out her glass for more. She watched the bubbles stream upward toward the surface for an interminable moment. Finally, she took a sip.

"No," she said. "I won't. Because I'm not running."

Julia had always thought spit takes were exaggerated movie-type riffs until she showered Claudette and Dom with the contents of her glass.

"I'm sorry. I'm sorry." She offered the obligatory apology, but as they mopped at themselves with their napkins, laughing, she tugged at Claudette's sleeve. "Leave it," she said. "What the hell are you talking about?"

"Leave it—no way. This is silk!" Claudette thumbed her phone. "There's got to be something here about how to treat this. Do I just splash it with water? Put salt on it?"

"Dishwashing liquid," Dom said authoritatively. When both women turned to him, he shrugged. "Susan had an array of silk blouses."

Claudette went to the sink and busied herself doctoring her blouse.

Julia followed her. "Claudette, what do you mean, you're not running?"

On the one hand she felt a bolt of relief. Claudette's job as prosecutor had put them at odds, and facing Claudette across a courtroom was nobody's idea of fun. But Claudette was her best friend, and she wanted what was best for her.

Which, Claudette proceeded to inform her, was not a permanent spot as the county's top prosecutor.

"This system is seriously fucked. I was on my way to a plea agreement that would send Belmar to prison on nothing more than circumstantial evidence for a crime he didn't commit because it would have been so very easy and it's what everybody expected. The usual suspect, right? And because it would make me look like the kind of hard-ass prosecutor everybody wants to see elected."

She sat back down and pressed a dish towel to her sopping blouse. She blinked hard and turned her head away. When she faced Julia again, she was dry-eyed.

"I almost stuck with it. The race, I mean. As a giant *Fuck you*. Because everybody hates the fact that the Black woman put the clean-cut White deputy away, right?"

Julia and Dom nodded reluctant assent. Maybe race wasn't as much of a factor as Claudette thought—though it probably was—but for sure, nobody liked seeing a rogue cop revealed. It messed with people's—at least, nice, middle-class White people's—sense of the natural order of things.

"But there's a better way."

The bottle of champagne sat ignored, slowly going flat.

"What way?" Julia and Dom asked simultaneously.

Claudette's disturbing smile softened. "Leslie Harper's way."

Had Julia's glass not been empty, Claudette and Dom would have received a second shower. "You're going to be a legislator?"

Claudette leaned back in her chair and roared with laughter.

"Oh hell no. I'd rather prosecute misdemeanors for the rest of my life than join that particular circus. No, this is something I've been looking into for a while, first as a legal adviser to Leslie, who was going to be the executive director. Now that she's gone, I thought, why not do it myself?"

"Do what?"

"Leslie wanted to start a nonprofit focused on criminal justice reform. You know, ending prison time for nonviolent crimes. Only misdemeanor charges—or better yet, just tickets—for low-level drug offenses, and no more over-the-top fines and fees."

Julia shook her head. "It's a worthy goal. But it'll take years to accomplish, if it can be accomplished at all. The system is so entrenched."

"Exactly." Hard lines furrowed Claudette's face. "It's why Ray ended up in jail for every least little thing, which in turn is what made him so believable as a suspect in Billy's and Miss Mae's killings. I don't care if it takes fifty years." She thought a moment and recalculated. "Well, let's say twenty. It has to get done."

"No." Julia shook her head. "This is crazy. I mean, it's a great idea. But why don't you spend a term as prosecutor and then do it? Think of the credibility you'll have."

Claudette lifted the champagne bottle to her lips, tilted her head, and chugged the remainder.

"Because that's the sort of play-it-safe shit that led me to stick with Ray as a suspect. Four years of waiting means four years of more people getting reamed by this bullshit system. I'm starting tomorrow. I've already got an office picked out." She flashed a look of wicked fun toward Julia.

"It's over Colombia. You can visit whenever you make a coffee run."

"I STILL CAN'T BELIEVE she dropped out."

Julia sat in the passenger seat of Dom's car, gazing at the empty lawns that had once displayed *Go With Greene for Prosecutor* signs.

"Made sense to me. Close your eyes. You promised. That's the only reason you're not blindfolded." Dom was taking Julia to see the house he'd picked out as the best candidate for one they'd share.

Julia complied, even as she mentally noted the turns the car was making. If she'd calculated right, they'd left Dom's neighborhood several blocks to the south of Beverly's and were now heading downtown, but—

"Hey! You just drove a giant square, didn't you? Are you trying to confuse me?"

"I see you peeking," he said, entirely too cheerfully. "Keep your eyes closed."

"What if I don't like it?"

"We've been over this. If you hate it, we won't put in an offer."

"Has Elena seen it? What does she think?"

"Seen and approved."

Julia didn't know if that was good or bad. Elena had veto power over Dom's choice, as did she. But she'd hate to start their new life by disagreeing with her—her what, exactly? A question she posed for the umpteenth time, getting Dom's rote response.

"If you'd marry me, she'd be your stepdaughter."

Julia folded her arms across her chest and didn't bother to answer.

Change, change, and more change, Claudette had said. She'd had enough change in the last few weeks to last a lifetime. Still, despite her caution against assumptions, love had somehow become a given, an unspoken steadying lifeline amid the chaos of recent events.

Dom sighed. "I'll try again in a few days. And again in a few months. But don't wait too long. Elena's got her heart set on being a bridesmaid, and she thinks Calvin would make the perfect adorable ring bearer."

"Don't you ever quit?" Julia launched a well-worn diatribe. "Can't things go along the way they've been?"

"No," said Dom.

"I think I get a say in the matter!"

But Dom shushed her. "I mean, no, they can't go along the way they've been, because we're at the house. Keep your eyes closed. Don't open them until we're at the front door. And seriously, Julia, if you hate it, I'll turn right around and walk away with you. The only thing I won't do is walk away every time you tell me you won't marry me. For that, I'll wait."

Julia wondered if he could see the exaggerated eye roll behind her closed lids.

His door slammed, and she heard his footsteps come around the front of the car to the passenger side. He opened her door.

"This is a lot of fuss for the kind of house we can afford." She'd done the math repeatedly, factoring in her own nearly nonexistent savings and the money from the sale of Dom's house, repeatedly pointing out the imbalance, only to have him repeatedly push back against her concerns.

"If you like, you can pay more of the mortgage. Or I'll pay the whole thing and you can pay me rent. Whatever makes you feel comfortable without bankrupting yourself."

He took her by the arm and led her up a walk, pausing to open a gate.

"Okay," he said. "You can look now."

Julia opened her eyes and beheld her own house, or at least, the house that had been hers until Caroline Harper, as admittedly was her right, sold it out from under her.

"Like it?"

"I don't understand. We can't buy this house. For one thing, we can't afford it. And for another, Caroline already sold it."

"I know."

He punched the door combination. "She sold it to me."

The door swung open.

"Surprise!"

Beverly and Calvin and Gregory, Ray and Angie, Claudette and Marie, and Elena and her new boyfriend stood just inside the door.

Maybe it was the pent-up frustration of the last few weeks. Of finding Ray charged on the flimsiest of pretexts. Of her boss taking her off the case. Of the inability to see Wayne charged with Leslie Harper's murder. So many things—so many wrong things—out of her control. This was a right thing, but . . .

"You bought it without asking me? For us, without even talking to me about it?"

Dom's cheerleading section fell silent.

Beverly, as usual, took things in hand. "Why don't you all help me in the kitchen? We need plates and forks for the cake."

"Cake!" Calvin and Jake led the charge to the kitchen.

Ray turned to go, but then leaned in close, his face—clean-shaven, with a whiff of aftershave—brushing hers.

"Don't fuck this up. You know, like I would do."

With a wink, he was gone.

58

"YOU COULD HAVE told me."

Dom reached for her, but she folded her arms across her chest and stepped back.

"I wanted it to be a surprise."

She aimed the kind of smile at him that she'd seen Claudette use on opposing attorneys, the kind that made them wish they'd chosen another line of work.

"You succeeded."

"It's just . . . you've been through so much lately. And I wasn't there for you for most of it. I wanted to make up for that. I know you love the house. And it's convenient. You can walk to work and Calvin's school from here, and of course I can walk to the high school."

Julia's fingers brushed the doorjamb. She did love the house. But . . .

"It's the principle of the thing."

Dom, who'd been deflating by the second, brightened. "Exactly. Which is why the sale is contingent upon your approval. I'm not a complete idiot. But Julia."

He took both her hands, not speaking until she uncurled her fists and entwined her fingers with his. "I know this is a big step for you. For both of us. For all of us—Elena and Calvin and even the dog. I promise to be better about communicating."

Julia tried hard to suppress a smile.

"What?"

She turned her head aside. Her shoulders quivered with held-in laughter.

"What, Julia? What's going on?"

She lost the battle and whooped aloud. She freed her hands and swiped at her eyes.

It was Dom's turn for the arms-crossed stance of disapproval, one he'd probably perfected as principal, a look that set her off again.

"I'm sorry," she said finally. "It's . . . communication. I could be better at it too."

Puzzlement warred with severity in his expression. "What do you mean?"

"You're wrong about something."

He uncrossed his arms and shoved his hands in his pockets. "Apparently I'm wrong about a lot of things. What now?"

The laughter threatened again, but Julia managed to restrain it to an impish smile. "I can walk to Calvin's school, but I'm going to have to get up a few minutes earlier each day if I want to walk to work."

He glanced through the window. "What do you mean? You can practically see the courthouse from here."

Julia put her hands on his shoulders and spun him around. "My new office is a couple of blocks in that direction."

He spun back even more quickly.

"What are you talking about?"

She bit her lip. "I didn't tell you. I, uh, wanted it to be a surprise."

"O ye who professes to hate surprises."

Julia knew she deserved that. But Dom awaited—and deserved—an explanation.

"You know how Claudette's starting that new nonprofit?"

"What about it?"

Julia looked skyward. She looked at her feet. She looked everywhere but at Dom.

"As executive director, a lot of her work will involve fund-raising. She can't handle the legal part all by herself. So . . . well . . . you're looking at the new legal director for Justice Rising."

Now Dom was the one laughing.

"You're right. We really need to work on communication. You comfortable doing that under the same roof? This roof?"

At which point, Julia did what he'd probably expected her to do as soon as he told her to open her eyes. She fell into his arms and, with eyes wide open, kissed him long and hard.

"Let's go get some cake," she said when she'd caught her breath.

"Oh, the cake's for everyone else," said Dom, and what he said next removed any lingering doubts as to whether she truly loved this man.

"For you, I got pie."

ACKNOWLEDGMENTS

THIS BOOK, MUCH of it written during an extraordinarily difficult time in my life, owes its existence to the compassionate guidance of agent Richard Curtis and Crooked Lane Books editor Terri Bischoff. Gratitude to the rest of the Crooked Lane team—copy editor Rachel Keith, cover designer Meghan Deist, marketing manager Madeline Rathle, and publishing and production assistant Rebecca Nelson—who work the magic that turns a manuscript into a book and get it out into the world. Shout-out to daughter-in-law and murder consultant Jessica Breslin. Deepest appreciation for Amelia Bateman at L'Appartamento Napoli artists residency, where this book was completed, and to Napoli itself, that beautiful, exuberant, chaotic city whose existence in the shadow of Vesuvius proves that life goes on, even after the worst disasters. And, as always, love to Scott, who saw me through to the other side.